Journey to *Where*

A CONTEMPORARY SCIENTIFIC ROMANCE

When a radical experiment into the nature of time is sabotaged, the scientific team finds themselves in an alternate universe where humans never became the dominant life force. Instead, dinosaurs evolved into intelligent bipeds, developing language and societal structures.

The scientists have to learn to communicate with this alien species, who view them as unusual pets, and figure out how to recreate the original experiment in a non-industrialized world so they can go back home—assuming there's a home or even a universe, to return to.

But the scientist who sabotaged them is trapped in this new world with them. And he's looking to rise to power, even if his quest means the death of his traveling companions.

Praise for
Journey to Where

"A deftly crafted, inherently interesting, and thoroughly entertaining read from cover to cover, *Journey to Where* impressively showcases author Steven Paul Leiva's genuine flair for originality and a distinctive, reader-engaging narrative storytelling style."
Midwest Book Review.

"The author's true strength is in storytelling. The attention to detail is spot on, providing just enough visual imagery to fill the reader's perception without diluting the setting with unnecessary clutter. Throw this in with a strong cast and a nicely paced plot, and *Journey to Where* by Steven Paul Leiva is a fun read sure to entertain fans of the classics."
Ricky L. Brown, *Amazing Stories Magazine.*

"*Journey to Where*—a truly wild trip. Recommended!"
Stephen Webb, Physicist, Author of *New Light Through Old Windows: Exploring Contemporary Science through 12 Classic Science Fiction Tales.*

"Science fiction can be a lot of different things: science-y, thinky, adventurous, fun, philosophical, bizarre, allegorical, and laden with commentary on current affairs, but rarely does one volume provide a dollop of all of these things while at the same time featuring realistic characters and realistic sentient dinosaurs. Recommended."
Donald J. Bingle, Author of the *Dick Thornby Thrillers*

"By the Sea: A Comic Novel is a delightfully engaging story about an eccentric community that resides in the foggy environs of Leech Beach...Leiva deftly interweaves characters' past and present to create a vibrant ensemble that is immediately engaging."
Literary Fiction Book Review.

"A novel that delightfully throws out all the conventions of what a romantic novel should be like...part farce, part seriocomic story, and all sexually motivated, *The Reluctant Heterosexual* is a riveting tale."
Stuart Nulman, *Montreal Times.*

"I've continued to enjoy thinking about the book long after reading it. *The Definition of Luck or The Post-Modern Prometheus* certainly gets a recommendation from me."
Andy Whitaker, *SFcrowsnest.*

"This brisk and touching comic novel (*Made on the Moon*) has mysterious and profound things to say about the price of freedom. Highly recommended!"
John Billingsley, Actor, "Dr. Phlox" on *Star Trek Enterprise.*

"*Creature Feature* is a weird, funny, twisty romp through the creepier parts of the American landscape. Highly entertaining and highly recommended."
Jonathan Maberry, NY Times Bestselling Author of *Rot & Ruin* and *V-Wars.*

"Leiva is witty and engaging, stylistically striking an immediate generational middle ground...*Creature Feature's* perfect mix of dynamic action and dry dialogue keep readers turning the pages."
Areyon Jolivette, *The Daily Californian.*

"Steven Paul Leiva is a very bad man. His version of U.S. politics (*IMP: A Political Fantasia*) Trumps anything the real world has to offer. Hell, you thought the orange one was the only homunculus America had to worry about. You thought wrong. There's always the nuclear option."
Steven Savile, *New York Times & USA Today* Bestselling Author.

"Ray Bradbury will be remembered as one of the literary giants of the 20th Century. Steven Paul Leiva's book (*Searching for Ray Bradbury*) is a perfect tribute to the life and works of this great artist."
Joe Mantegna, Actor.

Journey to Where

A CONTEMPORARY SCIENTIFIC ROMANCE

Journey to *W*here

A CONTEMPORARY SCIENTIFIC ROMANCE

Steven Paul Leiva

Magpie

Press

Los Angeles, California

ISBN: 979-8-218-44227-9
Library of Congress Control Number: 2024912061

Author Photo by Amanda Martin

Published in Los Angeles, California

For Jean Rabe

Who, in the dead of winter and the dead of night, is the living proof that a long-distance friendship can be just as close as the one right next door

CONTENTS

PROLOGUE

"In the first place, please bear in mind that I do not expect you to believe this story."

That is how Edgar Rice Burroughs, the master of pulp fiction and the creator of Tarzan and John Carter of Mars, began his 1914 novel At the Earth's Core. It was an account of an inadvertent trip to the true land down under, a land filled with dinosaurs, strange intelligent creatures, and the oppressed. I can think of no better way to start this account.

But Burroughs' account was fiction in the guise of non-fiction. Whereas this account is non-fiction in the guise of fiction.

I had no other choice. As true as this story may be, it is not my story. It is the story of my brother, Sam Reynolds. You may have heard of him. His fame in scientific circles leaked out into the general population early on. He was once dubbed the Rock & Roll Physicist when he was very young, charismatic, and wild in his theories. You haven't heard of him lately, for obvious reasons. But once upon…as they say. It is also the story of Sam's mentor at MIT, John Keegan, who was there and wasn't there. And the story of Lara Penrose, Sam's brightest grad student at Caltech; of Danielle Dorlac, a French national, a physicist and leading theorist on the Existentialism of Time, and of Bertram Brill, also mentored by John Keegan and who also was there and not there and may still be there.

How do I know this story? How can I tell it in such detail? Sam came to me. He brought John and Lara and Danielle with him. They told me their stories. They brought with them a piece of physical evidence.

Sam did not come to me with this story because I am his brother. We don't actually like each other much. Never have. Sam came to me because I am a social psychologist specializing in human deception. I study grand, eloquent liars and mundane tellers of white lies. I'm fascinated by self-aggrandizing liars. I have written a book—well, the book—on self-deception. I have appeared on local television—very local television—quite a few times. I am an almost ubiquitous expert on the subject in the little pond I live in. And yet, my brother made sure I remained humble, telling me for years that "Psychology is not really a science, just a form of philosophy, in a dress made of data."

And yet, who did he come to tell his story to? A story that seems so obviously on the surface a lie, an invention, a fiction.

He came to me—a man who can tell a liar from a truth-teller as easily as you can tell a cat from a dog.

And I believed him.

I would have believed him even without the physical evidence he brought with him, which I grew quite fond of. Other scientists have assured me that it is no longer extant in this world—or so they had always assumed.

I have gathered all I have learned, all the points of view of all the participants I have immersed myself in, all the facts, and all the emotions so that I can now tell their story as omnisciently as possible. But, as you will soon see for yourselves, I had no other choice.

Richard Charles Reynolds, San Francisco

ONE

STORMING THE DARK LADY

The solar-powered commuter dirigible moved slow and low over the Mojave Desert, heading towards the Engagement Ring. It was a nickname, of course, coined by a journalist from the United Kingdom during the first press junket to the VLPA (Very Large Particle Accelerator), arranged by the International Organization for Deep Particle Science (IODPS). She came up with the name partly because the scientists there would be *engaging* with the universe to unlock its darkest secrets but mostly because, from a satellite or jet flyover, the damn thing looked like an engagement ring.

Its sixty-mile circumference was prominently marked on the barren landscape by a circular two-story mound rising from the desert floor. One could see a slight sun glint at the east end as if a precious little diamond rested there. But there was nothing precious or little, relatively speaking, about the cause of the glint. Instead, it was a utilitarian, massive, domed dirigible hangar with a sun-deflecting reflective surface.

Of course, there were competing nicknames—everyone needs to be clever. The engineers who built it called it the Gigantron, a name that never really stuck. Opponents had called it the Great Money Sinkhole. The scientists who worked there, living in the covered, climate-controlled community thirty miles away, called it The Dark Lady because they were trying to unlock the mysteries of dark matter and dark energy.

But to most of the world—or, at least, those who cared or even knew it existed—it was known as the Engagement Ring and was one of the wonders of the modern world.

Sam Reynolds, who sat at the front of the passenger deck so he could be the first to see, the first to "be" there, didn't care what they called the super-duper, superconducting, super collider, as long as he got his shot at it. It was a shot that had been hell to arrange and one that would be shorter than he wanted, but it had finally, if grudgingly, been offered—with conditions. The conditions were more annoying than surprising, but he was willing to live with them to prove himself right— and nearly everyone else wrong.

There it was! From the airship's low perspective, you couldn't see the entire ring, just some of the flat-topped, curving mound and the sparkling hangar they were heading towards.

"We will be hovering here for a moment, folks, as the last group of staff takes off to ferry back to Tysontown," the pilot's voice came over the PA system. "In the meantime, if you look to the west, you'll see the beginning of a spectacular desert sunset."

Lara Penrose, Danielle Dorlac, and John Keenan, all members of Sam's team, did so. But Sam kept his eyes on the hangar dome as it parted, and a commuter dirigible lifted and emerged out of it, pointing itself north, and gracefully floated away.

"Okay, folks, here we go. Prepare for landing."

The rigid airship moved into position over the open hangar, then slowly descended to the floor, gracefully moving to one end until coming to a gentle rest on four hover-pads.

Sam and his team gathered the few bags they carried and exited the craft, moving into the huge cavern that was the hangar. It was the first part of the Engagement Ring, built so that the powerful cargo dirigibles could land and unload all the tunneling and building equipment and supplies it took to build the rest of the facility.

The pilot instructed them to stand in a circled area about a hundred feet away, which they did. Then, the dirigible lifted off and floated out of the hangar. The dome closed after it, and the efficient climate controls kicked in to make the vast space comfortable.

The four stood alone, feeling diminished by the vastness of the empty hangar. Not even another dirigible was in there for company.

"Well, I didn't expect a brass band, but..." John said, looking around.

"There's someone," Danielle noted.

Far away, a door slid open, and Dr. Bertram Brill headed toward the group.

Sam walked to meet him halfway.

As Bertram and Sam closed in on each other, there was something very *High Noonish* about them. Lara and Danielle could feel it, but John understood it.

It was a long walk for both, but they finally came together.

"Hello, Bertie!" Sam said, with a false chirpiness and a subtext relatively close to the surface.

Dr. Brill said nothing, just stared at Sam as if making an assessment.

Sam stared back as if unconcerned over any assessment Dr. Brill could make.

It was awkward for the remaining team members to witness the atmosphere thicken and chill.

A bit more sensitive than Sam, Dr. Brill looked beyond him and smiled at the other three to relieve the tension. "Sam knows I do not like being called Bertie."

"Oh, that's right, Ber*tram*, you don't like nicknames."

"But wasn't it you, Dr. Brill," Danielle said, as she stepped forward, "who gave Sam the nickname of *Rock and Roll Physicist*, by which he has become famously known?"

"I did, but I meant it as an insult."

"And a rather dunderheaded, atavistic one, Bertie, as no one has used the term *Rock and Roll* for decades."

Their shared mentor, John Keenan, moved forward, offering Bertram a big smile and hearty hand. "How are you, Bertram? It's so good to see you."

"I'm fine, Dr. Keegan, quite fine, thank you."

"Did you get the applesauce?"

"I did! Right on time, same as every year. Martha, in the commissary, was delighted."

"I didn't send too much?"

"No, not at all. We've got a lot of hungry scientists here."

"You send him applesauce?" Sam asked.

"Well, you're allergic to apples."

"But—"

"It's the only thing I know how to make and preserve."

"We'd better get you guys set up," Dr. Brill said. "You only have twelve hours." He turned and led them back to the door.

"Yes, thank you for making that stipulation, Ber*tram*. I *really* appreciated it," Sam said.

"It's twelve hours too long, as far as I'm concerned."

"Yes, you've made that quite clear in your obstructionist attitude, Ber*tram*."

The door slid open, and they passed through it into an empty reception area.

Dr. Brill stopped and turned to Sam. "I don't suppose you could do me the professional courtesy of calling me Dr. Brill, could you?"

"No, no, I don't think I could. I've seen you naked, you know."

Dr. Brill took a deep breath through flared nostrils, then released it in a puff through his mouth. "I am the director of the VLPA and the president and CEO of the IODPS, Sam."

"Only because you know how to *slap a-da-back* and *kiss a-da-ass*," Sam said in a bit of snotty stereotyping, flashing a slicing smile.

Dr. Brill did not smile back. "More importantly, I knew how to get this supercollider funded and built. Did you? I had to work the Congress, the Secretary of Energy, two presidents—not to mention their counterparts in twenty other nations—just so arrogant bastards like you could probe the mysteries of existence."

"Yeah, but you didn't get the funding by selling them on the beauties of pure science, Bertram. Like any tight-assed bureaucrat, you told them there would be practical, commercial, and, I'll bet you, even military benefits. *Especially* military benefits."

"There will be," Dr. Brill said as he escorted them to an elevator door.

"How do you know?"

"Because," Dr. Brill poked the down button repeatedly, "there always are."

Danielle turned to John. "Those two don't like each other, do they?"

"They used to," John answered sadly. "They used to be best friends."

"I'm sorry. When did our past become a topic of public discussion?" Dr. Brill asked.

"Why not?" John replied. "Lara here is young and innocent—"

"Hey!" Lara spoke her first word.

"And needs to learn that scientists are human and not demigods. And Danielle is French. There's nothing about human nature we can expose her to that she doesn't already know."

Danielle smiled as the elevator doors opened, and they entered the spacious vertical conveyance.

"So, why do they hate each other?" Danielle continued her inquiry as the elevator descended.

"It was a love triangle." John laughed.

"Ooo, so there was a woman involved." Danielle was intrigued.

John shook his head. "No, they were fighting over me."

The elevator doors opened onto a wide corridor, and Sam and Dr. Brill quickly exited.

"And it looks like Sam won," Dr. Brill conceded.

"No, Bertram," John led the others out and walked over to his two former students. "He did not. It was a tie. You were both the teacher's pet. You just never accepted that fact. Did you have a hard time sharing your toys as a kid?"

It was a question Dr. Brill was not about to answer. "I'll take you to the lab," he said coldly.

Lara walked quickly to catch up to the Director. "Dr. Brill, *uh*, we didn't seem to ride for long in the elevator," she said with a tinge of hope.

"We're only two stories down."

"Oh. That deep? And, uh, um, in case of emergency or power failure…"

"Lara has a slight case of claustrophobia," John explained.

"I do not. I'm just safety-conscious."

"Well, a power failure is unlikely. We are powered by a large array of solar panels and many storage batteries about three miles south. A rather hearty power cable brings us energy and is plugged into the ring right by the hangar. The cable is buried beneath the desert but has a protective covering. But, in case any emergency happens, we also have—spaced fairly frequently along our sixty-mile circumference— escape ladders, like this one here." He walked over to a metal ladder bolted to the wall. "Of course, it's a four-story climb, but we don't expect ever to have to use them."

"I thought you said two stories."

"The ladders take you to the top of the hump, so that's two stories underground and two stories above ground."

"What's the reason for the hump?"

"It houses our cooling systems. One for normal climate control. One for the liquid helium to cool the collider equipment. It's my own design."

"I always said you were more of an engineer than a scientist," Sam said, twisting an old, familiar knife.

Dr. Brill turned to Sam. "And I always said you were more of a fantasist than a scientist."

"Okay, guys," John brought up a natural authority he rarely exploited, "let's cut the banter and get to work."

///

The sign on the door read: *LAB STATION SCORPION.*

"Scorpion?" John asked as they walked into the lab.

"We have several stations that headquarter various experiments. They're all named after creatures indigenous to the Mojave Desert."

"Physics paying homage to biology?" Sam asked accusingly.

"Same molecules, Dr. Reynolds."

"Well — at least it's not psychology."

Despite its romantic name, Lab Station Scorpion was a familiarly inelegant physics workspace dominated by computer stations and ugly instruments. It seemed very much lived-in or, it would be better to say, *worked-in.* On one wall, a giant blow-up of a satellite photo of the desert showed the circular hump of the facility. Someone had handmade a red cardboard arrow that pointed to an area down a ways from the glint of the dirigible hangar. There was, of course, an accompanying sign that read *YOU ARE HERE.*

"The computer stations have your nameplates on them," Dr. Brill said, "which reflect the assignments in your proposal. Each assigned computer has been loaded with the software you've asked for. If you get hungry, the commissary is five doors to your right. I couldn't justify the expense of keeping a night staff on, especially on a Friday, so you're on your own there. But it's all user-friendly. Help yourself to anything. I will be in my office. If you need to communicate with me, each station has an intercom."

"The atomic clocks?" Sam asked.

"They've been placed, per your proposal. Three at the designated spots within the circumference of the collider." He walked over to the aerial photo and pointed out, "Here, here, and here. And three outside the circumference, here, here, and here."

"Excellent," Sam said sincerely. And yet, the creep of arrogance was still in his voice.

"Do you truly think you're going to find a fifth force, this *chrono* of yours?"

"Hey," Sam smiled with professional pleasure, "you've got to admit that, as a hypothesis, it's a beautiful idea."

"As a hypothesis, it's *Alice in Wonderland*."

"Bertie, everything in science is *Alice in Wonderland*. Until you find the evidence."

"And you make a damn fine Mad Hatter," countered Dr. Brill. "Who's loading the material?"

"Lara will be handling that," John said.

"Fine. I'll take her to the loading station."

Lara grabbed the container they had brought and prepared to follow Dr. Brill.

Before they left, he turned to Danielle. "Dr. Dorlac?"

"Yes, Dr. Brill?"

"I read your book, *Time's Broken Arrow*, with interest."

"Did you? I'm honored."

"I found it fascinating."

"*Merci.*"

"Wrong—but fascinating." Dr. Brill turned to Lara. "Ms. Penrose, I'll take you to the loading station now," he said as he moved toward the door.

"Well," Danielle said, once she and Sam and John were alone, "he's a bit of a *petit merde*, isn't he?"

STEVEN PAUL LEIVA

TWO

DOWN MEMORY LANE

Dr. Bertram Brill entered his office and immediately felt the cool comfort of returning home. That is what his office was for him, the only real home he knew. He did have a residence in Tysontown, but as he was unmarried and divorced from a woman who had never understood him, that well-appointed place was only where he slept on occasion. But his office, which he had designed himself, was the physical manifestation of the "I" he knew he was. Its enclosed space provided the most breathable atmosphere he could imagine, the only landscape that truly inspired him.

It was the office of an important man; no one could ever perceive it otherwise. The walls were paneled in a vintage dark wood reflecting the occupant's serious demeanor, and the bookcases, built of a complementary wood, were tall and imposing and held books that had been organized rationally. There were framed photos and documents well-placed on two walls. All the images were of Dr. Brill with people of some note—presidents, prime ministers, atavistic yet wealthy royals, leading scientists, garage tinkerers who had become billionaires, and even a movie star with a well-known interest in science. The framed documents attested to his superior education and celebrated his headline accomplishments.

His desk was large and dominated the center of the room. Also designed by him, it was both traditional—almost antique looking, in its well-crafted mahogany—and yet slickly utilitarian, with all its accommodations for modern technological tools. A long, luxuriously upholstered couch along one wall begged to be allowed to comfort. The one disjointed inclusion was a dry-erase board on wheels shoved to one end of the room. Written on it in Dr. Brill's tight and precise handwriting were notes and equations for something he had been musing on. For anyone who understood it, there was some incomplete excitement there. But nothing had been added to the board for quite some time, like a hobby put aside for lack of time or inspiration, but a hobby one couldn't abandon.

Dr. Brill walked over to his desk and turned on his computer, which lit up a large, widescreen monitor. The image emerging was a split-screen with square panel views of various locations around the facility. He sat at the desk and replaced the split-screen view with his computer desktop. He had work to do, important stuff. As important as anything Sam Reynolds was doing. He opened a document. It was a letter in mid-draft. He read it through. It was more routine than important, necessary but essentially inconsequential. His draft would suffice. And yet, he could not let it go in this state; he could make it better. *But now? Tonight?* No. Monday would be soon enough. In any case, the recipient wouldn't get to it until Monday.

He closed the document.

He looked at his desktop files. There were other things he could do, but...

He opened a file marked *MIT_pics_and_docs*.

He may well have known that he was being masochistic. He may not have given a damn.

One after another, he opened the pics and PDFs and scans.

There he was, a young grad student. So good-looking. He had always been so good-looking. His mother always told him this. But he was smart enough—after all, he was a genius—to know his mother may have been biased. But all the girls who giggled after him in high school, could they have been wrong? Could his college dates, hookups, and near-engagements have all been wrong? Even the several male acquaintances who had hoped to hell that he was bisexual—could they have been mistaken?

His attractiveness assessment was purely objective, based on long-term observation, solid anecdotal evidence, and a fine sense of aesthetics. He was fortunate to have matured at a time when being smart was considered sexy, but he knew damn well that it was his good looks, combined with his smarts, that had really made him popular. Even heterosexual men, despite their protestations, were not oblivious to the attractive ones among their own gender.

He was also a natural leader—you could see that in the photos as well. It came easily to him. The irony about being a leader, being out in front of the pack, was that it often placed one precisely into the center of the universe—quite comfortably so. The discomfort came when natural followers did not follow.

There was Sam. Sam with his nice head of hair, always worn long to flaunt it. But it could never really distract from his essentially misbegotten face, so long and narrow, yet with this odd lantern jaw and a nose with a bump in the middle. And shorter than him. Not by much, but still, Bertram Brill had won the height race, and he had always taken pride in that.

Why had he kept this photo? It had always irritated him like a torn cuticle. It could have easily been dumped into the digital trash bin. And yet there it was, taking up zeros and ones in Bertram's computer; Sam surrounded by a group of undergrads hanging on his every word, his odd face making no difference to—and this had challenged Bertram's imagination, a challenge he had lost—his natural charisma. Not that Bertram believed in charisma. But still, if it did exist, it obviously had a mass greater than good looks, causing a stronger pull of gravity. *Everything was physics.*

He had a nice photo of John Keegan laughing, possibly at a joke he had told himself. Bertram had always thought Dr. Keegan looked like Jack Lemmon, a 20th-century film actor few remembered. But Bertram had discovered him hidden in his grandmother's vast collection of dusty DVDs when he transferred them all to digital files. There was something about Dr. Keegan sharing Lemmon's open, boyish, pleasant, essentially unserious face that Bertram had, at first, found disconcerting. What could this face teach anyone?

And yet, John had been a revered professor long before Bertram had shown up at MIT. Bertram soon realized why. The man was brilliant. And he was open to the brilliance of others, finding it and nurturing it. Which is what he did for Bertram and Sam. He had never mentored two students at once before; he had always worried about not doing justice to either. But a three-way bond had formed, a loop that fed itself. Their times together had been grand. But not without some darkness on the horizon.

Dr. Brill scanned through photo after photo after photo; so much captured light documenting the three. But then they had lived at a time when every human life, or nearly so, was equipped with a camera, one element of the newest human appendage provided not by evolution but by

technology, which was produced by human brain power, which

was, of course, a product of evolution. How could there not be photo after photo after photo of youth budding so successfully into maturity?

He turned to actual documents. Published papers of fine science authored by the three in various collaborations. Some by all three together, many by just one of the protegees with the mentor, only one co-authored by Dr. Brill and Dr. Reynolds. PDFs of news accounts of breakthroughs, of awards, even of a breakup. The last item: a scan of the front page of the New York Times, the last paper to use print. It featured a photo of Keenan and Reynolds above an article covering Caltech's granting of a special lab for Dark Matter and Dark Energy research for Doctors John Keenan and Sam Reynolds. *Just* Doctors John Keenan and Sam Reynolds.

Not a good trip down memory lane.

And yet, he had felt compelled to make it. *Why?*

That was a question he did not think science could answer.

Dr. Brill closed the MIT file and then replaced his computer's desktop with the split-screen views of the facility. He looked at the Scorpion Lab view. Lara had returned and was at her station. Dr. Keegan and Sam were busy at theirs.

He initiated a link with Dr. Keegan's intercom. "How's everything going in there, Dr. Keegan?"

John stopped a review of his monitor to answer. "Anybody who loves my applesauce can call me John. And everything is going just fine, Bertram. This is a superb facility. You should be proud."

The compliment pleased him. "Thank you. Look, I've been here all day, so I'm going to stretch out on the couch and try to get some sleep. But call me if you need me. I'm a light sleeper."

"Will do, Bertram, but I'm sure we'll be fine."

Dr. Brill got up and went to the couch, picking up a folded throw from one end. He unfurled it, kicked off his shoes, laid down, covered himself, and was soon asleep.

THREE

DOWN THE RABBIT HOLE

Having slept through time lost, Dr. Brill woke up in temporal confusion, not knowing where in time he was. Fifteen minutes from the last time he was aware of? An hour? Three hours? A not unusual state of being, but one rarely pleasant. Still not fully awake, he leaped off the couch, the throw dropping to the floor, and quickly crossed to his computer. The computer awoke—brighter for the moment than he was—showing him the multiple views within The Dark Lady. He checked Lab Station Scorpion, but the four visitors were not there. He looked to corridors, the loading station—nobody. The commissary, ah, there they were. The four were sitting together, relaxed, at a table. They seemed to be finishing up a meal.

Fully awake now, Dr. Brill turned on the speaker.

"Well, are we ready to do this?" Dr. Brill heard Sam ask the others as he stood up.

The others, all obviously agreeing, stood up as well, and moved to leave, leaving behind dirty dishes and open containers.

"*Belle compote de pommes*, John," Danielle said as they exited.

"They could have cleaned up after themselves," Dr. Brill said to himself, disgusted over this minuscule malfeasance.

He switched to the view of Lab Station Scorpion and watched as the four entered and went to their assigned computers. He brought that view to full screen, opened his menu, and clicked on DIRECTOR'S ACCESS.

Four windows opened, each displaying exactly what was on the screen of the four Scorpion Lab computers being used. He enlarged the windows one by one and studied what he saw.

He saw brilliance. Possibly. He was studying John's computations for the energy to be used when he heard Sam say, "All right.

Everybody, make a last check of all your computations, then give me the high sign."

"I'm good," Danielle said.

"Me too," John announced.

"John, can you double-check me?" Lara asked, feeling the excitement of the moment more intensely than the others, who were business-like in their deep concentration.

John got up from his station and went to Lara, looking over her shoulder, and read.

On an impulse, a moment directed by emotions, Dr. Brill, who could not only view what was on John's computer but could command it, highlighted a number—one small number—in John's computations and changed it for another.

"Lara's fine," John said as he returned to his station. "As we would expect."

Sam positioned a finger over the ENTER key on his computer keyboard. "Then let's go to Wonderland."

Sam put pressure on the ENTER key. And existence blinked into nothingness.

///

Lara Penrose was the first to awake. She had fallen out of her chair and found herself sprawled on the floor, face down. Certain contact points along her body, the ones most pressed into the floor, were sore, and she was confused. She raised her head, looking along the floor and slightly above it, and noticed that not much was illuminated. It was like her childhood room at night, under the protection of her moonglow night light. With some painful exertion, feeling surprisingly weak, she got herself into a sitting position, propped up against a leg of her desk.

"What...?" finally rose out of Lara's foggy confusion.

"What?" she asked again, as if repetition would provide an answer.

She looked around and could see that John was slumped at his desk, that Danielle had also fallen to the floor, and that Sam was leaning back in his chair, his butt slid forward, his head back, his face facing the ceiling. All were unconscious. At least, she hoped it was just unconsciousness and not the unbearable other.

"Sam," she said as she pulled herself to her feet...

"Sam," she repeated as she went over to him...

"Sam!" she screamed as she shook her mentor violently.

16

Sam started to wake, as did the others.

"Christ almighty, and son-of-a-*bitch,* have I got a headache," John said as he rose from the keyboard that his head had been pressed into.

Sam caught himself before he fell out of his chair, and stood, looking around, assessing the information surrounding him. He turned to his desk, found the intercom switch, and engaged it. "Bertram! Are you there?"

"Some kind of accident, maybe? Something to do with the ventilation system?" John proposed.

Danielle had remained on the floor but had moved onto her back. "I'm hungry."

Sam turned to her. "Is this really the time—"

"No, I mean, I'm famished, *affamé.*"

"Yeah, me too," John said offhandedly as he scrutinized Sam's face and reached for his own. "Sam—feel your beard."

Sam did. His beard was rough and scratchy, about three days' growth, he figured. "Odd."

"Odd? It's a tonsorial anomaly."

"All right. Something happened, something major. An earthquake?"

"Terrorist attack," Lara said, as if certain.

They all considered the possibilities for a moment. Then Sam hit the intercom button again. "Bert! Dr. Brill!"

There was no response.

"Any idea where his office is?" Sam asked.

"Yes!" Lara said. "He pointed it out to me."

"Okay, let's go" Sam said, letting Lara take the lead.

///

The corridor was also dimly lit, which was fortunate but not reassuring.

"If it was an earthquake or an attack," Danielle asked, "why hasn't somebody come to rescue us?"

Sam, following closely behind Lara, considered the two options and found the absurd in any conclusion he could come up with. "Maybe it was a very big earthquake. Maybe California has fallen in the sea, and we're sitting on beachfront property."

"Well, there goes our tenure at Caltech."

"Or the terrorists finally got the bomb," Danielle considered

Armageddon as she walked shoulder to shoulder with John, who gave her a look.

"Gee, thank you, Little Miss Sunshine."

Lara stopped abruptly, bringing the other three up short, and turned to them. "Look. I know it's helpful for some people to relieve tension with humor, but as we have no idea what really happened, I would prefer to remain tense!"

That she was quite agitated was clear to Sam. He smiled at her, not in amusement but in concern. "I want to say, *calm down*, but observation compels me not to. Still…"

Sam almost reached out to lay a reassuring hand on her shoulder or offer a hug. But Lara stood like a steel beam to deflect any patronizing.

"Dr. Brill's office is over here," she said, turning to start the march again.

They found Dr. Brill unconscious and slumped at his desk, his head resting by the intercom.

Danielle checked for a pulse and communicated the results when relief crossed her face.

"Light sleeper, huh?" John said, then shook the director. "Bertram."

Dr. Brill woke, yawned, stretched, and then looked up at the four surrounding him. "I'm sorry. I guess I fell asleep again." Then the quality of the artificial "dawn" dawned on him. "Why are the emergency lights on? And why am I so hungry?"

///

It was obvious to all that the first thing that needed to be done was to eat. They made their way to the commissary. Danielle went straight to the refrigerator and opened it, revealing dark and releasing stench.

"Crap!" John covered his mouth and nose with his hand.

"*Merde!*" Danielle concurred as she slammed the refrigerator door closed.

"Sounds so much better when she says it, John."

"Excuse me for not being French, Sam."

"Plenty of food in the pantry," Dr. Brill said as he pointed it out.

Lara went over to it, opened the door, and entered to explore the wonders within. "Well," she reported shouting out, "there's lots of applesauce. Crackers. Beans. Vienna Sausages. Both healthy and sugary breakfast cereals. And…" She came out bearing an excited smile and three cans that she held aloft. "Spam!"

///

Spam was their entrée, rounded out by John's applesauce, some still-good bread, and cold canned peas. They dined in low light, feeling no romance, just the joy of satiating hunger.

"You know my mother used to make fried Spam sandwiches," John said as he finished. "I love Spam,"

"I hate Spam," Sam said, leaving no room for doubt.

"I've never had Spam." Danielle poked at the remains of her meal. "Tell me, I will never have to have it again, *s'il vous plaît*."

"It was a staple in my home. You people have no taste." Lara took her last bite and smiled.

Dr. Brill speared his last bit of Spam, ingested it, and then cleaned his plate of applesauce with his last piece of bread. When he looked up from his meal, he found four expectant faces. "I am totally indifferent," he said. "It provided sustenance, which I think was its purpose."

The dim emergency lights flickered.

Dr. Brill looked at the lights. They flickered again. "Ah. The emergency generator is giving out."

"How long is it supposed to last?" Sam asked.

"Three or four days."

John stroked his chin. "Seems about right."

The lights flickered again, and Dr. Brill stood up. "There are flashlights and lanterns in the back of the pantry. We'd better get them, fast."

///

They retrieved the flashlights and lanterns just as the generator died, and the dim illumination retreated, allowing the dark to enfold them. Small switches were engaged, and beams of light streamed out. What could now be seen was seen mainly in snatches, thin slices of a larger reality.

"We better get up and leave here and see what's going on," Dr. Brill said. The closest ladder is this way."

Dr. Brill said when they got to the ladder, "Leave a couple of the lanterns lit on the floor. If we come back down, we'll need them to stay oriented."

No one questioned that Dr. Brill was in charge. "I'll take the lead. Then Dr. Dorlac and Ms. Penrose. And then Dr. Keegan, if he feels up to it."

"Well, I'm not going to stay down here," John protested.

"It's four stories."

"I can do it. A lot of walking, a lot of swimming, I'm in shape."

"Okay, but Sam will be behind you to offer support. Right, Sam?"

"Sure. However, John is probably stronger than I am. I *don't* do a lot of walking and swimming."

"You're younger than Dr. Keegan," Brill said, frowning. "Just call on your youthful vigor. Okay, let's go."

Vigor was needed from all—male, female, elder, younger, especially as the fourth story loomed. But they finally reached the top and found themselves in a small, enclosed space, a box really, extending above the roof of the hump. By the time all five were off the ladder, it was a very cramped box. At one end was a door with a simple handle. Dr. Brill opened it, and daylight streamed in, not quite as harsh as one might have expected.

They walked out onto the top of the hump, which had a flat roof, and faced the interior of the circumference of the Engagement Ring. There was the Mojave Desert in all its parched, patchily vegetated, unwelcoming glory. But the sky was thick with grey clouds, which explained the less-than-harsh light and the surprisingly temperate atmosphere.

Sam looked around the immediate vicinity and then off into the far distance. "I don't see any problems. There are no earthquake fissures or anything like that. I didn't know it got this cloudy in the summer."

"At least they're not mushroom clouds," John said with a bit of wit and much relief.

"Clouds in the sky are not our concern right now." Dr. Brill appreciated neither the wit nor the relief. "The lack of a dirigible in the sky is."

"Maybe it's around here." Lara moved around the exit box to see what was outside the Engagement Ring.

Her gasp was loud and alarming.

The others quickly followed, and all may have gasped as well, for they did not see a dirigible hanging in the sky over a dry, arid landscape of patchy vegetation. Instead, there was a forest. A vast, dense, lush forest with some of its trees tall enough, it seemed, to reach the clouds. Not one of the five had anything to say. Or could they have if they did. They just walked to the edge of the hump, looking out. There was a breeze, and trees rustled, making an incongruously pleasant sound to accompany the cold coming together of the real and the surreal. Then, they heard more natural music as the sound of a rapidly flowing river reached them.

Their eyes confirmed their ears as they glimpsed views of the river beyond the immediate trees. Suddenly, another sound muted the music of river and trees: the thumping, crashing sound of something significant, or some things many, or some frightening combination of both, progressing through the forest.

Breaking through the trees, onto a path of bare ground that ran alongside the hump, came a herd of creatures, around nine feet tall, fifteen feet in length, moving with alacrity on two legs. They leaned and stretched forward as they rumbled along as if trying to get ahead of the game; their stubby arms, if they were arms and not just little legs, dangled uselessly from their torso.

They were two-toned. That's the thought that hit John. *Brown with white spots along their backs and green on their undercarriage.* And they were bald. Or, more accurately, they had domed heads, like they were wearing helmets. There must have been thirty to fifty of them streaming by, oblivious to the two-story structure to their right and the little *Homo sapiens* who stood upon it.

Lara began to hyperventilate with a strained rasp, with the panic they all felt to different degrees.

Danielle gently took her in her arms and whispered soothing sounds into her ear. "It's okay, it's fine, *ma chérie*. You're in no danger. Breathe now, breathe deep, slowly. *Bien. Bien.* Walk with me. We'll go back— back down—hide in the dark for a while."

FOUR

?

They returned to the commissary, set one of the lanterns in the middle of a table, and then took seats around it. It was unintentionally eerie, with only their faces illuminated, seeming to hover in a circle. They were quiet for a while, some thinking, some trying to come out of shock, and some feeling numb. Breaths could be heard but were not noted.

There was the subtle rustle of clothes as Sam moved in his chair. "I don't think it's useful to answer the question on everybody's mind. It would only be speculation."

"Sam," John said to the younger man, "in a situation like this, a little speculation can't hurt. We *need* to try to grasp what happened."

"We time-traveled," Danielle said, in such a matter-of-fact manner that she made it sound normal.

"I'm not ready to accept that," Sam said.

"That's because you're too much of a theoretical physicist, Sam," John said. "The core of science is observation, and we have observed dinosaurs quite happily sauntering by. The last observation I made on this matter, in the mid-twenty-first century, was that dinosaurs were evident only in fossilized remains, indicating that they all became extinct sixty-six or so million years ago."

"*Oui!*" Danielle leaned forward, illuminating her hair, which was thick and lovely. Sam observed this and thought it was weird that he was doing so. "And what did we observe within the circumference of the hump? The Mojave Desert, as would be expected. And outside the circle of the hump? A forest with dinosaurs. *Pardon,* but that does not even need a leap of imagination to conclude that we somehow turned this Dark Lady into a time machine and have traveled back sixty-six or more millions of years. It…it's exciting."

"It's fucking frightening," Lara said, her face still stone-like with shock.

The other four looked at her face hanging in the dark.

"Lara!" John registered the mutual shock. "That's the first time I've ever heard a curse word coming from you."

"Fuck! Shit! Hell! Damn!" Lara's voice boomed out and echoed down the corridor. Then her face fell, as did copious tears.

Danielle put her arms around Lara again, concerned but also amused. "It is okay, *ma chérie*. No one in the twenty-first century can hear you. Here, drink some water."

Lara took the offered bottle of water and drank it dry.

Sam stood up and started to pace, leaving the light, then returning, then leaving again, his footfalls, though, ever-present. "But the experiment was not fundamentally different than experiments in colliders have been for years."

"But they were dealing in matter, and we are dealing in time," Danielle, the philosopher of time, said.

"Yes, to find a force that *is* time, that defines it, but not to…to travel along it. Our calculations were precise, and the amount and kind of particles we used were exact. The amount of energy we needed was huge, I grant you, but we had determined it after how many computer simulations? The design of this experiment was perfect. All that should have happened was the stopping of time, within the circumference, for a few nanoseconds, as measured by the atomic clocks within the circumference, against the atomic clocks outside of the circumference. If we had done that, we would have shown evidence of chrono."

Lara, John, and Danielle knew this. Dr. Brill knew it as well, it had been in the proposal, although he had not considered it a serious hypothesis. But…considering… What if…?

"Bertram," John called for his attention, "I have rarely known you not to weigh in on a scientific controversy."

Dr. Brill—or perhaps, we should call him Bertram from now on, doctorates being quite meaningless in the age of dinosaurs, even if the knowledge behind the doctorate wasn't—Bertram's thoughts and demeanor re-joined the others. He smiled. "I have nothing to add to this discussion. Maybe I've been a 'tight-ass bureaucrat' for too long, but my mind right now is more on survival. The air in here will not last long. There is no way we can get the generator going again without fuel. However that we got here, here we are, and we are going to have to survive."

Lara, who was quite calm now and her normal Midwestern self, saw the wisdom in Bertram's words, but the question remained, "How?"

"We have to go out into that forest. Find food, shelter."

"Explore!" John said with a sudden excitement.

"*Oui!*" Danielle agreed.

"What? No! Survival is all, Bertram declared. We no longer have the luxury to satisfy our minds. It's our bellies you are going to be worried about real soon."

"The Spam won't last forever," Lara said, presenting the reality.

John and Danielle turned to the sound of Sam's footfalls.

"Sam?" Danielle asked.

"Yes, *mon capitaine*, what do you want to do?" John finished the question.

Sam came out of the dark and sat down again. "All I really want to do is figure out what the hell went wrong. I want to check our calculations. I want to check my hypothesis. But how? By standing on the shoulders of giants who haven't been born yet? We can't get our computers running. Plus, you know me, I'll get obsessed, I'll forget to eat unless someone feeds me. But that presupposes there being something to feed me with. So, survival, yes, we must survive. But only that? We're scientists, Bertram. Which means we're explorers. Even locked away in a lab, we're explorers. But we won't have a lab, so we might as well explore what we do have. I don't want to go out there just to survive, which is a mundane existence at best. I want to see this world, to observe. We can start science all over again."

Bertram let out a guttural groan. "Listen, *Alice*, we would be much wiser to stay close to the collider so that if we need to, we can escape back into it as a sort of cave. Plus, the river we saw will be a consistent water source."

"Ah, come on, Bert*ram,* where's your sense of adventure?"

"In the twenty-first century—where it belongs!"

STEVEN PAUL LEIVA

FIVE

LEAVING THE DARK LADY

It was time to leave, whether to live a life of just trying to live or to live a life of the mind and not only of the belly. First, they went through the labs and offices and, of course, the commissary and pantry and even the restrooms and gathered up anything they thought might be useful: flashlights, batteries, food, bottled water, knives, tools, a pair of binoculars, the first aid kit, and toilet paper.

"Toilet paper?" Sam questioned Lara, who had gathered up ten rolls.

"I'll put off as long as possible the use of…leaves or whatever."

"Well…I hope it's biodegradable."

It took a while, hours, poking through the dark with handheld illuminations. They gathered everything together at the foot of the escape ladder, along with anything they could carry the stuff in—canvas bags, briefcases, a backpack left behind by one of the staff scientists who actually liked the desert. They packed the best carriers with the most essential stuff. Bertram found some rope to tie the bags onto their bodies, leaving their hands free to climb the ladder—except for himself. He took the backpack. Lara took on the extra burden of a large canvas bag with images of Las Vegas on it to carry her ten rolls of toilet paper.

"The rest of this stuff, we'll come back for when we can," Bertram said as he took the lead.

With the added weight of the clumsy bulks tied to them, Sam and his team had a difficult time following their leader, especially as the air was growing thin. But eventually, they emerged out of the exit box on top of the hump, surprised to find the sun rising. They realized that they had lost the concept of time, having been enclosed in the dark interior, not knowing it had been dark as well outside for hours. After catching their breaths and resting, Bertram took them to the forest side of the hump, to the escape ladder leading down to the forest floor.

"Oh, God!" Lara said, stepping a bit back from the edge.

"It's only two stories this time," Bertram assured her, "and with gravity assist."

"It's not that, it's…it's…it's… *That.*" She pointed straight out in front of her. "The forest…the primeval world we're about to just casually walk into."

"Walking casually is the last thing we are going to do. Perk up all your senses, be constantly aware of your surroundings, and look out for dangers. It will probably exhaust you more than climbing the ladders, but it's essential for survival."

"A bit melodramatic, don't you think, Bertram?" Sam smiled.

Bertram did not. "Do you have any grasp of reality at all, Sam?"

"Spent my life looking for it."

"That life is over. The privilege you enjoyed, looking into the mysteries of the universe, has been revoked. Now you are just a weak, defenseless biped with a radically reduced life expectancy."

"Guys!" Danielle interceded. Stop the stupid rivalry and take a moment to look at the sunrise. It is *magnifique.*"

Bertram slowly dropped his mouth. "We don't have time for sunrises. Or is that some French irony?"

"No. I like sunrises."

"When we enter the forest, will you stop to smell the flowers?"

"*Oui.* If there are flowers, I shall smell them."

"Jesus Christ!"

"Oh, come on now, Bertram," John said, placing a fatherly, calming hand upon his former student's shoulder. Sam and Danielle are just trying to keep some sense of the usual, okay? Some grounding in what they know while facing so much that they don't. It's understandable."

"Jesus Christ!" Bertram exclaimed in frustration.

"Bertram, we are very much in a B.C. situation. Calling on Christ seems somewhat premature."

"Try fuck, shit, hell and damn," Lara advised. "It actually works."

Bertram looked at Lara, somewhat disappointed. Then, saying nothing more, he started down the ladder.

///

They entered the forest and were surrounded by sounds. The breeze in the trees. The flowing water of the river they were heading towards. A loud buzzing that gave premonitions of oversized insects. The strange calls of birds. Even their own feet, falling on a forest floor of fallen leaves and dead twigs, and the skittering footfalls of the company that they could not see, for they couldn't see much besides the trees, except for one bird in the sky, a red and orange, elaborately feathered bird.

When they reached the river, they set their bags down. It was a narrow river, flowing rapidly over outcroppings of boulders near the center. But the water near the shore was calm, pooled, and clear. Danielle kneeled and dipped her hand in the water, bringing some to her mouth to taste.

"*Bien.* It is good. And I see fish down there. Weird fish, but fish."

Lara came up to the river and looked deep into it. "Do you think we can take a bath in it? We haven't had a bath for days."

"We haven't had a bath for over sixty-six million years," John corrected.

"Now, John. You know that, like all things, time is relative," Sam said.

Bertram, ignoring the banter, looked around the immediate area, deep into the forest and back towards the hump of the Dark Lady, which could still be seen in breaks between the trees. "I think we should make camp here, by the river, as we figure out shelter. I grabbed the fire ax. Maybe we can chop down some of those smaller trees and construct huts, or lean-tos, or something." He was ignored as much as he had ignored.

Danielle answered Lara. "I would use the river water to bathe, but I wouldn't go into the river. Who knows what would want to eat your toes? Plus, you don't want to lather up in the river—we would be the world's first polluters."

Bertram continued his investigations and moved over to a smallish tree as a possible candidate for chopping. "Dr. Keegan?"

"Bertram, my doctorate means nothing here. Call me John."

"Do you recognize any of these trees?"

"Nor is my doctorate in paleobotany."

"That's my point. Don't these trees look—modern to you?"

The question caught everybody's attention. They looked, considered, and touched.

"Well," Sam finally said, "they certainly don't look primordial, if that's what you mean."

Lara was examining a large tree with a massive trunk, one of the trees that reached for the clouds. She found moss on the lower trunk and a trail of some ant-like insects when she heard a scratchy-scurrying sound around the other side. She moved around the trunk slowly, and the scurrying occurred again. She stopped, leaned her body around the trunk, and found a tiny foot with grasping claws. She moved the rest of her body forward, and a furry, foot-long creature blinked at her. It was brown, except for its face, which was white. It had a long tail that reminded her of an opossum's tail. Many whiskers were exploding from its long snout and above its eyes. It was extremely ugly and yet still cute.

"Hey, look what I found," she called out to the others.

They gathered around her. The creature did not stir, seemingly unafraid—or unimpressed—by these visitors to his forest.

"John, what is it?" Danielle asked.

"How would I know? I'm not a paleobiologist, either."

"Damn specialization!" Sam lamented.

"It's a mammal," Bertram said.

"*Évidemment.*"

"Primitive," Bertram continued, "no competition to the dinosaurs. The kind of life that could survive but not thrive."

"Can we eat it?" Danielle asked.

"What?" Lara was shocked by the French pragmatism.

"I'll give you all my Spam." Danielle offered.

As if offended by the mention of processed meat, the creature shot up the tree—very far up. But the actual reason became apparent when the ground shook with nearby pounding, accompanied by the violent rending of unseen branches. Out of reflex, they turned toward the disturbance and were more than disturbed to see a dinosaur, forty feet long, with tons and tons of flesh being supported on two tree-trunk-sized legs, emerge from the trees. Its long-snouted face was extended towards them as it looked at them with some consideration.

No one moved. Whether by choice or not is debatable.

"Maybe we're too small, not worth its while," Sam mused quietly.

"You're assuming it's a carnivore, then?" John asked.

"Oh, yeah. And one which is looking for a big meal, not merely appetizers. The thing is not to panic."

"Can I faint?" Lara asked as the monster snorted a hot wind at them and moved forward.

Panic was now a good option if it spurred flight, which, fortunately, it did. The five turned and ran as fast as they could.

"Stay together! Stay together!" Sam yelled out.

"No! Different directions!" Bertram countered. "He can't go after all of us."

"If we're going to die, let's die together. Does anyone want to be here alone?"

Sam prevailed, and they all ran close together, even Bertram, who took the lead. Sam grabbed Lara's hand and dragged her faster than she had been running alone. Danielle fell but recovered and was back on her feet quickly. John, a dedicated walker who had always declared that he would only run if he were being chased, proved as good as his word and was not left behind despite his sixty-plus years.

And the creature, the monster? It lunged after them with large and long and slamming steps but found the randomly spaced trees a constant impediment that slowed him down.

The five suddenly found themselves in a meadow. It was beautiful, which was none of their concerns. However, its openness worried them.

Then Lara spotted something at the far end. "Look!"

A pile of felled trees formed a fortress with ample nooks and roomy crannies. They ran for it, reached it, climbed onto it, and descended into the nooks and crannies. They controlled their rapid and loud breathing and looked out between the fallen trees at the giant monster, which seemed to be wondering—if its tiny brain could wonder—where its prey had gone.

Suddenly, the creature roared in irritation and anger and whipped around to face the source of its consternation. Several large spears were sticking out of its lower back. The beast tried to shake them loose. Then, a barrage of arrows and spears flew out of the forest from several directions. They rained down upon the creature, many of them hitting their mark, others falling to the ground. The beast roared in anguish and turned and turned again, trying to find something to attack. Loud voices flowed out from the forest, shouts of command in a language unknown. A second barrage flew. The creature was becoming a pincushion and again roared its dissatisfaction. But finding nothing to hurt back, it escaped out of the clearing, back into the forest, back toward the river. Indecipherable shouts and commands followed and soon faded.

Silence returned—or the peaceful sounds more typical of a forest. The five slowly emerged from the fortress of fallen trees and walked to the meadow's center, to the crop of sharp instruments stuck into the ground.

Using two hands, John pulled a long spear out of the ground. It was heavy and well-crafted, with a thick shaft and a strange metal head honed to a fine point. "Despite not being a paleontologist, I do know there were no humans around to hunt dinosaurs."

"Humans?" Bertram tried to grip the shaft. His hand, which was not small, could not completely encircle it. "Look at the size of this."

"We *need* to get away from here!"

They looked at Sam. His voice had grabbed their attention as much as what he had said. It had quivered. They would later swear that Sam was shaking as if his whole body was tight with the sudden grasp of reality.

SIX

A WIDENING VISTA

"We need to get our stuff," Bertram said, starting back the way they had come.

"No!" Sam stopped him. "We need to get away from…from them. We need to think this out."

"There is nothing to think about, only things to do."

"Yes, later. Right now, we need a safe haven, and I don't think we will find it with whoever the spear-throwers are. And they are between us and the river."

Danielle moved to block the stare-down between Sam and Bertram. "Sam, where do you see a sign pointing to SAFE HAVEN? *Où allons-nous?* Which way do we go?"

"Let's start with the opposite direction from them."

"We still need our stuff," Bertram insisted. "How can we survive without it?

"Bertie! The potential of our survival is probably so low that a few batteries and Spam tins will not make a difference. Get the stuff if you want. You'll have it all to yourself."

Sam turned, walked to the fortress of fallen trees, and started to climb over it. He stopped midway and turned. John and the two women had not left their positions, which surprised him. Bertram stood beyond then, waiting for the three to join him.

"Guys, make a choice," Sam said.

Lara was the first to break. Abandoning Sam was, for her, unthinkable. John followed, then Danielle. Bertram stared after them, disgusted. He then bent down and gathered up as many fallen arrows as he could carry. Like the spears, they were oversized, almost spears themselves. He then looked toward the fallen fortress. The others were all at the top, making for the other side.

Idiots! All of them, he thought, and yet...

He headed towards them, offering the arrows when he got to the base.

Sam and the others grabbed two each.

Sam looked down at Bertram. "That was smart of you—and stupid of me. Let's go."

"Yeah," Bertram said as he began to climb. "Let's go."

///

It was a long trek, deep into a forest that seemed to get thicker and darker as they went along. The ground was undulated with gullies, bottomed with streams, and dotted with rises covered with strange vegetation. The surrounding sound was more intense now, as if captured in an enclosed space, causing tiny echoes. They were right in thinking the buzzing would be insects, as several—as large as they had feared—flew by but, thankfully, did not choose to bother them.

John tripped over an exposed root and tore the knee of his right pants leg, scraping the skin beneath, but declared himself okay. Lara cut her upper arm on a sharp branch and cried a little. Danielle tore a strip from the bottom of her shirt and tied it around Lara's arm to stop the bleeding and protect the cut. Bertram stepped into a large pile of something disgusting. Sam noted some more small and benign animals and took what comfort in them he could.

They knew the day was soon to end, and despair began to hit them when they saw light penetrating the trees ahead. They pushed forward and through until they emerged out of the forest and found themselves on the wide edge of a cliff, looking out upon a vast vista of cultivated fields. There were fields of grain in square patches on one side of a broad, flowing river (possibly their river?) and orchards with several types of trees on the other side. There were workers in the fields and the orchards—two-legged men, it seemed, from what they could see. And there were large beasts of burden, pulling wagons, which the men were loading with whatever they had cut or gathered.

They followed the river with their eyes to the horizon, noticing what looked like a city but one in decay. And yet, the odd thing was, there seemed to be something futuristic about what architecture they could make out. There were tall, narrow buildings, their top stories connected by bridges, some only partial, with sections missing, some still intact. Following the river well beyond the city, they could see a forested green hill. On top of the hill was a massive structure with what seemed to be towers, gleaming and glittering as the sun descended behind them.

Then, through the forest behind them, sounds came of voices like those of the morning. Having nowhere to run except off the cliff—the five slowly turned around. A band of bipedal creatures came out of the forest, upright, lightly clothed, and carrying spears, bows, and arrows. Some were well over eight feet tall, some maybe twelve feet. Some were only six or seven feet tall. The taller ones had multi-colored, scaly skin. The shorter ones seemed covered in something softer but also multicolored. Their faces were almost human-like but without prominent noses.

The tall ones were initially stunned, then disbelieving, then fascinated by the five small, weird-looking creatures before them. One of them began to bark out orders, both verbally and through gestures, indicating that his fellows should surround the creatures slowly, not frightening them but definitely with the aim of capture.

Sam turned his back on them and whispered urgently to his companions, "Don't talk! Don't let them know we have language!"

"Why?" Lara whispered through tight lips.

"They think we're dumb animals and no threat."

"But we have clothes," Danielle pointed out.

"Hide or loose skin for all they know. So, act dumb."

"We have four doctorates and a master's degree among us," John said. "It ain't going to be easy."

Sam turned back to the bipeds and cautiously approached one of the smaller ones (although it was still much taller than Sam). Sam made a display of sniffing it and looking it over with harmless curiosity. He saw that its soft skin seemed downy with something between feathers and hair. The creature reached out and took from Sam's hand the two arrows he had been carrying, but he had forgotten that he was holding them.

The Downy took Sam's hand gingerly. Sam offered no resistance. The Downy then led Sam towards its companions. Others came forward and took Bertram, John, Danielle, and Lara in hand after having gingerly relieved them of their arrows, as one would a child. Lara started to shake. The Downy that had taken her seemed concerned and began to pet her hair, finding its smooth strands interesting.

The one giving commands gave more, and the mixed group—the Scaly, the Downy, and the Skins—moved to the far side of the cliff and started to descend a trail hidden from view.

SEVEN

CARAVAN

At the bottom of the cliff was a caravan of large wooden wagons and carts on wooden wheels, each hitched to a large, bulky quadruped with forelegs longer than hind legs, making its upper body higher than its lower. The quadrupeds had greenish skin striped like tigers' fur but with the texture of a Komodo dragon. Their heads, partly red, looked like blunt instruments, like elongated stones with small eyes on either side, a wide puppet mouth full of flat, masticating teeth, and no visible ears. Each stood about six or seven feet tall at the head and were maybe nine or ten feet in length, including a not long, possibly superfluous, tail.

Most of the enclosed wagons were packed with chopped wood or wild vegetation. Two of the wagons—somewhat disturbingly—were dripping blood on the hard, packed ground below, with large, black insects flying around and sauntering upon what looked like a canvas covering. None of the five doubted that those wagons were filled with the remains of their pursuer from earlier.

The carts were essentially four-wheeled cages made of closely spaced wooden bars. They contained living creatures of various kinds, some of whom were obviously insulted to be so contained, and some of whom seemed acclimated to or uncaring about their lack of freedom.

The leader of the Saurs *(we might as well dub them this, for they were obviously descended from the creatures they hunted and utilized)* shouted out commands. Several Saurs quickly emptied one of the cart cages of its living contents. They then stuffed them into the next cart cage full of various creatures, causing a momentary ruckus. The empty cart was quickly swept clean. Another command from the leader and the Saur holding onto the four PhDs and one Master's led them to the empty cart cage, gently prodding them into it.

Still following Sam's lead, no one spoke, leaving them alone with their thoughts. They were apprehensive, curious, confused, fearful thoughts—thoughts on the verge of tears, thoughts that wanted to shake, thoughts that struggled to make sense, thoughts that were calculating.

The leader, who had taken a position at the head of the caravan, gave more commands. Certain Saurs scrambled to take charge of the bulky quadrupeds; others fell behind the wagons and carts in a loose grouping. Then, the caravan moved forward along a rough road. The cart cage the five small exotic captures were in shook enough to make it prudent not to stand, so all five sat and held onto the wooden bars.

Soon, they were traveling a road that cut through the fields of grain and the orchards. They got a close-up view of the work in the field, which was being done by other Saurs—horrible-looking ones, smaller, emaciated, and exhausted. They were dressed in yellow, in what seemed to be simple pullovers that ended at the knees. Some of them were Scales, but most were Downies.

The caravan came to a stop for an unknown reason. One of the workers in the field looked up and noticed Sam and company in their cage. He stood up and gasped, grabbing the attention of the others, who all stood to gape, their eyes wide with wonder. But most of those eyes quickly returned to being downcast at the shout of a large Scale, mounted atop a beaked creature, balancing high in a bipedal stance. There were several of these mounted overseers throughout the fields, and they all looked as mean at a distance as this one did up close. One of the emaciated Downies had continued to stare at the five strange animals in the cage, and the Scale overseer, enraged, ordered his mount to lower and secure itself on its smaller forelimbs, allowing for a short drop when he jumped off and stomped over to the infringing Downy. He gave him no second chance but began to beat him viciously with a club he pulled from his belt. He may or may not have taken pleasure in the beating, but it was obvious it would only end with the death of the Downy.

John started forward as if he was going to stand and shout, but Sam grabbed his right arm and whispered, "*Don't,*" as Bertram grabbed his left. Danelle remained unmoved or pretended well. Lara averted her gaze as subtly as she could.

The caravan moved forward again, and soon they were beyond the scene and out of the fields and orchards, traveling through an uncultivated landscape that, while not lush, had no hint of the desert they had come to three or four days before—relatively speaking. Sam raised as if stretching to look ahead as the caravan curved to the right. He could see the ruined city and the river cutting through it. It was a safe assumption that this was their destination.

///

The caravan entered the city, traveling down what must have once been a central boulevard. Sam looked at the high-rise buildings they had seen from afar. Now, he thought they were not so much futuristic looking as alien. They were not made of concrete or covered with stucco, wood, or even metal. The building material seemed somewhere between plastic and ceramic and was smooth and of a piece. The tall sides of the buildings had not been constructed with many individual bricks or sections fitted together, but only a few.

The buildings were not faced in neutral colors, grey, sand, or beige, but what must have once been vibrant reds, blues, and yellows—once vibrant because now the colors were obviously faded. There were windows, some with convex glass, some open as if the glass had been broken, shattered, or removed. And huge, great chunks seemed to have been cut out of many of the buildings, leaving gaping holes through which you could see that the buildings were deserted.

But the boulevard was busy, with many Scales and Downies going about their business in what looked to be a makeshift village built along the side of the skyscrapers out of various materials. Most of which, it seemed apparent, had been torn or removed from the skyscrapers themselves. It was a marketplace—that was clear—with goods and services being offered and haggled over. But it was not a prosperous marketplace. Neither the sellers nor the buyers seemed joyful in their transactions. It was desperate commerce, with both ends of the dealmaking just trying to make do.

They all looked haggard. Their clothes were ragged. Their eyes were deep pools of resignation. Also, in the marketplace and on the street, various incogitant dinosaurs could be seen (mostly work animals, but also small ones just running through the street), dashing around market stalls, looking for, most likely, a meal.

And then there was the two-foot lizard with long legs, three-fingered arms, and smooth scales held by a Scale child accompanying a parent. A pet? Future food? No, the child was petting it, not eating it, so it was a pet.

As the caravan moved along the boulevard, the village Saurs got out of the way or stayed clear of its path, except those who noticed the wheeled cart cage with Sam and the others inside. With open mouths and wide eyes, they stopped whatever they were doing and moved forward, curiosity being a powerful force. But they were yelled at by a big caravan Saur and pushed away by other caravan Saurs, with dire warnings.

Then, the caravan stopped, and the leader came to the cart cage. He took a considering look at Sam, then John, then Danielle, then Bertram, and then finally Lara. He conferred with another Scale. They seemed to agree and were happy with the agreement, as they both smiled—a disconcerting sight for Sam and company. The leader gave orders, and the cart cage was pulled out of the caravan and taken down a narrow, dark side street, then out onto another wide street of what seemed like makeshift homes.

The day's light quickly faded, and great bonfires, spaced along the road, were lit to provide illumination and warmth. The cart cage turned to go down another street of homes, which led them to an open square about half as large as a baseball field. It was filled with cages filled with animals of many sizes and kinds; quadrupeds and bipeds, fierce and gentle, and flying creatures, with elaborate feathered or leather-looking wings, a range of beaks, and not happy attitudes.

The cart cage was directed to a large cage, empty except for a couple of small animals hiding in the dark off to one side. It was backed up to the cage's door, which an attending Downy opened. A Saur, a Scale of great bulk, who seemed to be in charge, opened the cart cage and encouraged Sam and company to vacate it for the comforts of the large cage. Still playing dumb, they did so, huddling together in the center of the cage.

The Saur looked at them, taking in these strange specimens for a moment or two. Then, he ordered the cart cage away. He stared at the five some more. Whether out of curiosity, disgust, avarice, or something genuinely alien, Sam and company would never know. Then, he turned and left.

EIGHT

A NIGHT BEHIND BARS

The last of the day's light was gone, and the five moved their huddle to the back of the cage, where they thought they would be able to talk and not be heard by the Saurs. The only illumination came from a series of bonfires in the middle of the square. Smaller fires were dotted here and there, where food was being prepared for the contingent of Saurs, who seemed to be the caretakers of what Bertram thought might be a zoo of sorts, and Sam thought was more of a holding station.

Sam and company were debating the different merits of their positions when John suddenly told them to shut up as two Saurs bearing baskets approached the cage, opened it, and walked in. They dumped the contents of their baskets—what seemed to be fruits and vegetables mixed with leaves—into the middle of the cage. A third Saur, an eight-foot Scale, entered, dragging a long, thick log, with several thick leafy branches shooting out of it. He took it over to the other two occupants of the cage, then left with the others.

Lara and John went over to the pile of food in the middle and rummaged through it, picking out what they thought was edible. While there, John noticed that the log was now occupied by the two animals, who were happily clinging to the branches. John could just make out the creatures in the weak light from the bonfires. They were not small dinosaurs, as would have been easy to assume, but rather something more like the little mammal they had seen that morning on the tree and others that had scampered along the trail. They were both fur-covered and seemed *warm*, which was the only way John could put it.

One was about three feet long, with a brown fur-covered compact body of some bulk, no tail, and a long snout of a face with beady eyes. Ridiculously, John thought it looked like one of those realistic puppets sold in Natural History museums. It was slowly picking leaves from the branches and chewing them. If it noticed John and the others, it didn't deign to acknowledge them.

The other was not more than a foot long with grey fur streaked with black lines and delicate looking with big, pointed ears and a short face dominated by large, perfectly round eyes. It had those eyes on John and seemed reluctant to take them off him. Its saucer eyes followed John as he and Lara returned with their bounty to the others. Or was it the bounty the creature was following?

John decided to test the hypothesis, tossing something that seemed to be like a large berry toward it. The little creature jumped off its branch, scurried to the berry, and grabbed it. Then it returned to its branch and began to eat the berry while keeping its two round eyes on John.

"Cute critter," John said.

"It's the big, round eyes," Bertram offered. "Activates the protective parent in you. I noticed you didn't throw any of this feast at the other one."

"He looks like he can take care of himself."

"Exactly."

Some of the food was sweet, some bitter, some pulpy, some soft, some fibrous, but all was eaten. No one had complained about being hungry while on their trek; the day had been too radical of a reality shift to make their empty stomachs of concern. But once they started eating, they ate voraciously—like the animals they were.

III

The five sat in a ragged circle after the meal, digesting, waiting to see if anything they ate would make them sick—or worse. They were all quiet with their thoughts, if they were even thinking. But how could they not have been, being the people they were? Still, a simple white noise in one's head might have been welcomed.

Lara looked to a group of Saurs beginning to bed down around a dying but still effective bonfire. "I wish we had a fire."

"Dumb animals don't use fire," Bertram said.

"But I'm cold!"

"Come here, sweetie, gather by Papa," John said.

Lara gratefully scooted over to John and his waiting arm and burrowed into him for warmth. A way off, saucer-eyes gathered in enough light to see this.

"Danielle," Sam looked down at the French woman, who had

decided to lay her head on Sam's thigh and stretch out, "I'm going to guess we didn't time travel."

Danielle adjusted herself for comfort, then looked up at Sam. "Worse. Except, if we had time-traveled, we would be dead now. How we ever thought we could have survived that forest is, you know, *au-delà de la raison*. We are all brilliant individuals. But—*évidemment*—not always smart. You should apologize to Dr. Brill, Sam."

Bertram snorted.

"What's wrong, Bertie, you think I can't apologize?"

"No, it's not that. I'm now in agreement with John. Academic designations are a bit superfluous in this here-and-now. Not that we know what *this* here-and-now is. But if you want to apologize, stop calling me Bertie."

"Well, I do apologize—Bertram. You were right. Maybe we should have gone back for our stuff."

"I appreciate that, Sam."

"This is all very civilized of you two, but I think the critical thing Danielle said was that our situation is worse than if we had time traveled," John said. "Sorry for being such an old academic, but I'm more curious about what she meant by that than thrilled that you two are kissing and making up. Something happened, or we are sharing one hell of a nightmare. You have some idea about this, haven't you, Danielle?"

"Some thoughts, John, *oui*."

"Well, let's share them, shall we?" John's authority asserted itself, and Lara adjusted her snuggle to pay attention to Danielle.

Danielle did not move. She was comfortable with her head on Sam's thigh and her eyes on the field of stars above. "Whatever we did, we did not travel through time at all. It is, I think, in one sense, still the twenty-first century, although probably not counted as such. I think our experiment altered time, changing events, possibly billions of events throughout the universe. Or maybe just one event. Maybe this twenty-first century is a time on Earth where, sixty-six or so million years ago, an asteroid did not slam into it, a gigantic cloud of smoke and debris and dust did not surround the planet, cloud the sky, and shield the sun. Vegetation did not die; the food supply was not cut off, and the climate did not become *inhospitalière*. And so, *ce qui suit?* The dinosaurs did not become extinct. This means that they've had sixty-six million years more of evolution. Certainly, that is more than enough time for one or two of their kind to evolve into bipeds, with opposable thumbs and big brains full of *cogitations complexes*."

"This would mean," Sam continued the thinking, "that mammals never got their chance to evolve into anything but secondary life on Earth. And certainly, no primates developed beyond the primitive."

"Like the ones sharing our cage," John added.

"And we—humans—never came into existence," Bertram said, almost to himself.

"Which means," John sat up straight, moving Lara to sit up, "we just wiped out over eight billion humans."

"More." Sam hated the thought but could not avoid it. "We wiped from existence every human who ever lived."

Lara leaped up, wondering how the others could remain seated. "How—how are we going to live with that?"

"Sit down," Bertram ordered, and Lara dropped to obey. "That's a useless question. The real question is, how are we going to live— period. Reality has changed, no matter how it came about. At this moment, in this world, in this existence, we are considered nothing more than caged, dumb animals. Luckily, these—these creatures who captured us, seem to consider us more curiosities than food. We can't philosophize over what happened. We must consider how to use this to our advantage."

"I agree," Sam said.

"Well, that's the first time in a long time," John declared.

"I agree, in the short term. But in the long term, we must figure out how to get back to the collider and rerun the experiment—maybe backward. We have to try to reverse what we did."

"You're kidding," Bertram said, dumbstruck.

"I am not. Despite your insistence on focusing on the here and now, I don't want to be known as the man who wiped out humanity."

"Known by whom?"

"Known by me!"

"This is now our existence!"

"No! This is not *our* existence. Think of me as a *Homo sapiens* chauvinist. We must reverse what we did."

"Sam, look around you. Sixty-six million years of further evolution and history. Why does it look like the Dark Ages out there? Have you been paying no attention? Their fuel and light come from fire. And yet this place was obviously once very advanced. These people have already had their golden age of science and technology. I built The Dark Lady; I can tell you, she takes electricity to operate—a lot of electricity."

Sam was not daunted. "Look behind you," he said, indicating something the others had their backs to.

They turned together and saw—looking down the broad boulevard at the other end of the square and off into the distance—the massive, towered structure upon the hill, glittering with a bright, steady, golden illumination.

"I don't know what's illuminating that," Sam said, "but it's not fire. It is some form of controlled power. Whatever it is, we need to get it to the collider."

Bertram turned back to Sam and shook his head in disbelief. "You're crazy! You're a complete idiot! We'll be lucky if we can ingratiate ourselves among some of these—these creatures here and lead pampered lives as glorified pets!"

NINE

THE SHINING CITY ON THE HILL

Dawn found the five a huddled mass of sleep. Lara was no longer in John's arms but in Sam's. Danielle was snuggled up to Bertram, who was snuggled up to John, who awoke to find saucer-eyes burrowed into the crook of his right arm.

"Well, hi there, little guy." John looked up to see where their other native cage mate might be and saw the beady-eyed creature clinging to his branch, staring at them with offended disapproval—or so it appeared to John.

Suddenly, the sound of wooden wheels rolling intruded upon the dawn's calm, waking the rest of the humans. They stretched and stood up. John slipped saucer-eyes into the right leg pocket of his cargo pants.

Two Scales were positioning a cart cage in front of their cage door, shouting commands to the beast pulling, or rather, at the moment, backing up the conveyance. One of the Saurs entered the big cage with food in his hands, more fruits and vegetables. He spoke to the five in the common low-pitched voice of the Scales they were now familiar with.

Although they could not understand what he was saying, he was clearly doing his best to talk to them, as one does to incogitant animals or very young children, in a cooing, coddling voice, trying to convey no threat, only a benign intent. The Saur held out the food to entice them, then started to back up toward the cart cage, hoping these five strange, previously unknown specimens of fauna would follow.

The five strange, previously unknown specimens followed, having no other choice. Their instinct was that the cooing and coddling might become harsh and harmful if they did not fulfill the tender expectations of the Saur.

The Saur was delighted with his success. Once he got to the cart cage, he quickly opened it and threw in the food. The five dashed in after the food, continuing to play the role. The Saur closed and secured the door. He then joined the other Scale at the beast, and together, they pulled it into action. The cart cage moved slowly across the square to exit along the boulevard that led to the river.

The five sat together, as far to the back of the cart as possible. John pulled saucer-eyes out of his cargo pants pocket.

"Ahhh!" Lara said, in a near silent breath.

"He adopted me. I think I'll call him Cuz."

"Why?"

"Because he's the closest relative we've got around here."

///

They were taken to a long, wide wooden pier on the river, where several large flatboat barges were moored. The cart cage was unhitched from the beast, with the five still in it, then was taken on board one of the flatboats and secured with ropes and blocks. The flatboat had already been loaded with cargo, packed in various types and sizes of receptacles. Their two minders came on board to accompany them and sat down by the cart cage, resting their backs against one large receptacle.

It was a leisurely trip along the river, and the five kept quiet and ate their breakfast, sharing some with Cuz. They took in the passing landscape, which became lush with greenery as they approached the hill upon which loomed the reflective structure—the obvious destination—they had seen from the cliff. It was hard to look at if the sun was hitting it just right, which it almost always was. The reflection stunned the eyes, forcing them down in self-preservation and the appearance of deference. But they briefly looked at it when a cloud obscured the sun. It was golden everywhere, walls and towers, and even more massive than they had perceived it from a distance.

Soon, they came to an array of docks at the foot of the hill. The flatboat was negotiated into a slip. Workers came forth, all Scales, all large, ten to twelve feet tall, and of muscular bulk and strength, as they proved when they started to unload the flatboat without the aid of tools.

The cart cage was gently moved off the flatboat and hitched to two beasts. The handlers had a quick conversation with several Scales who were dressed alike, and then one of them mounted a creature similar to the ones the overseers had ridden in the fields and rode swiftly up a wide path leading, they assumed, to the golden structure. The handlers took control of the beasts and moved the cart-cage slowly along the same route.

///

When they reached the top of the hill, they came to the open gates of the golden structure. There, they were met by a contingent of Scales uniformly dressed, carrying long spears, with swords attached to their belts and dark lenses extending down from headbands to cover their eyes. All this the five could see only through squinty, smarting eyes. As they began to pass through the gate, though, a cloud covered the sun again, and Sam looked at the side of the structure. It was covered with square panels of pounded, thin sheets of gold, attached by crude, iron nails. They were raggedy without precise meetups between panels, and the pounding had not been enough to create anything fine and smooth and attractive but rather knobby and rough.

Once through the gate, their eyes adjusted, and they could see that this was not a single structure but a great walled city. It was filled with buildings finely crafted in a gray stone, with some rising to three stories. And yet, there was an overpowering sense of space. Space dominated by an exceptionally tall, pyramidal structure in the center. There were gardens everywhere, and what they first thought were streams but soon realized were canals, flowing into large pools where Saurs (both Scales and Downies) fished, hooking and pulling up odd-looking swimmers, which delighted them.

As they moved into the city, now accompanied by soldiers, they passed an opulent and elegant marketplace selling often unrecognizable yet unmistakably luxurious wares. Most Saurs teaming about the city for business or pleasure were dressed in long, colorful robes, some encrusted with colored stones or jewels.

Sam and company noticed more females than they had seen before while trying to decide how they knew they were female, as there was no difference in dress. But there was something about them, some grace, some smoother movements, both macro and micro, that seemed to be the telling factors. And there were children in half robes, some in the care of adults who were most likely their parents, for there was a sense of affection between them. Other children were in the care of subservient adult Saurs, mostly Downies, dressed in the identical sack-like dull yellow pullovers that the workers in the fields wore. No love seemed to be lost here. The contingent of soldiers led the cart cage down the main thoroughfare. The teaming Scales and Downies along the road stopped their goings and doings and gathered along either side of the road, taking in the strange creatures. The robed ones and the yellowsacks became one in awe, fascination, and wide-opened mouths.

Some children tried to get a closer look. Those with their parents were pulled back and disciplined. The children in the care of the yellowsacks had more freedom and could only be pleaded with by their minders to return to the side of the road. One soldier took it upon himself to scare those children back, telling them something fearful in a loud voice.

They continued along the boulevard until they came to the grand pyramidal building. Its sides were terraced from the ground level up. Every other terrace was a garden, and all the remaining terraces were battlements. The walls were embedded with colored stones and nuggets of gold. At the center of ground level was a tall, wide door covered in beaten gold, which opened and released another contingent of well-armed soldiers. They quickly lined up along either side of the door.

Then, a magnificently robed Downy, about eight feet in height, emerged, followed by the Scale soldier who had carried the message up from the docks. The magnificent Downy approached the cart cage slowly for a closer look at Sam and company. His mouth did not fall open, like the mouths of the street Saurs. However, his eyes widened as much as he could let them while still maintaining dignity, for he was a creature who consciously walked with dignity and with the flow of a perfected attitude, denoting great importance, possibly coming from a great office. He took a moment to study the five, revealing nothing of his thoughts.

Then, he had the two handlers brought to him. He addressed them, and they spoke with excitement and gestures, telling a story. When they concluded, they waited in silence for a response. The magnificent Downy said nothing at first but looked at the five again, up and down, from one to another. After some time, he turned to the handlers and spoke. The handlers kept nodding until the magnificent Downy had finished, and then they clapped their hands three times in unison. The

Downy of great importance turned and walked back to the grand building's entrance, stopping to say something to one of the soldiers, who turned and ordered several under his command to stay behind.

Once the Downy and the rest of the soldiers were back inside and the door shut behind them, the remaining four soldiers lined up behind the cart cage, two-by-two, and the handlers moved to the beasts. They led them away down a narrow street parallel to one side of the grand building, the four soldiers following several steps behind.

"Quan," Danielle whispered.

"What?" Sam and Bertram both asked.

"I listened carefully. It is a strange language. But then, I suppose any language is strange if you don't understand it—except for French."

"It's a pretty stupid time for nationalism," Bertram said. It's a good time for you to explain what you mean."

"Quan?"

"Yes?"

"It was the most repeated word."

"Ah."

"Significant, I think."

"Unless it's a verbal punctuation mark," Sam said, "or something like the Japanese *so desu ne,* which they pepper a lot in normal conversation."

"*Possible.* But I think not. The word had weight. And it was said with a certain reverence."

"I didn't get any of that," Lara said.

"Of course not, *ma chérie*, it comes from experience."

"Hey!"

"Stupid time, you guys," Bertram admonished again.

John looked down at the furry, saucer-eyed critter in his lap, happily munching on leftover breakfast. "What do you think of your cousins there, Cuz?"

TEN

THE LIGHT AT THE END OF THE CORRIDOR

Just before they came to what the five assumed was the rear of the building, the handlers stopped the beasts before a plain door. One stayed with the beasts, while the other went to the rear of the cart cage and opened it up after the soldiers had placed themselves in a semi-circle around the back. The handler addressed the soldiers in a quiet voice, then turned to Sam and company and made a simple, non-threatening gesture that could only have meant that the five should come out. They did so, knowing this was the only course to take. The soldiers closed ranks around them, cutting off any path of escape.

The handler reached out, took Sam's hand, and led him to the door. Sam quickly grabbed Danielle's hand, and Danielle grabbed Bertram's hand. He grabbed John's hand, and John grabbed Lara's, and they all followed in this chain. In viewing this, one of the soldiers made a vocalization that, to the humans, sounded every bit like a chuckle or possibly a giggle. But it certainly couldn't have been that.

The door was opened, revealing a long, narrow, dark corridor. The Saur handler led them along it, the soldiers following. At the end was another door. The handler made a sudden, loud growl of a sound, announcing them, the five assumed. After a moment, the door opened, and light—artificial light—streamed into the corridor. A Downy, in a simple, colorless, unadorned robe, stood there, at first annoyed, then quickly amazed once he caught a glimpse of Sam and the others behind him. The handler pushed his way in, bringing along his contingent, as the Downy backed up into the room.

The room was high-ceilinged, spacious, and cluttered with books, what seemed to be various instruments of possible utilitarian value, and charts and maps that were laid out on tables and pinned to walls where wall space was available. Where it wasn't, tall cases of cubbyholes took up the space. The cubbyholes were filled with rolled-up papers and stacks of books.

As they were led into the center of the room, Sam glanced at an open book on a table. It was larger than what the five would consider a normal book, with a long rectangular shape bound on one of the long sides. The pages were covered with markings and illustrations.

There was another Downy in the room, similarly dressed, but there was an obvious contrast between the two. The first Downy was the elder. How they perceived this was a mystery. Maybe it was because he was bulkier than the other. Maybe it was because his down did not seem as…fresh? Smooth? Thick? Maybe it was his air of both authority and irritation.

The Scale handler spoke to the elder, giving him instructions. The elder seemed to only half-listen, as his eyes never left the five. He suddenly burst out in objections, but the handler stood his ground well, being conveniently backed up by the soldiers. The elder seemed to sigh and acquiesce. Then, the handler and the soldiers left, leaving Sam and company with the two Downies.

The elder stood back from the five, who gathered themselves in a line-up. The younger was free with his amazement, letting his mouth gape open and his eyes widen not just with awe but with curiosity and excitement. He very gingerly moved toward the five. The elder at first seemed to caution the younger, then seemed to encourage him. The younger moved forward, coming up to John. John smiled, showing teeth, which made the younger recoil slightly.

But as the smile did not lead to any further aggression, the younger moved forward again, and reached out to touch John on the chest, laying his hand flat against it. John did not recoil. Then, the younger moved his hand up to John's face and was taken aback by his scratchy whiskers. A soft sound came from beneath John. The younger looked down and saw Cuz poke his head out of John's cargo pants pocket.

John reached down and took Cuz out of the pocket and brought him up. The younger found no delight in Cuz and tried to take him away, but John protested by holding harder onto Cuz and going, *"Uh-uh!"* exactly as his Uncle Ray had done when he was very young, and his uncle had caught him sucking his thumb. That memory flooded John's brain and turned a surreal situation somewhat sad. But the younger seemed delighted to see the bond between John and Cuz. He turned to the elder and commented on it. The elder, bolder now, moved forward and went to the next one in line, who was Lara.

Lara took in a deep breath of fear. Danielle, who was standing next to her, took her hand and squeezed. The younger turned to Lara and looked closely at her face, then stroked it, confirming the report of his eyes. He started to talk rapidly to the elder and had him touch John's face, then Lara's, for a bit of compare and contrast. The elder became fascinated with what he took to be Lara's hide, but which he soon realized were unnatural coverings. He pulled at them rather crudely to get them off. Lara screamed and flew into John's arms, disconcerting Cuz, who climbed onto John's shoulders.

"Oh, come on!" Danielle broke their silence pact impatiently and loudly. "They are obviously scientists of some kind, *érudits* at least. *Mon dieu*, let them investigate." She casually began to strip. "They're our kind of people. Cooperation may lead to communication. It is our best hope." Once fully naked, she opened her arms to the Saurs and addressed them. "Come on, *messieurs*. *Un regard*. If you're like everyone else who has, you'll fall in love!"

The elder and the younger, both stunned (but not over Danielle's nakedness), turned to each other, neither being able to speak.

So, Sam spoke. "Yes. We can talk. We are intelligent, as I hope to hell you are."

The younger burst into excited chatter at the elder, then turned to Sam and chattered at him, wanting so desperately to communicate. The elder was desperate in another way, desperate to have his sane, comfortable assumptions restored. In a panic, he pulled the younger away from the five and admonished him. The younger put on a good display of reasoning, but the elder would not have it.

They talked back and forth for quite a while. Danielle noticed, then pointed out to the others, that the word or sound of *"Quan"* was heard frequently again. Finally, the elder forcefully stopped the conversation, then seemed to strongly lay down the law to the younger. The younger stepped back and quickly clapped three times. Satisfied, the elder turned and headed toward the door, moving rapidly.

"Hey, wait!" John yelled out after the elder.

The elder stopped and turned back to the five. He had not, of course, understood John. And yet, John's intent was not a mystery to him.

John took the opening and slowly walked to the elder, speaking calmly. "Look, we're not dangerous. We are rational, thinking creatures like…like you."

John gestured toward the elder, and the elder moved back half a step.

"Look…" John turned and surveyed the room, then headed to a table, passing Danielle, who still stood unselfconsciously naked. "Maybe you ought to at least put your shirt on, *Dr. Dorlac,*" John whispered to her in passing.

Danielle did so, slipping her pants on as well.

John arrived at the table, which was covered with documents, maps, writing paper, what looked like crude pencils, and books. There was also a big bowl of the fruits and vegetables they had become familiar with. He placed Cuz on the table, giving him a small fruit to occupy his attention. Then, he carefully and with respect, moved the books and papers to the sides of the table, stacking them as neatly as he could, retaining one sheet of blank paper and one of the pencils.

He placed the paper on the cleared surface and briefly wrote on it. Finished, he turned and addressed his companions. "We always said that if we ran across aliens, our common language would be math. So, let's try this—something simple." He held up the paper. On it, he had written **2+2=4** in bold, thick lines.

"Yes," Bertram said, "But it's not likely they would know our Arabic numerals. We need to be even simpler." Bertram went over to the table and pulled several items from the bowl. He laid out two round edibles, two cylindrical ones, and then four of the mix.

The two Saurs had come forward, curious as to what this strange life form was doing. When Bertram turned around, he was almost face-to-face with them.

"Oh! Good. Look," he addressed them. "Two…" He picked up two of the edibles and presented them to the Saurs. "Uh…" He turned to his companions. "What are these, apples?"

"Just call them round," Sam suggested.

"Right." He held them again in front of the faces of the Saurs. "Two round fruits," he placed them side-by-side on the table. "Plus two," he picked up two of the long ones, "uh, cylindrical fruits—"

"They could be vegetables."

"John, please…" Bertram chided, then turned his attention back to the Saurs. "Two round fruits *plus* two cylindrical fruits…" He placed them down, a little off from the round ones. "*Equals* four…" He grabbed the remaining four fruits, two of each kind, and gathered them together about a foot to the right of the two plus two. "Fruits!"

Then he grabbed John's piece of paper and showed the calculation to the Saurs, pointing to each digit and symbol as he enumerated, "You see, two *plus* two *equals* four."

The Downies, both elder and younger, looked at the markings on the paper, then at Bertram's arrangement of fruits, and then back to the paper. The younger got it first and started to nod his head vigorously. He rapidly began to talk to Bertram as if he would be understood.

Bertram just nodded his head in return.

The elder gasped, possibly in wonder, but it sounded more like fear. He grabbed the younger and pulled him away from Bertram, talking to him as he had before, with admonishment, warning, and strict commandments. He put his hand over the younger's mouth and held it there tightly for a moment. He spoke harshly one last time. The younger stepped back, stood straight up, and clapped three quick times. Satisfied, the elder gave Sam and company one last, not-happy, not-friendly look, then left through the door.

This seemed to bring great relief to the younger, who turned to the five and gave them a very happy and very friendly look. He looked them over from head to toe, allowing the full force of wonder to delight him. But this was no time for glee—first things first.

He walked up to Sam, pointed to himself, and said, "Lodak—Lodak."

"Lodak," Sam repeated, pointing to the young Downy. Then, he pointed to himself. "Sam."

"Saammmm."

Then the others introduced themselves.

"Danielle."

"Dan-el."

"Lara."

"La-ra."

"John."

"Jaa-on."

"Bertram."

"Bert-rie."

All but Bertram laughed, which fascinated Lodak.

"No, Lodak—Bert-*ram*."

"Bert-*ram*."

Bertram smiled.

Lodak smiled. Then he made a face, an awful face. He tried to explain, but their communication was still too rudimentary to convey his message. Deciding to rely on body language, Lodak stuck two fingers into his nostrils.

"I think he's telling us we need a bath," Danielle said.

"Oh, God, yes!" Lara exclaimed.

ELEVEN

BATH TIME

Lodak gestured to them to follow as he moved to one of the tall cases of cubbyholes. Taking a firm grip on it, he slid it to the right, revealing a dark corridor. They traveled the corridor only a short distance but long enough for them to perceive other connecting corridors, equally dark.

Then, Lodak turned them to the right into another corridor, which ended abruptly. He opened a door and ushered them into a large room with a square pool in the center. The room was lit naturally via shafts of light that descended from several circular openings in the high ceiling. On shelves, there were various implements of cleaning and glass jars containing powders, oils, and liquids. Off to one side, a six-foot-wide stream of water poured out of a slit in the wall about twelve feet high and descended like a waterfall into a twelve-by-twelve depression in the floor and drained away.

Lodak worked hard to make them understand that they should use the waterfall to wet themselves and the stuff in the jars to clean themselves before they could relax in the pool. Once he was convinced they understood, he gestured that he would leave now but that he would soon return.

Sam nodded and did his best to let Lodak know that they understood, but he wasn't sure that Lodak did understand. So, he stood up straight and quickly clapped three times.

Lodak was delighted and he confidently left by another door to another corridor.

"Very *Japonais*," Danielle said, looking over the situation.

"Huh?" Lara asked.

"Have you never been to Japan, *ma chérie*?"

"I've never been anywhere but home in Ohio and Caltech in Pasadena."

"And here," John said, "here in a whole other world. I think that qualifies you for being well-traveled. Well, let's get to it." John began to strip.

"All of us? Together?" Lara asked nervously.

"Well…" John was down to his underwear. "We've already seen Danielle as her mother first saw her."

"Actually," Bertram started to unbutton his shirt, "she probably first saw her in swaddling clothes."

"Bertram, do you always have to be so technical?" Sam started with his shoes and pants.

Danielle began undressing again. "I should have just stayed naked."

Soon all except Lara and Cuz (who snuggled himself into the pile of John's clothes) were enjoying the waterfall, which the four found to be warm but not hot. Danielle had brought over a jar of powder and it proved to be a kind of soap. A not particularly fine-smelling soap, but it did generate a bit of lather. She also brought over what looked like scrapers, something like the ancient Romans had used in their communal baths, but these had very small fine teeth. Nevertheless, they seemed to remove the grime.

Lara did not join them. She occupied herself looking around the bath, keeping her eyes away from the pool.

The others were now using the scrapers on each other's backs.

"How simian of us," John said.

Lara heard the sounds of the four leaving the waterfall *(the return of a steady flow rather than the chaos of interrupted flow)* and entering the pool *(splashes from subtle to extreme)*.

"La-ra?" Danielle's chiding/kidding/pleading voice came through after the four settled down into the warm water. "La-Ra come on. It is *magnifique*. You are the one who so wanted a bath."

"Well…"

"You are going to be so envious of our squeaky-clean skins and fresh scents."

"Um, maybe after you guys are done?"

"I can never get used to *les Américains puritan*."

"I'm not a puritan! Just—just shy."

"Lara," John said, "we five seem to be the only humans in all of this existence—what is there to be shy about?"

"Well—cover your eyes, then."

"You are kidding, are you not?" The femme from Paris wanted to know.

"We will, Lara, we promise," Sam said.

Lara slowly turned and saw that all the men had complied. But Danielle stood up in the bath, proudly female, with her arms akimbo. "I am not covering my eyes."

"Well, okay—you're a girl."

Lara removed her clothes, entered the waterfall, and was delighted by it. She luxuriated in the flow, the soap, the scraper, the washing of her hair. Then, she joined the others in the pool and sunk down to her neck.

Danielle, who had watched Lara with a certain amusement said, "Ma *chérie*, you have nothing to be shy about."

Lara smiled. Whether from the bath or from the complement is unknown.

"Can we uncover our eyes now?" John asked.

Lara, now accepting the situation and how silly she had been, splashed John and laughed at her action. John splashed her back, Danielle splashed Sam, who retaliated, and then laughter and splashing went all around, excluding Bertram, who moved as far away from the others as possible and wondered with no delight over how frivolous humans could be when anything but was called for.

For the others, though, tensions were released, and the respite was enjoyed.

III

Later, relaxed, they sat in the pool leaning against edges, each having thoughts they were keeping to themselves—until Bertram spoke.

"It's all that movie star's fault."

"*Quelle?*" Danielle said it for all of them.

"You know that movie star you hang around with," Bertram addressed Sam, "who has this 'great interest in science'."

"Xander Fitzgerald."

"Yes, that's the one."

"A good friend. Very smart."

"You only think that because he always agrees with you."

"He always agrees with me because he's very smart."

"Boys…," their former mentor admonished.

"*Oui, continuez*, Bertram. What do you mean?

"Well, if pretty boy Xander hadn't called the president of the United

61

States, supporting Sam's application, I would have successfully turned it down for the fourth time. And right now, you would be sitting in some café in Paris, no doubt. Sam would be sitting in his office, spinning his empty theories. Lara would be sitting by his side, mooning over him—"

"Hey!" Lara's cheeks—the visible ones—reddened.

"And John would be sitting at lunch with the president of Caltech. Instead, you are all sitting here together in a damn big bathtub, and so am I, while I should be sitting at my desk in The Dark Lady, happily overseeing some real science."

"Yeah, overseeing but not doing," Sam said.

"You don't know that."

"John, do you recall any major papers authored by Bert here in a while?"

"It's easy to be prolific when all you've got are theories." Bertram defended himself.

"Bertram, that's why Sam needed the collider—to test the theory."

"*Oh, tais-toi, hommes stupides!* Do you think any of that matters now?"

Lodak entered and expressed satisfaction that they had bathed. He was followed by two thin yellowsack females, their heads down in subservience. One carried a stack of plain Saur robes, and the other carried a stack of something for them to dry off with.

Once they were out of the tub and dried, the two yellowsacks started measuring them head to toe while never once meeting their eyes. Then they were allowed to put on the greatly oversized robes. But the yellowsacks quickly began pinning them up here and there until the five could walk with some grace and no fear of tripping.

As they started putting their shoes back on, Lodak shouted a command to the yellowsacks, and they snatched the shoes from the humans' hands. It was startling and not a little bit scary.

"Maybe so we don't run away?" John posed the theory.

"I don't think so," Lara said. "Look how they are looking at them—so intently."

"Well, they are curiosities to them. Until this moment, I hadn't even noticed that they don't wear shoes." Sam said.

"Who would if your feet were tough enough?" John asked.

"Well, ours aren't, so we need them back," Bertram said.

"Okay, Bertie. You attack Lodak, and the rest of us will subdue the slaves."

Somehow, the use of the word *slaves* sobered them beyond a concern for their shoes. But there was no time to think about that, as Lodak was questioning the yellowsacks loudly. One looked to the other with a silent question, then looked up to Lodak and said something to him that was satisfactory.

John turned away from this scene and gathered Cuz. He petted the small creature before returning to his companions.

Lodak called Sam and company to follow him, then led them out of the bathing room and down another dark corridor. The cold stone floor was uncomfortable but not dangerous to their bare feet. Eventually, they found themselves in a large, open room covered in bed-sized cushions and centered with a big, round, low table laden not only with fruits and vegetables but also cooked meat.

"I hope we can digest it," Bertram worried.

"I am willing to try," Danielle said as she picked up what may have been a rib and began to gnaw. The others followed, even Bertram.

"I wonder what we're eating," Lara said between bites.

"Well, I hope it's not one of Cuz's cousins," John nodded to the little creature munching on a piece of fruit and looking at the five—they all would have sworn—in a somewhat askance way.

"*Idiot végétarien!*" Danielle said with a smile.

Lodak addressed them gently as if he were saying, "Eat, sleep, I'll see you in the morning." And who's to say he was not?

TWELVE

QUAN

Shafts of natural light streamed down from the ceiling, just waking up the five when Lodak and the elder burst into the room. They were followed by the two thin yellowsack females, carrying stacks of clothes, still keeping their eyes on the ground. The five stood, naturally apprehensive but just as naturally curious in anticipation.

Lodak spoke briefly to the elder, then pointed to each of the humans in turn and named them for the elder's benefit. "Saammmm, Dan-el, La-ra, Jaa-on, Bert-ram." Addressing the five, he then introduced them to " Cornar—Cornar."

"Hi, Cornar!" John said jauntily.

"*Bonjour.*"

"Good morning, Cornar," Lara said.

"Thank you for your hospitality," Bertram said.

"Yes, good morning, and thank you." Sam was cut off when Cornar's large hand was slapped across his mouth.

The Saur was not impressed by this display of civility and was, in fact, greatly disturbed by it. He spoke severely, gestured with his free hand wildly, and stomped his left foot several times. Then, staring down deeply into Sam's eyes, he slowly removed his hand.

"Okay," Sam said and shook his head, "no talking." Then he clapped three times quickly.

"Why not?" John wanted to know.

Cornar turned on John rapidly and slapped his hand over John's mouth.

"Okay, okay," John muffled out, "no talking."

Satisfied, Cornar released his hand. He turned to Lodak and gave instructions in terms the five could not understand but were no less certain for that. Lodak stood up straight and clapped three quick claps. Cornar, dressed in a deep black robe with four golden bands encircling the upper arms, slapped his hand across his own mouth, looked deeply at each one of the five in turn, and then left.

Lodak, also dressed in a deep black robe, but with only two golden bands, closed his eyes for a moment, and sighed a Saur sigh. Then, he ordered the yellowsacks to give the clothes to the five and indicated that they should change into them.

The multicolored robes, with various sizes of circles throughout, fit each of the five perfectly. There were no undergarments, which allowed for a certain freedom that Danielle was used to. This was liberating for the men and embarrassing for Lara. But even Lara had to admit that they all looked rather handsome in their robes.

A male yellowsack entered, carrying a large box, which he set down before Lodak. Lodak reached in, pulled out a pair of what looked like booties made of some strange material, and looked them over. He handed them back to the yellowsack and pointed to Sam. The yellowsack hurried over and dropped to his knees before Sam, lifting Sam's leg and putting one of the booties on his foot, then repeating the action with the other leg.

"They're warm," Sam said with surprise.

The yellowsack then began what Sam thought at first was a foot massage. But he soon realized that the yellowsack was molding the bootie to Sam's foot, all the while blowing on it as if to cool it, then repeating his actions with Sam's other foot. When the yellowsack was done, Sam leaned against a table, lifted one foot, and examined his new footwear.

"It's soft, yet seems tough—durable, I'm guessing."

"Yeah, but are they comfortable," John wanted to know.

Sam stood upright and walked around. "Yes! Like walking barefoot, yet I feel support."

Soon, the others were also happily well-shod

III

Lodak escorted them through corridors and out of the building. They found themselves standing before another wide boulevard crowded with Saurs, both Scales and Downies. Right before them was what they later came to call a street barge resting on the shoulders of four large, yellowsack-dressed Scales. There were five seats on the barge, and it was colorfully decorated with flowers and leaves. The barge was surrounded by soldiers holding back the crowd and a group of very grand-looking Scales, all topping ten feet, in jeweled robes.

Lodak led the five to the side of the barge, where a twelve-foot soldier stood at attention. Lodak said something to him and he preceded, one by one, to grab the five, lift them high, and place them on the barge. Unfortunately, Lara was the first one he grabbed, and she screamed in shock and surprise.

Danielle stepped forward to go next and quickly got to Lara, coming up close and whispering, "Are you okay?"

"Yes, fine," Lara whispered back. "Kind of fun—like a thrill ride." She laughed a small laugh.

Danielle gave her a subtle smile and gentle pats on her head.

The three men were elevated and joined them. Once they were seated, orders were shouted, and the street barge moved forward. They soon realized that they were part of a grand procession—a parade through the city—on display, so the populace could get a good look at them.

And the five got a good look at the city. Which seemed like a paradise, especially compared to the ruined city where they had spent their first night. The Saurs that lined the various boulevards and streets they traveled, Downies and Scales alike, seemed prosperous and satisfied—maybe self-satisfied—and looked upon the five as delightful curiosities. But way back in the crowds, and poking out of some doorways and windows, spots of yellow could be seen. How satisfied they were, the five had no way of knowing.

III

It had been Sam's experience that when any institution—churches, universities, corporations, governments, the gilded rich—wanted to impress, they often did it with greatly oversized buildings, with at least one public area or space (for 'space' was the operative word), voluminous in scope, as presented before you and behind you, and to your right and to your left, and also, most importantly, above you, with very high, often vaulting—not to mention vaunting—ceilings. The reason for this, although never admitted by the institutions or individuals, is to make the average feel not just average but small. Average can always be debated, but small is small, and there is no room for contention about it. By contrast, this made the institutions and individuals well above average and large, thus superior, and graced by a god or intelligence or fortune, or—rightness. All of which, in the minds of the institutions and individuals, was proof positive of their own feelings on the matter.

The central building of Saur city, the hub of everything, was certainly oversized to Sam and company. How could it not be, as it had to accommodate creatures so much larger than they? But after their circuit of the city, as they were taken into the pyramidal building—still carried on the street barge—it was easy to see that it was grandly oversized for the Saurs themselves.

They entered a massive hallway with floor, walls, and ceiling decorated with colorful, abstract shapes. The five noticed immediately that the shapes seemed to be made of the same material that fronted the buildings in the ruined city. There was a contingent of Scale soldiers lining either side of the path through the hallway, and every sixth soldier along the way shouted out the same statement, the word *"Quan"* prominent among the words the five did not understand. The shouters were, of course, heralds, sending the message of the procession's arrival down the line, all done with voice. No horns or any musical instruments were seen or heard. They were hardly necessary. The voices of the Scales were loud and melodious, and the hallway was a perfect echo chamber, so the first herald's shout was just on its last echo when the next designated herald raised his voice, continuing the announcement like a series of progressive waves.

They came to the end of the hallway and entered a vastly greater space. It was crowded with elegantly-robed elite. The majority of them were Scales, but there were also a not small number of Downies. The space was rectangular with a curved ceiling, higher than the hallway's, which was all of one piece, with no evidence of pillars or beams supporting it. There were a series of openings in the ceiling and shafts of natural light descended from them, illuminating the floor and those standing on it. But that illumination flowed only weakly to the sides, giving the illusion of ethereal walls somewhere off in the shadows.

There was one other beam of light coming from the ceiling. It did not descend straight down as all the others did but at an angle directed to the far end of the space. It was brighter than the other beams, obviously not natural, and illuminated a massive individual sitting on a high throne, dressed in a robe sparkling with colored stones and spots of golden reflections. As the procession got closer and closer, this individual loomed larger and larger. Even sitting, the five could tell that this Scale was the largest Saur they had yet seen. A male, he must have been fifteen feet tall, with an enormous head that rested on colossal shoulders. His face was passive, but his eyes were lively with interest, and followed the procession until it stopped. He scrutinized the five on the barge as the yellowsack bearers lifted it up and placed it on a large wooden block about eight feet high.

Two Saurs stood upfront before the high throne, facing the barge. One was the magnificent Downy of great importance, who had greeted them at the foot of the pyramidal building the day before. And the other was Cornar, in his black robe with the five gold bands along the upper arm. Cornar stepped forward, then turned, and, looking up to the massive individual as if looking up to heaven, he gave an address. He delivered it in a singsong, declarative voice, accompanied by many elaborate gestures, some of which referred to the five, some of which seemed to refer to himself. But most of which referred to the massive individual, always punctuated by the word, "Quan."

So, this was Quan. Officially, the Great Quan, Sam and company later learned. The king, or ruler, or despot, or 'god' of this land. He was undeniably impressive. And unnervingly frightening.

As Cornar continued to drone on, Sam caught a glimpse of Lodak off to the side. He could not hide from his face that he was unhappy with what Cornar was saying, nor a strong opinion that his elder was a pompous old windbag.

Beyond Lodak, something else caught Sam's eye, something sitting in a shadow to the side of the throne. It was a block of some material, with an indentation in the top—unless that was another shadow as well? It was hard to tell. On the floor below it, something caught what light it could and glistened, something wet. Despite Cornar's drone, which reverberated throughout this great space, Sam could just make out the very small sound of buzzing.

Finally, Cornar finished, and the Great Quan stood and slowly walked down several steps to the barge on its pedestal. It was like a damn Macy's parade balloon floating their way, Sam thought, with the passive face in the huge head dominating. Then it arrived, and that face had to be faced. It looked closely at them. The Great Quan's head tilted to its right, his eyes squinted, then widened, and then the head returned to an upright position. Slowly, the sides of the Great Quan's mouth rose, and soon, a huge smile sat on his face. He reached out to the five, singling out Danielle to pet. Danielle stood still, unflinching, then smiled herself and started to coo.

"Ha!" the Great Quan exclaimed, then said something to the assembled elite that must have been witty as they laughed heartily *en masse*. Then he called some of them up to the barge, offering closer looks at the five anomalies of life, the five previously unknown specimens, and the five latest delights in the Great Quan's collection.

Lodak could take it no longer and shouted out. It was immediately evident that he had breached a great matter of courtly etiquette, for the assembled was shocked; gasps and high-pitched squeals of offense echoed around the space. He, a mere assistant, a server to one higher, had spoken without being invited to, rising above his station, causing consternation to the Great Quan, who turned to stare at this little Downy with only two bands on his robe. But Lodak continued to speak, to explain. Cornar rushed to him and tried to shut him up, but Lodak would have none of it, pushing Cornar away violently as he continued to speak.

With furious rage, the Great Quan screamed out a command. Several soldiers rushed to Lodak, grabbed and dragged him to the block in the shadows. It was suddenly illuminated by another beam of artificial light, which showed the wet to be a bright red. Lodak was picked up and slammed down to the ground; then, his head was positioned on the block. A burly Scale came forward out of a shadow and raised an immense blade over Lodak's neck with both hands.

John lurched forward, but Sam grabbed and held him back while shouting "Stop!" to the assembled.

And the executioner did, as did everyone.

Sam leaped off the barge and fell hard on the floor, but he rolled with it and got up and over to Lodak. "Why are you killing him? I don't care what society it is; a good mind is a terrible thing to waste."

Cornar turned to the Great Quan and addressed him rapidly, but the Great Quan cut him off with an angry shout and smacked him across the face, knocking the Downy to the floor. Then, he said something to the executioner, who quickly got Lodak onto his feet and brought him to the Great Quan. Lodak looked up and waited. In a measured, almost quiet voice, the Great Quan talked to Lodak, mentioning Cornar, seemingly seeking truth.

Lodak answered with a calm, if still shaky, voice.

The Great Quan flared angrily and turned to Cornar, shooting a condemning hand at him. Soldiers gathered Cornar up, ran him to the block, and kicked his legs out from under him. They slammed his head on the block, and the executioner severed it with a swift cut. The head rolled a bit before coming to a rest.

The only sound was an anguished squeal from Lara, which caught the Great Quan's attention. He turned to the four on the barge and talked to them quietly.

"I wish we could understand you," John addressed him, "but we can't. And I wish I could ask you why it was necessary to kill that man."

"John, don't be naive," Bertram said.

Danielle came up to John and placed a hand on his shoulder. "John, this—this—" She turned and looked straight at the massive creature before her. "Quan?"

The Great Quan was delighted to hear his name come from such small lips. He turned to the assembled elite and smiled to share his delight, and they shared it, acknowledging how wondrous it was.

"I think the Quan is a near god to these people, John. It would be best not to question him—even in a language he does not comprehend."

The Great Quan listened closely to Danielle and was amused by her verbal abilities but seemed frustrated that he could not understand. He turned to Lodak and spoke briefly but pointedly. Lodak stood up straight and clapped three times quickly. The great Quan then shouted out loudly into the air, and shortly, the magnificent Downy of great importance came forward, bearing the folded black robe with five golden bands on the arms and only a little blood stain around the collar. The Saur of great importance seemed to apologize for this as he handed it to Lodak.

Lodak looked up at the Great Quan, then bowed his head. The Great Quan returned to his throne, sat, and waved for whatever was next.

Lodak said something sharply to a soldier nearby, who immediately ordered the barge off the block and set down on the ground. Lodak called Sam, still by the executioner's block, over and gestured for Danielle, Lara, John, and Bertram to step off the barge. He then led all five out of the great space.

THIRTEEN

BACK TO SCHOOL

Without leaving the pyramidal building or traveling through a labyrinth of dark corridors, Lodak led the five back to their communal room. Cuz, who had been left alone, jumped immediately into John's arms, then scurried onto his shoulders.

As the five gathered around the central table, which had been laid with fresh food, Lodak began to pace. Agitated and excited, confident and anxious, happy and fearful, he rapidly spoke to himself through a mutter that would have masked what he was saying, even if the five could have understood him. It was amusing to watch, and Sam and Danielle chuckled as they started to eat. Bertram was more interested than amused, and he also began to eat.

John and Lara stood there with their mouths open, but not to receive food.

"How can you guys eat?" John asked, perplexed. "We just witnessed an execution, a murder, a beheading?"

"It was horrible!"

"So is my hunger," Danielle said. "I wish they made bread. Do you think we can teach them?"

"Yes," Sam addressed Lara, "it was horrible but—"

"But at least it wasn't one of us," Bertram interrupted.

"Or Lodak." Sam filled his statement with meaning. "Who may become very important to us. I doubt that Cornar would have been."

"But he was still a—a person," John protested.

Sam looked at John and considered what he had said. He wondered how to answer John's strange concept.

"Here, let me help." Lara moved over to Lodak, who had stopped pacing and was now naked. He was trying to put on the black robe with the five gold bands, but he had gotten caught up in one sleeve. Lara grabbed the garment, assessed the situation, and straightened it out. Soon, Lodak was fully clothed and looking quite pleased.

"Cunie," Lodak said to Lara.

"You're welcome," she replied reflexively.

They looked at each other, realizing together and sharing the delight of having just communicated. Lodak was thrown into quick thinking. He looked around the room—looking, looking—then spotted Cuz on John's shoulders. He rushed over to John and Cuz and pointed to the little creature. "Skeen."

"Skeen?" John questioned.

"Skeen," Lodak confirmed.

"Cuz is a skeen," John announced proudly to the others.

Lodak was pleased and tapped his chest three times quickly. He went to the table and picked up one of the fruits or vegetables. "Stoll—stoll," he said while holding the item up high.

Sam took it from Lodak and repeated, "Stoll."

Lodak smiled and tapped his chest again three times.

Then Sam gathered up two other items from the table, held all three in the palms of his hands, and questioned, "Stoll?"

Lodak ran his hand from left to right over his chest once, which clearly meant no. He took the three from Sam and held them up one at a time. "Stoll—carlex—fordar." Then he placed all three back on the table in a close group and waved his hand over them all, saying, "Potan—potan."

Sam nodded, then separated the potans and pointed to each sequentially. "Stoll—carlex—fordar." He pushed them back together, waved his hand over them, and said, "Potan."

This time, Lodak slapped his chest three times quickly. He seemed gleeful as he picked up two other items from the table. Holding up one, he said, "Glan." Then, holding up the other, he said, "Ormon." Then, putting them together, he said, "Keepnar."

Sam turned to the others. "Okay, everybody, all together now." He pointed to individual items and led a human chorus: "Glan and ormon are keepnar; stoll, carlax, and fordar are potan."

Lodak, refusing to contain his delight, drummed upon his chest.

"Kids," Sam said, "I think we're going back to school."

///

The whole city became their classroom.

First, they learned the city's name was Quannak, the equivalent of a city name like Jacksonville. "Or more to the point, I think, Alexandria," Bertram said to no argument.

Their communal room also served as their classroom, where they sat in tailored, non-ceremonial brown robes under the tutorship of several young Downies that Lodak had brought in. They may have been teachers of young children, for they used props and crude illustrations that they drew on the spot—and after using, immediately destroyed by fire—to teach Sam and company individual words, concepts, and eventually sentences and paragraphs. But, towards the end of each day, Lodak would arrive, and he and the tutors would take them on a field trip throughout Quannak, filling their heads with words and words while showing the five the objects, the animals, the substances, and the situations those words named. Over months of this daily routine, they became more and more confident in the language of the Saurs—and increasingly hirsute.

There was no word for shaving as the Saurs did not shave, so there were no shaving instruments. The men's beards quickly went from stubble to full to ridiculously long, and their hair kept apace. The women had no real facial changes—neither had been radical eyebrow-pluckers—but their legs and underarms became rather furry. Danielle lived with this with equanimity; Lara was disgusted daily. The longer the hair on their heads grew, the harder it was to maintain and the more annoying it became. They could wash it, of course, but as there did not exist in this world, as far as they could discover, combs and brushes, and as the slightly combed bath scraper proved to be of no use, their hair became unruly and often matted messes. Lodak, the tutors, and the citizens of Quannak who spied the five on their daily field trips were all fascinated by this continuing growth. However, as it did not seem to diminish the five's health, they all just took it as the alien phenomenon that it was.

Their study of the Saur's language and the field trips also gave them an education in the culture of the Saurs. Or, at least, of the Saurs living in Quannak. They saw commerce in the marketplace, amusements in the streets, and familial love and affection in the elegant homes they were taken to. They saw showing off and primping and the Saurs' great concern with robes and the wearing of them. They saw contests of strength and skill, most edged with violence. They heard laughter and angry voices, calm conversations, and agitated arguments. And always and everywhere, there were yellowsacks, both Scales and Downies, tending to, picking up after, serving the needs of all, slight of frame with eyes cast down and quiet, always so silent.

Being trained observers, they did not just see all of this; they took note, contemplated, analyzed, and talked about their findings among themselves in the evenings when they had been left alone to have their meal.

"The field trips have been good. Much to *apprendre* beyond language. How else would we have learned that they make bread?"

"Not very good bread," Lara said.

"*Oui*, it is hard, *grossier*, and so far, we have found no *fromage* to go with it."

"You have this annoying obsession with food."

"I am French, Bertram."

"You are French, and there is no longer a France."

"As long as I am alive, France exists."

"Christ!" Bertram exclaimed.

"You know, that's something I've noticed," John said. They don't seem to have any religion. At least, we've seen nothing resembling churches, priests, icons, or reverent ceremonies."

"Would we be privileged to them if there were?" Bertram asked.

"Well, possibly not. But you would think we would see some evidence."

"The Great Quan *est leur dieu*. I've thought so from that first audience."

"But where does he get his authority?" Lara asked. "I mean, in societies such as this, you know, primitive, the ruler—kings, emperors, despots—usually claim some grant of authority from something larger than themselves, a god or gods. Otherwise, what makes him so special?"

"Well, he's larger than everyone else."

"No, seriously, John, it's something to think about."

"What you are forgetting is that this 'primitive' society," Bertram said, "is part of a dark age, obviously from the evidence of the ruined city, that follows what may have been millions of years of civilizations. They may have gone through their—supernatural stage, for lack of a better word—eons ago."

"What you are all forgetting," Sam, who had been silent all evening, as he was most evenings, spoke up, "is that the only thing truly interesting about this place is that they seem to have some form of energy. How else do you explain the artificial light? And how do you explain that the artificial light is only seen in the great throne room, in Lodak's study, and illuminating the outside of the city walls at night? Otherwise, it's just natural light or fire. That's what we must find out. That's what we must get our hands on. Everything else is completely superfluous to our mission."

"*Our mission?*" Bertram repeated the words with questioning disdain. "Our only *mission* is survival, and we're doing a pretty good job so far. Don't you dare muck it up, Sam."

"But we have to—"

"You know," John said with a raised voice, stopping Sam with a touch of his hand on Sam's arm. "Sam's point about the artificial light might be germane to Danielle's. Outside of Lodak's use, artificial light is used only to illuminate the Great Quan and his city. If that isn't pointing to yourself as a god, then I don't know what is."

"But Lodak does have it as well."

"Yes, Lara, he does. And exactly why and how that relates to Quan's use is something to ponder while falling asleep, which I am about to do. So, goodnight, everybody, and shut up."

Another evening's conversation ended even less amicably and had been set in motion by Danielle.

"Have you all noticed a real absence of something?"

"You mean besides other humans?" Bertram asked.

"No, Bertram, I mean art."

"Art?" Lara not so much asked, as joined Danielle in the pondering.

"In all our travels around Quannak, have you heard any *la musique?* Have you seen any statues? Even statues of the Great Quan?"

"The Great Quan is a statue of the Great Quan," John commented.

"That's truer than you probably meant," Bertram added.

"Or paintings? Even in the homes we've been brought into. Or even illustrations?"

"There were illustrations in some books in Lodak's—"

"Or books!" Sam's reminder was added to Danielle's list. "Have you ever seen a book outside of Lodak's? In homes or hands?"

"The robes," Bertram said. "Some are beautiful and quite elegant."

"That's *mode,* um, you know, fashion. Art is about self-expression. Fashion is about self-aggrandizement."

"Well," Lara said, "how about those designs on walls, the colored circles, and other shapes."

"*Exactement, des dessins!* Nothing but abstract designs. Nothing *humain* about them."

"Well, they aren't human, are they?" Sam pointed the question sharply. "They're damn lizards and birds."

The other four looked at Sam. His statement had such a hard, sharp, dark edge that it revealed something the others had not previously seen. Or it had always been there, and they had been oblivious to it, which was understandable. They had been living, breathing, traveling, eating, sleeping, and questioning in such a—to them—surreal world that the real was easily lost.

John, the elder, the mentor, and the surrogate father, said. "Sam, that's a stupid thing to say."

"Why? Why is it stupid to realize that we are in a completely alien world, a nightmare world, an un-human world that we do not belong in? Oh sure, we must survive. Survival is so damn important. So, we wear their clothes, learn their language, and try to analyze them to understand them. But what right do we have to understand them? What right do they have to exist? They are an accident. An accident we caused."

"Speak for yourself," Bertram said sharply.

"Shut the fuck up, *Bertie!* You people don't get it. You haven't gotten it from the beginning. This is not supposed to be. How can we live here—and be us? What are we supposed to do? Just be the Great Quan's pets, that Bertie seems to want us to be?"

"That's not—"

"He says we must survive. But what about thrive? What about growth in knowledge? That's what we humans do. Do you see any evidence of that here? What are *we* here?"

"Talk about *angoisse existentielle.*"

"Danielle, hush," John admonished. And then he turned calmly to Sam. "Sam, I see what you are saying. We are in a nightmare of sorts. And it may well be of our own making—Bertram excepted. But far from surreal, it is the only real we have. Our whole—universe, it would seem—has changed. But that doesn't mean we have—or have to. But we are still just children in this world, trying to grow up, to learn, to master enough information so that we can—integrate, I suppose, ourselves into this universe. Once we have, then thriving will be up to us. Remember our instincts when this first happened? Yours, mine, Danielle's? To explore, to find out, to gain knowledge. Well, once we are ready, what's to stop us? It may not be our universe, but it's still a universe. And as knowledge seems to be in short supply, we have much to offer by adding to it."

"Is it in short supply?" Sam asked John. "Is it?" He asked the others. "Or is it unwanted, unnecessary, unwelcome? They have a nice little community here. Happy, gaily dressed, comfort-loving creatures with one hell of a father figure, or god, or what have you, to thank for it, I guess. What more do they want or need? No books, no art, no questions. Oh, a little bit of fear, maybe. I've seen it, have you seen it? I've seen it in their eyes whenever, oddly, the name of their daddy god is mentioned. But it's just a little fear, nothing compared to what I bet are in the eyes of the yellowsacks if you could ever get them to lift their heads so you could see. A nightmare it is; a nightmare, I say, unworthy of humans."

"Why?" Bertram's face had set hard. "Do you think they are so different than us? You were always so damn naive, head in the clouds, Sam. *Your* little perfect world or universe may have been destroyed, but don't claim that for the rest of us. Maybe for us, it's just a variation on a theme. Maybe we can live with it. A pity you're not as adaptable."

"Okay, guys, it's of no help to any—"

"John, stop!" Sam said harshly. "You don't always have to mediate. You are not our father, you know."

All could see how that hurt John. And Lara, for some reason unacknowledged by her and unrecognized by the others, could feel it.

Sam turned, walked over to his sleeping cushion, and laid down. "If you're all going to continue this discussion, please keep it down. I'm going to try to sleep."

FOURTEEN

GRADUATION

After a couple of months, just as the five felt comfortable and competent with the Saur language, their lessons suddenly stopped without explanation. One of the tutors told them that Lodak had said that the five should remain in their communal room until he came to them, and then she said what was obviously a final farewell.

It was unnerving.

They did not leave the communal room for five days except for escorted trips to the bath. Their meals, as always, were brought in, and the only Saurs they saw were the yellowsacks who brought them. However, the yellowsacks were unwilling to engage in conversation or even look at the five, so Sam and company could only continue practicing the language by speaking it to each other.

But, on occasion, English just had to be used.

Walking by Bertram, struggling to untangle his beard, Sam looked at him and said, "You're looking quite *Rock 'n' Roll*, Bertie."

"Oh, shut up," the unappreciative Bertram said.

Danielle started listing things she missed. "Chocolate. Swiss, of course. Georges Simenon's *Maigret* novels—they are my secret vice. The Amalfi Coast—we vacationed there once when I was ten, and I had a crazy two-week love affair there when I was seventeen. Paris, *naturellement*. Hotel minibars. Riding my *bicyclette* in the country. Wine, of course, but really, *café*, but that goes without saying."

"Then, why say it?" Lara snapped as she twisted a long strand of her hair.

"*Excusez-moi, ma chérie.*"

John's usual genial demeanor was beginning to irritate everyone. So, he put on his stern professor's face and, to pass the time, started quizzing them all on the fundamental truths of physics, world capitals, and movie trivia until they begged him to be genial again.

Unnerved and getting on each other's nerves, it was not a pleasant time for them.

Then, on the morning of the sixth day, Lodak entered, not unhappy, not dour, and not concerned about a pending disaster. This relieved the five, as theories of negative turns in their fortunes had been flying the past five days in between the irritations.

Lodak was not only his usual, excited self; he also seemed as genial as John. And he was wearing his official black robe with the five gold bands.

"Saammmm, Dan-el, La-ra, Jaa-on, and Bert-ram, I have just come from an audience with the Great Quan. I gave him a full account of your education, lessons, and progress. He was quite pleased and has declared you Honored Guests of the Great Quan."

"What were we before?" John asked.

"Specimens."

"Oh."

"There was the possibility that, at some point, I would have had to dissect one or two of you."

"Ah."

"But, no more. I have convinced the Great Quan that you are almost as Saurian as a Saur."

"Almost?" John asked.

"Well—you can never be fully Saurian. That is just a physical fact."

"That's absolutely true," Sam said.

"So, there will be no more lessons—except for me. Now that we can communicate, I hope you will tell me about your people and land and how you got here. The Great Quan is quite anxious to know."

"I'll bet he is," Sam said in English.

"We will be pleased to inform you of this," Bertram said in Saurian.

"But, for now—" Lodak's glee became even more excited. "I have a surprise for you all. Follow me. Come on, follow me."

He took them down a dark corridor, as they had usually traveled within the pyramidal building, but then out into a wide hallway, lit by natural light, and through various rooms, all filled with natural illumination, that Lodak explained the purposes of: "Here, we have great banquets. Here, soldiers display feats of strength. Here is the gossip room, where the challenge is to reveal something about someone else that will truly embarrass them. Here, children are disciplined. Here, the makers of robes compete to please the crowd.

82

Here, mass sexual congress takes place for the Great Quan's pleasure. Here, the Great Quan approves of and dissolves marriages." And finally, "Here are your new living quarters."

It was much larger than their communal room and divided into two sections.

"La-Ra explained how the males and the females should be in separate areas," Lodak said.

Sam looked at Lara and smiled.

Danielle also looked at Lara and smiled, but her smile was somewhat lopsided.

"You'll find these sleep cushions so much more comfortable than the ones you had and designed more for your size. You now have a separate table for eating and various other tables for whatever you might want to do at them. They are easily moved. I had two extra light holes created, so, as you can see, it is almost as bright as the outside here. And here's the best part, especially ordered by the Great Quan himself." He looked to the back of the room, which was still in the shadows despite the two extra light holes. "Come forth—come forth!"

Emerging from those shadows were five yellowsacks: two females and three males. They were skinny, of course, and only their yellow sacks kept them from seeming emaciated. Of the females, one was a Downy, and one was a Scale. The males counted two Downies and one Scale among them. As was typical of yellowsacks, they came forward with their heads down.

"Now you each have a yellowsack of your very own! Which is quite a privilege. I am, myself, three years away from having my yellowsack. Danielle, the Great Quan gives you Avar." Lodak gestured for Avar to come to Danielle, which she quickly did, as did the others to their new owners when they were called forth. "La-ra, the Great Quan gives you Sencee. Saammmm, the Great Quan gives you Guien. Jaa-on, the Great Quan gives you Nob. Bert-ram, the Great Quan gives you Agfa."

The five were astonished—a subtle mental storm that often leads to speechlessness. But something had to be said. And Bertram, who had talked to presidents, prime ministers, constitutional monarchs, and billionaires, was just the man to do it.

"Lodak, please convey to the Great Quan, with excellent wishes for his health, our most deeply felt appreciation, and gratitude for his most generous gifts."

Lodak was pleased with that. He said his goodbyes for now, then left.

The yellowsacks all stood by their new masters, waiting for instructions.

"I don't want a slave," Lara said with disgust. She stepped away from Sencee, not realizing that her expression of disgust was taken personally by Sencee, who stayed in step with Lara while hanging her head lower.

"Yeah, I'm pretty uncomfortable with the idea," John said.

"I know what you are saying, but it will make life *beaucoup plus pratique.*"

"Practical?" Lara's shock did not silence her. "You want to oppress a person for your personal convenience?! I thought you were an existentialist, not a pragmatist!"

Bertram turned to Lara, withholding most, but not all, of his exasperation. "Lara, stop being childish. It's not our place to fight their social norms."

"*It's not our place.* That's an understatement," John said with a short laugh. "This is certainly not our place."

"Look at them," Lara pleaded. "It's obvious they've been abused. They look half-starved."

"Which is the reason to keep them," Sam said, eliciting Lara's open mouth of non-understanding. "Are you planning on abusing them?"

"Of course not."

"Then life with us as their masters is going to be a hell of a lot better for them than any other situation."

Sam turned to his assigned yellowsack, Guien, and said, "Follow me."

Saying nothing in response, Guien did as Sam moved to the dining table, which was laid out with a meal. Guien immediately filled a plate with a selection of food and then handed it to Sam, keeping his head bowed and his eyes on the floor.

Sam took a bite from a stoll. Then, he took Guien's chin in his free hand and raised his head just enough to face him. "Cunie."

Guien did not know what to do.

But Sam just smiled at him and said again, "Cunie."

Guien hesitatingly returned the smile and said, "Ta—Tamash."

Sam handed Guien the plate, and Guien began to set it back on the table, but Sam stopped him. "No, Guien, please have some."

Guien looked at Sam with disbelieving dismay.

"Go ahead, eat," Sam urged. Guien picked a piece of potan from the plate and slowly raised it to his mouth, looking to Sam for further urging, which Sam gave him.

Then he ate it with relish. "Cunie! Cunie!" Guien said between bites.

"Tamash," Sam said, then turned to the others—all the others. "Now, everyone over here. Let's have a feast!"

Lara, Danielle, and John escorted Sencee, Avar, and Nob to the table.

Bertram did not move. And so, Agfa did not move. "This is a big mistake. In this society—"

"Oh, shut up, Bertie!" Lara said, with a mouth full. She surprised herself enough to laugh, spraying out bits of food, which caused the other humans at the table to laugh, which fascinated the yellowsack Saurs.

Bertram sighed, shook his head, sighed again, and then turned to Agfa. "Well, we might as well follow the crowd." Master and slave joined the others at the table.

FIFTEEN

QUESTIONS AND ANSWERS

As honored guests of the Great Quan, the five were now completely free to move about the pyramidal building and the city as long as they were attended by their yellowsacks, who had been ordered not only to serve their human masters but to protect their diminutive selves from a world built to suit taller, larger, stronger beings. They had to inform Lodak of their specific personal plans each day, and if Lodak thought it necessary, he would also assign a soldier to accompany them.

But in the first weeks of this freedom, Lodak monopolized much of their time in conversation, in Q&A really, as Lodak wanted to know about the land they came from.

Knowing this was coming, the five had devised a story that they could all tell, one that contained some truth, so they could tell it comfortably using their memories, but one that left out the actual means of their travel to Anaraquan—Where the Great Quan Rules.

"There are lands beyond Anaraquan. We know this," Lodak said one afternoon to the five, who had been invited to join him in his study. It had changed a bit since their first day in Quannak. It seemed neater and more ordered, as if something systematic was going on, something needing order to find order. Lodak was the master here now, comfortable in the room and a good host, using the five's yellowsacks as his to command while they were there, to serve him and Sam and company, refreshments, cool them with fans and bring them whatever they might need. He spoke to them sharply and with a guttural voice, which he used at no other time.

Guien, Avar, Nob (all Downies), Sencee, and Agfa (Scales) kept their eyes lowered and mouths shut, as all good yellowsacks did, and moved with alacrity to fulfill Lodak's every request. Sam and company had decided upon this after Bertram insisted that while it was fine, he supposed, for them to treat the yellowsacks in an egalitarian and fair manner while alone, out in Saur society, they'd better be as "masterly" with their slaves as was the norm, or they would bring suspicion upon themselves.

Lara and John did not like the idea. But Sam pointed out, and Danielle agreed, that the consequences would not be dire for them but might be for Guien, Avar, Nob, Sencee, and Agfa. The yellowsacks agreed vigorously. So, Sam and company learned to speak in a guttural manner.

"There are lands beyond Anaraquan. We know this, but we know nothing of them. As you are the first of your kind ever to be seen in Anaraquan, I assume you are from one of those lands and traveled a great distance to be here. Can you deny this?"

"Lodak, you are quite perceptive. We come from a land called Amerifrance," *(this, of course, had been a compromise)*, "which is far, far away, beyond a great body of water," Sam gave the party line.

"A great body of water!" Lodak became excited. "I have read of great bodies of water but almost thought they might be legends."

"They are not," John said. "They are many miles across and deep, and great creatures roam them."

"And you crossed this great body of water in a barge?"

"No," Bertram said, "we flew over the great body of water."

"Flew? Flew? Like air creatures? But how? You do not have wings or bodies that would accommodate such locomotion? And if you can fly, why haven't you flown away?"

"We do not fly ourselves." It was Danielle's turn. "We flew in great, floating barges—like street barges or river barges—that move through the air."

"How? How do they move through the air?"

"On the winds," John said.

"But how do you get up to the winds?"

"We are carried there by huge sacks filled with a gas lighter than air, so it lifts us," Sam said.

"Why—why would you do this? Leave the solid land for something so—so slight, changeable, unpredictable as air?"

"To explore," Lara said with a smile and a light in her eyes.

"Ah, yes, of course. Explore what?"

"The whole world!" Now, Lara was getting excited. "We wanted to take our barge of the air, the—the Nautilus we called it, and go completely around the world, all around it, seeing what we could see, strange new lands and peoples, and we were going to try to do it all in eighty days!"

"What do you mean, *around* the world?"

Five mental *uh-ohs* dashed around inside five skulls. Possibly, the simple truth, as seen with one's own eyes, was too strong here to buck.

"Are you saying that this, which we stand on, is not flat but round, as if we are all living on a fordar?" The fordar was a round potan.

"Well, uh, yes." John took the leap. "That's right, that may come as a—"

"I knew this," Lodak whispered as he gestured for the five to draw near. "I knew this because it is in the books. Cornar did not believe it; Cornar said I was being a fool to deny my senses. But I believed it, for the books showed how it is possible. But I am the only one in Quannak who believes it. Or, rather, the only one in Quannak who knows it, who has ever been presented with the idea of it, for Cornar would not let me report it to the Great Quan. And if I had, the Great Quan would not have let me tell anyone else."

"Why?" Danielle asked.

"What?" It suddenly seemed like Lodak realized he should not have revealed this.

"Why would the Great Quan not have let you tell anyone else?"

"Because—" Lodak thought momentarily, pondered for a second, and searched for the right words. "Because the Great Quan loves his people and would never want them discomforted. And the idea that one is standing on a spinning fordar, traveling through the sky, is, you must admit, a very frightening idea."

"It's spinning? And traveling?" The humans perceived Sam's mockery but did not seem that Lodak had.

"Yes! Oh, does that disturb you too?"

"Well, it will take some time to get used to it, but—"

"I have books that tell me why and how, and it all makes sense—I have made observations. But I don't tell anyone else. Possibly, I should not have told you. I even hid these books from Cornar, for he would have destroyed them. You must not talk of it."

"I assure you," Bertram, the administrator, said, "that we will not." And all agreed.

"And now, I have a 'why' for you, and I hope you won't take offense."

"Lodak," John said, "You could do nothing to offend us."

Lodak nodded, a habit he had picked up from the humans. "Why—why are you so small?"

It was a question they had not prepared for, and it tied the tongues of four of them, but the fifth, Lara, spoke right up. "Because we are aeronauts, wind travelers, specially bred to be small so that our air barges have less weight to lift. All other…humans—that is what we are called humans—are every bit as big as most of you Saurs."

Sam looked at Lara and smiled, admiring the quickness—and delight—of her mind.

"Oh. And are all you humans all of one kind?"

"One kind?" John asked.

"I am Downy. The Great Quan is Scale. We live together but are not *of* each other. Do you humans have any others?"

"Many years ago, yes. But not now. Now we are all one."

"So, you can mate among yourselves?"

John laughed. "Yes, we can do that."

"Are you going to?"

"Well, um…" Bertram did not know how to finish.

"Because you will be honored guests of the Great Quan for the rest of your lives. Your air barge has been, I assumed, made inoperable."

"Why would you assume that?" Sam was truly curious to know.

"Otherwise, you would want to leave, return to it, eventually fly again over the great body of water, and return to France. You can't be fully comfortable here. And yet, you have settled in. I assume it is because you have no other options."

Sam looked up at Lodak, scanned his Downy face, looked into his inhuman eyes, and said, "Lodak, you are truly a formidable scholar and seeker of truth."

"Cunie, Saammmm."

As the five returned to their quarters, John whispered to Lara, "Albatross."

"What?"

"You should have named our air barge the Albatross, not the Nautilus."

"Oh, of course, darn! That was stupid."

"Well, don't beat yourself up. Lodak will never know the difference, and I'm sure Jules would forgive you."

SIXTEEN

THE GREAT HUNT

TWO days later, Lodak informed the five that the Great Quan had bestowed upon them another great honor. He had invited them to accompany him—and a hundred elite Saurs—on a great hunt for the geter, a massive beast covered with armor and notoriously hard to kill. He ordered Guien, Avar, and Nob to fashion hunting robes for the five and Sencee and Agfar to pick up some hunting weapons, made to human scale, that he had ordered. The hunt would take place in two days. Lodak was excited. He had been invited as well, although he would not be hunting.

On the day of the hunt, Lodak came to collect them at dawn, admired them in their hunting robes, and took them to the open city gates. Beyond them was a long row of land barges, three times as big as street barges, elevated upon the shoulders of twenty yellowsacks each. Upon the barges sat and lounged—for there were both seats and couches—beautifully attired elites, both males and females, about two-thirds Scales and one-third Downies. Some were in hunting robes; the rest were in simple but resplendent robes. A legion of yellowsacks was attending to them.

As the sun was not yet high, there was no blinding reflection from the golden city walls, and all the elite held their heads high, even the lounging ones, and chatted and laughed and seemed very much in a holiday mood. There was also a land barge for Lodak and Sam and company. Lodak took them to it and walked them up a ramp so that they could take their places on the barge. Their yellowsacks, who were already there, were preparing everything for their morning meal. The five still gathered looks of awe and interest, causing a buzz of Saur talk to surround them. John was sure they were eliciting tickled-pink delight over how *cute* (the Saurian language did not have an equivalent word,

91

only an equivalent expression) they were in their little hunting robes, looking just like the big Saurs. He mentioned this to the others, then noticed how Bertram straightened his back and stretched himself taller.

Behind the caravan of barges were many wagons with supplies, including tents, tables, and food. And behind them were soldiers on foot and mounted on the creatures they had seen previously, which they now knew were called suunars. There were no flags or banners and no contingent of hornblowers, all of which the five, being humans who had seen old movies about olden times, felt the absence of.

But suddenly, among the soldiers, a melodious relay call went up, announcing the arrival of the magnificent Downy of great importance, who was, of course, the Great Quan's right-hand Saur, something like a prime minister, except there were no other ministers for him to be the first of, no governing body of senators or lawmakers at all. There was only a bureaucracy, overseen by the magnificent Downy of great importance, whose name (or the name of his office) was Savaan. He rode on a suunar and traveled from the back of the caravan to the front, greeting the elites with words of official acknowledgment of their existence.

Then an even louder, grander, more melodious relay shout sprang into the air, announcing the arrival of the Great Quan. He came out of the city gates on the largest suunar they had ever seen, but it had quite a weight to support. All the elites got off their seats or couches and stood to greet the Great Quan. Lodak and the five, of course, did the same. All the yellowsacks, except those holding up the barges, prostrated themselves and seemed to melt into the decks of the land barges.

The Great Quan surveyed the caravan slowly, spotting the land barge with Lodak and the five. He then rode over to them.

Towering above them, as he sat most comfortably on his suunar, the Great Quan looked down upon the five humans and smiled a razor-sharp smile. "My honored guests," he addressed them, "little and strange and amusingly weird as you are, welcome to my hunt. Do you think you will bag a geter today?"

No one quite knew what to say. Except for Bertram.

"Great Quan, if we do, we will dedicate the kill to you and your magnificent hospitality, from which we have so benefited."

"Ah. Appropriate. You know there is no meat as sweet as geter meat."

"If we prove worthy enough to bring down a geter, it will be our pleasure to serve you, its meat."

"Ah. Doubly appropriate."

He turned to Lodak. "You have done well, Lodak. I am pleased. I look forward to more time with these little ones." Then he moved his great Suunar forward to the head of the caravan

"Kiss ass," Sam said quietly to Bertram.

Bertram was not upset nor surprised, considering the source. "I'd rather kiss ass than kiss my ass goodbye."

///

Their trek was slow, being powered by the trudging steps of yellowsacks. But the elites on each land barge did not seem to mind as they ate, drank, laughed, and played games of strength and skill. They threw dart-like projectiles against a square-colored panel with various abstract targets on it, which was held up by a yellowsack. Yellowsack hands were, now and then, pierced. They held jumping contests and leg wrestling contests, where opponents would lay flat on their backs after hitching up their robes; they would then put their arms to their sides, onto the barge floor, palms down, and try to best each other using only their legs.

Both activities must have caused the yellowsacks upon whose shoulders the barges rode some discomfort and pain, but complaints were never heard as the yellowsacks concentrated on the next step—and then the next, then the next.

This caught John's attention—and his disgust, but he knew he could not complain. Instead, he huddled with Lara to discuss it and disgust together—to coin a verb.

Most of these contests were among the Scales, with very few Downies involved. Most of the Downies, like John and Lara, were huddled in conversation, although not in disgust, or, like Bertram and Danielle, were looking out at the changing landscape.

At first, that landscape was the hill upon which the golden city stood as they traveled down a well-worn road on the side of the hill opposite the river. It was, on occasion, steep, and the Saurs held on tight as the yellowsack carriers gingerly negotiated gravity, loose dirt, stones, and pebbles. But there was not one misstep or moment of danger, as the yellowsacks demonstrated great skill. There was, however, much complaining from the riders of the barges.

The landscape flattened, and they smoothly moved through a dry land of scrubby bushes, skittering little creatures, and swirling dust of their own making. But, far in the distance, a great, snow-capped mountain range could be seen, and it was lovely to look at. After an hour or so, they came upon a lake fed by a small river, on the other side of which was farmland that seemed to be between harvest and planting. A long curve to the left took them to a forest of sparsely spaced trees they had not seen before, and there, after journeying deep enough into the forest to be surrounded by its environment, the caravan came to a halt.

During the trip, Lodak had invited Sam to a set of couches, upon which they lounged and talked, probing each other for answers to questions they had. Lodak wanted to know something about Amerifrance, and Sam had fun portraying it as a land of freedom, cooperation, community, and curiosity. He told how some people lived in vast caverns cut out of mountains and which extended deep into the ground, while others lived in giant trees, in structures built of wood, and still others were helium farmers, living by vents in fields from which the helium expelled.

"Amerifrance has no leader," he said, "like the Great Quan, but rather a Council of the Wise, which everyone is required to be a part of for at least one year of their lives, as everyone is wise."

It was all silly and fanciful, and it amused Sam that Lodak took it seriously.

And Sam asked Lodak, "Scales and Downies are very different from each other, yet live together in harmony. Has that always been true?"

"As long as anyone can remember."

"There seem to be more Scales than Downies."

"Yes. In Quannak. But outside of it—and remember you have not seen it all—it is more—even."

"And Scales and Downies cannot mate?"

"No, of course not. The idea is quite repugnant."

"But—do—they—ever…"

"Well, Saammmm, that is a different question. Are you truly that interested to know?"

"Would you prefer that I not be?"

"It is rarely spoken of."

"Ah. So, let us not speak of it. But we can talk about what seems to be another difference between Scales and Downies."

"What is that?"

"Scales seem more—well—physical—than Downies."

"They are bigger, usually, and stronger. They like to fight, sport, and—"

"Not think too much?"

"Well—not about anything that matters."

"But the Downies—"

"Have a capacity just to sit and—mentally arrange things."

"And so, Savaan is a Downy."

"And those that help him, yes."

"And you are a Downy."

"Observably so, yes."

"So, the Scales and the Downies have a reciprocal relationship."

"That is so, yes, but I'm not sure anyone thinks of it that way. It is just—the way."

"May I ask a question?" John wandered over to them with Lara and listened to this part of the conversation.

"Of course," Lodak said.

"There are both Scale and Downy yellowsacks."

"Naturally."

"Naturally?" Lara questioned a bit self-righteously. "There is nothing natu—"

"Lara!" Sam stopped her rudeness.

"Yellowsacks are yellowsack first, Scale or Downy second."

"I don't quite understand—" John started.

"The Great Quan tells us who are yellowsacks. Once he does, they are yellowsacks and nothing else."

There was a redness coming to Lara's cheeks. "But—"

"Speaking of yellowsacks, you should be asking yours to lay out our next meal. Shortly after that, we will be at the hunting ground."

///

The hunting ground was a large square field, obviously cut out of the forest, with all the trees (sparse though they may have been) removed completely, not even stumps remaining. The ground was hard and compact, with only minimal, low-lying, new-to-life vegetation to be seen here and there. The caravan had stopped along one side of the square with a small but rapidly flowing stream just beyond the beginning of the trees on this side. The yellowsack barge-bearers gently placed the barges on the ground in a semicircle, leaving an ample space halfway from the first and last land barge. They then ran to the wagons and retrieved rods and materials to construct a tent over each barge, fully open on the side facing the square. And one set of yellowsacks erected a huge ground tent for the Great Quan and Savaan in the space in the middle. The Great Quan and Savaan dismounted from their Suunars once their yellowsack attendants filled the tent with furniture and luxuries.

After all that was done, many of the yellowsacks went off into the forest, while Scales from each of the barges emerged from their tents, resplendent in their hunting robes and fully armed with spears, bows, and arrows.

"You must join the hunt," Lodak told the five.

"Must we? Really?" John asked.

"The Great Quan demands it."

"And the hunt happens on foot, not from the barges?" Sam asked.

"Yes."

"But, Lodak, we have neither the height nor the strength of Scales to bring down a massive beast."

"I mentioned that to the Great Quan, and it seems that this is what amuses him about your joining the hunt."

"But we might get in the way, get underfoot of—"

"It is what the Great Quan wants, Saammmm. So, you must all grab a weapon and stand before your tent for inspection."

"Why can't we be like the Downies, who don't seem to be hunting?" John asked.

"We Downies have already done our jobs—we have devised hunting strategies. Have you devised hunting strategies?"

"Well, no, of course not," Sam said.

"Then, you must hunt."

With concern in their eyes, Guien, Avar, Sencee, Nob, and Agfa brought the five their custom-made weapons.

"The females have to hunt, too?" Lara asked in a panic.

"Of course. Females are no different than males."

"How enlightened your society is," Danielle said, managing as much irony as she could in the Saur Language.

Melodious calls from soldiers announced that the Great Quan, followed by Savaan, had begun his inspection. He could not help but be awe-inspiring, this largest of the Saurs moving slowly down the line, looking down on one and all, exchanging pleasantries. But the awe was doubled, possibly tripled for the humans, as the Great Quan truly towered over them.

When he got to them, at the end of the line of barge tents, he stepped back and smiled his scaly Saur smile, and the massive orbs of his eyes seemed to beam. "You are perfect, little hunters, quite perfect. I like your little spears and little bows. Quite funny, and yet very pleasant to look upon. I want you to join me in my tent. I have had special furniture built for you." He then signaled to the soldiers; five of them came forward and picked up Sam, John, Lara, Bertram, and Danielle, and carried them like babes in arms, with their arms (their customized spears and bows and arrows), following the Great Quan back to his tent, where, indeed, they were placed on five elevated chairs that surrounded the massive seat of the Great Quan.

The five were startled by this event but relieved. Their joining the hunt had obviously been the Great Quan's little joke. But how funny was it to be dressed up in little hunting robes, given diminutive weapons, and put on display? Not like trophies—more like knickknacks.

A cry came out of the forest, then two, then a chorus of cries. Then, the sounds of beatings and pounding feet. Kicked-up dust was seen in the distance. This continued for a few minutes, and then a small herd of geters, six at the most, ran out of the surrounding trees, driven by screaming, arm-waving, ground-beating yellowsacks. The geters were the size of African elephants, except with much shorter legs, so they had difficulty moving fast to escape. They were armor-plated and had wide flares of skin-covered bone extending from each side of their reptilian heads.

Once the herd was entirely in the square, the yellowsacks surrounded them, linking their arms, forming a living pen to hold them in. The geters were confused and panicked and wanted to break out of the screaming, yelling, yellowsacks surrounding them. They pushed forward against the chaos of yellowsacks, sometimes catching a fallen yellowsack under their big, flat feet, often impaling them with claws. The screams of the dying yellowsacks joined the screams of those struggling to contain the beasts in the circle.

It was as horrible a sight as the five had ever seen, yet they stared at it, their wide eyes fixed on the scene.

The hunters came forth and took positions around the surrounding living fence.

"Watch this," The Great Quan, who remained in his massive seat, told the five. It is most fun."

The hunters threw spears and shot arrows at the frightened creatures, most of which bounced off their armor but panicked them even more until they broke through, crushing a mass of yellowsacks, but no hunters, all of whom had wisely moved back and concentrated all their efforts on one lagging geter, a smaller one, possibly a youth, allowing the other geters to escape back into the forest. The hunters closed in on the geter and rained spears and arrows upon it until one spear found an exposed part of its neck and pierced it, which staggered the creature and caused a most pitiful, tortured moan to project from its open mouth.

More spears and arrows headed for the same vulnerable area, many of them hitting their marks, until the creature collapsed in a heap and began to writhe. Then, everybody stopped. The remaining yellowsacks retreated, and the hunters gathered around the geter, which was now whimpering, although it sounded as if it was coming from a bullhorn. None of the hunters now raised their weapons but turned to face the Great Quan, inviting him into the hunt. The Great Quan, acknowledging the invitation with a nod, stood up, was handed a long, thick spear by Savaan, and walked over to the writhing creature. A mass of hunters grabbed the poor creature by the back legs and rolled him so that his chest and stomach were exposed.

The Great Quan then poised the massive spear over the exposed breast of the beast and delivered the death blow in one swift, powerful thrust. The hunters and all the Saurs on the barges began to beat their chests with their right hands in appreciation of the Great Quan's fabulous hunting skills.

The Great Quan was pleased with himself.

///

Before the butchering of the geter could begin, the dead yellowsacks had to be removed from the field. They were dragged by their living companions a short distance into the forest, out of sight of the hunting party, and left for scavengers.

Lara was in tears, and John had set his jaw hard enough to remove the boyishness of his face.

"Lara, stop it," Bertram whispered urgently, afraid the Great Quan would see her when he returned. "Get hold of yourself, for Christ's sake."

"Shut up, Bertram!" Danielle, upset but in control, reached out her hand to Lara, hoping not to fall off her high chair. "M*a chérie,* the *imbécile* is not wrong. You must not show this."

"But—"

"Hush. You know I'm right."

Lara regained control of herself, breathing deeply, wiping tears vigorously, and forcing herself to smile as the Great Quan returned triumphantly.

"Now," the Great Quan said, "we will feast on geter meat!"

///

The process of gutting and butchering the geter was a complex one, with its thick hide needing to be cut into, although that part was easy as the yellowsacks who did it wielded long knives—swords to the Sam and company—that sliced deeply and smoothly, with minimal effort. This seemed unusual to Sam (who, along with the others, had been carried back to their barge). He took up one of their "cute" spears and looked at the head closely, remembering that it had caught his attention that first day. It was made of a material that was not quite metal. It had that ceramic aspect that the ruined city walls had and some of the abstract wall hangings they had seen. It was honed to a very sharp blade.

John noticed Sam's concentration and joined him in the examination. They did not need to speak to share their curiosity. Then John gestured with a quick nod toward the butchering work by the yellowsacks and their knives and said quietly, "It's a wonder they don't turn them on their masters."

Sam looked at John and saw more upset in his mentor's eyes than he thought healthy. "John, there's nothing to be done about it—by us."

"Yes, pity that."

"You're going to have to be dispassionate about this."

"Dispassion is for science, Sam, not for humanity."

"What humanity? Except for us five, I see none around here."

John returned Sam's meaningful look. "Yes, pity that as well." Then he walked over to Lara, lying on a couch, her right arm flung over her eyes, trying for unconsciousness.

The real complexity came in the butchering. It all had to be done through the stomach and chest, as the thick scales that were its armor plating could not be cut through or removed. So once the beast had been sliced open from thorax to genitals, a team of yellowsacks, some working from on top of the felled creature, some from the ground, pulled in two directions and separated the hide from the flesh and innards.

The guts and organs were then pulled out and laid in an orderly and, it seemed, ritual manner. Then flesh was cut away and then cut into small—relatively speaking—steaks. This took approximately two and a half hours, by which time twilight had arrived. A contingent of yellowsacks built fire pits in front of each barge tent and a giant bonfire, equidistant from the first and last barge tent, directly facing the Great Quan's tent.

Once the fires were roaring, yellowsacks divided up and delivered the cut meat and organs to each fire pit, laying them out in preparation for cooking. As night descended, the fires provided light and warmth, with the colossal bonfire spreading out an overall base illumination.

When total darkness was upon them, outside of the flickering firelight, a harmonious chorus of chanting began among the soldiers surrounding the Great Quan's tent. The Great Quan came out of his tent, Savaan having moved deep into the back of the tent. The chorus ended. All eyes were on the Great Quan. The only sounds were the crackling of the many fires and a few quiet noises emanating from the forest. Otherwise, all was still.

The Great Quan looked to the barges on his right, then to the barges on his left, and then, eyes straight ahead, he threw up his arms. A great white, clean, steady illumination then emanated from within his vast tent, backlighting him and making him seem even larger and more formidable than he already was. The Saurs—Scales and Downies alike—slapped their open right hands upon their chests and continued for some minutes as the Great Quan took it all in and let it please him.

Sam was stunned. It was the artificial illumination seen rarely in the pyramidal building, rarely but always effectively. This meant that the power source—and, of course, there had to be one—was portable. That meant it was possible to get power back to the Dark Lady. Sam, his chest pounding with a powerful heartbeat, his breath coming in short in-and-outs, closed his eyes and imagined the accelerator sitting alone in the distance, waiting. Then, he saw numbers and symbols to be forced into meaning. He visualized his home, his large house in the hills above Pasadena. He even, oddly, traveled in his mind along the 210 freeway, with its mix of self-driving cars and well-maintained classic cars, which demanded humans be in charge. He had one, a Tesla—silver and sleek and so much fun to drive.

"Sam. Sam!" It was Bertram.

"What?"

"We are being invited to split up and join others for the meal."

"We are being parceled out to the Great Quan's favorites, like party favors," John said with some sting.

"John, please," Bertram admonished.

"I want to stay with Lodak." Sam moved over to Lodak, who was talking to the soldiers who had come to collect the five. "Lodak, can I stay with you?"

Lodak, one side of his face illuminated by firelight, turned and looked at Sam, not unaffected by Sam's unexplained heightened state. "You are being summoned to join Savaan in the tent of one of our most important couples. I and Bert-ram are going to be in another. The others are all—"

"Bertram should be with Savaan. They would have much more in common. Bertram is fascinated by him, admires his—his bearing."

"Well—" he turned and talked to the soldiers and found that they had been tasked with dividing up the five as they saw fit among the Great Quan's favorites, so changes meant nothing to them. "It is settled. You and I will eat with a most amusing Scale and his family, some brothers, and a few cousins. They are all excellent leg wrestlers. Good fun."

Lara was frightened. She wanted to stay with Sam or John, but Lodak convinced her that the Downy family he asked the soldiers to take her to would treat her with kindness and genuine interest.

"Besides, young Hunar, their son, will soon join me in my study. He is to take my place, as I took Cornar's. This will give you a chance to get to know him."

Lara felt better. Downies did not overwhelm her the way the Scales did.

Danielle was the guest of a group of male Scales who were among the top officers of Quan's soldiers. They introduced her to an intoxicating Saur drink called numb, a rather apt nomenclature, Danielle later thought, given her condition after consuming much of it, in a challenge she was destined to lose.

John was the guest of an extended family of Scales, who were particularly crude in their manner, as they ate geter meat with abandon, drank to excess, found John's long grey hair and beard uproariously funny, and couldn't stop touching it in turns and laughing, and took some offense that John did not want to consume a copious amount of numb. Nevertheless, they plied him with it. A puddle of the stuff formed on the ground right by the barge's edge where John sat. He had a miserable time.

Bertram, however, had a fine time. He found much to talk to Savaan about, and Savaan found him companionable and wise. The couple, whose tent they were the guests of, sat and watched them, listening to them, as they all ate their meal and imbibed modestly—not numb but something closer to a wine, called lidenunchnon. The couple sat, feeling honored, looking honored, and pitying those not so honored.

Sam and Lodak faced a considerable meal and much numb, as they provided an audience for their hosts, who concentrated on beating each other silly with skillful and painful physical competitions. But Sam did not mind. It allowed him to talk to Lodak as they kept their eyes on the games, smiled, slapped their chests in appreciation, and toasted the winners.

"Lodak, the light…the special light that shines on the walls of the Golden City and illuminates the Great Quan—I'm just wondering where it comes from."

Lodak had just taken a large bite of geter meat and chewed it slowly, saying nothing, just continuing to look at a leg wrestling contest that had turned fierce. A scream pierced the air as one combatant applied more and more pressure on one leg of his opponent until a loud snap was heard.

"Oh, that will have dire consequences. Breaks are not allowed. And they are cousins from two different branches—"

"Lodak—"

"That's going to lead to a feud. But possibly, the Great Quan will not allow it."

"Lodak?"

"But then again, on occasion, he finds feuds funny, so—"

"Lodak, the light, the special light, where does it come from?"

Lodak turned his head and faced Sam. "How can you ask such a question?"

"Well, I was just—"

"It is clear where it comes from."

"It is?"

"It emanates from the Great Quan."

"Well, it often illuminates him, but it is clearly not coming *from* him."

"Sam—the Great Quan is light. He creates the light. He can make it shine on who and what he pleases. He can make it seem to come from above or below or behind. This is all that is to be known about the light."

"But you have the light in your study."

"Ah, yes, I do," Lodak said, hoping he would have to say no more. But the question in Sam's eyes was relentless. "A gift, you see, a gift from the Great Quan to Cornar. Cornar performed many fine services for the Great Quan."

"But—"

"Ah, good, they have called Downies who know how to fix broken bones, and they are here. There aren't too many of them, you know. I wasn't aware that any had come on the hunt. This is good. Now they will not have to kill him."

"Kill him?"

"What else could have been done if he was suffering without relief?"

"Well, I suppose it might have been…kind—"

"Yes, it would have been kind to all of us because his continuing screams would not have allowed us to get any sleep tonight."

There was no more talk of the Great Quan's light. Sam looked to the Great Quan alone in his tent except for attending yellowsacks, sitting at an elegant table. He was occupied with consuming much geter meat. But no numb or lidenunchnon. Instead, he drank a drink reserved only for him, which none were allowed to name. He sat there, ripping into and masticating geter meat, well illuminated and so clearly defined that all could see and admire him, his bulk, his brilliant dining robe encrusted with nuggets of gold that glinted in the light, and his massive head, which remained a solid and sharp presence, as all other Saurs began to fade into the insubstantial, as the light of the fires in front of their barge tents slowly died.

The Great Quan was all.

///

Sleep was heavy on all as dawn broke the following day. The five and Lodak had been returned to their barge tent, where they were grateful to find sleeping cushions laid out by Guien, Avar, Sencee, Nob, and Agfa. The night grew bone-chillingly cold, but plenty of thick coverings were laid on them by the yellowsacks before they left to sleep outside on the ground. John had difficulty falling asleep, as he had not brought Cuz with him for fear he would get lost. He missed the warm little mammal's presence in the crook of his arm. What he thought about that night as he lay awake will never be known. Sam later imagined that John must have had disturbed thoughts, black-lined, infused with anger and frustration. But John did eventually fall asleep and was one of the first to wake to the sound of trooping feet as soldiers, bringing a contingent of fresh yellowsacks to replace those that had been killed, marched into the square. It was intelligent planning. The safety of the land barges on the trip home could only be maintained with a full complement of twenty yellowsack bearers per barge.

SEVENTEEN

HAIR, HOVELS, HISTORY, AND HYDRO

In the time after the Great Hunt, the five spent their days more often apart than together. It was a natural part of becoming acclimated, if not fully acculturated, and having separate interests. And, of course, the fact that they were becoming somewhat tired of each other's company could not be discounted.

Bertram found himself a welcome guest in Savaan's offices and home. He was an eager student of Saur governance, the virtues of the Great Quan, the logic behind Saur social standing, and the workings of the Saur economy, simple though they were. He was a small and refreshing presence of empathy for Savaan, who was delighted that Bert-ram had a natural grasp of the complexities of effective administration, which hardly anyone else, including the Great Quan, understood.

Danielle became a lone wanderer of Quannak—except for being followed everywhere by Avar, her eyes appropriately always on the ground. When Danielle spoke to the yellowsack, it was sharply said and always with throat-straining irritation over Avar's slowness or stupidity. She never hit Avar, only threatened to time and time again, Avar collapsing into a cowering pose most satisfying to her mistress as it was to all the Saurs in the street, inside buildings, or in private homes that Danielle had been invited to, who happened to witness the strange, small alien from a far-away land acting just like a Saur of high status. They found it amusingly charming.

But it was all an act to deflect from the reality that Avar and her four companions in service were possibly the healthiest yellowsacks any Saur had ever seen. Avar's yellow sack helped in this, being baggy and formless and the perfect garment to hide her now not-emaciated body. It was possibly unnecessary, as "seeing" yellowsacks was not often done by the elite, but Danielle and Avar did not want to take any chances. Indeed, Avar insisted upon it. And they both decided to have fun with it, finding satisfaction in their fine performances.

John and Lara had become a team (along with Cuz), doing most things together. It was a father-daughter dynamic. It was two like minds banding together for comfort and defense. And a bit of defiance. After Lara had drawn out of Sencee something about herself, she discovered that her family had become yellowsacks after the Great Quan had lopped off her father's head, once a member of the Great Quan's guards. This was after he had protested, as gently as he could, the Great Quan's use of Sencee's mother for certain pleasures that Sencee would not name.

Lara was appalled, of course, but she could only sympathize. When she learned that Sencee's mother, who was now too old to be of service to anyone, lived alone, seeing her children only when their masters allowed them some time away, Lara decided that now there was something she could do. So, drawing John, not unwillingly, into a conspiracy, late one night, they had Sencee and Nob take them to Sencee's mother. They traveled down narrow backways carrying bundles, with Nod lighting the way with a torch, into an area of Quannak far from the pyramidal building and close to the city wall, that they had never been to before. In a dark hovel among hovels, they found Sencee's mother and some of her neighbors, including Nob's sisters, huddled around a tiny fire. They were all city yellowsacks: garbage collectors, street cleaners, vermin catchers, and laborers at dirty and often dangerous work. Sencee had gotten word to her mother to gather them and no one knew why. They were awed to see the two humans and wanted to reach out and touch them, but they were too scared to do so. And they were shocked over the—to them, abnormal—healthy, full flesh upon the bones of Sencee and Nob.

Sencee and Nob just smiled and introduced La-ra and Jaa-on.

Lara and John greeted them, opened their bundles, and pulled out potan and keepnar, various types of meats, and some bread, which they distributed among the gathered.

"How often can we do this?" John asked Lara.

"Every night? They give us so much food, and much of it is going to waste, so why not? Sencee and the others can take turns delivering it."

"They should have been stealing it all along."

"Too scared, John. Fear kills action."

"You're maturing into a wise and clever little *Homo sapiens*, aren't you?"

"I guess experience will do that to you. Isn't that what you always told me?"

"Sure. Didn't have this kind of experience in mind, though."

Sam attached himself to Lodak. He did not believe Lodak's explanation of the artificial light and was determined to find the truth. But he knew he couldn't push Lodak on it, not just yet, not until a relationship was built. To do that, he presented himself for study, spinning tales of Amerifrance and its history, society, and knowledge. He let Lodak examine his human body, on occasion in the presence of Saur healers. He asked in return to learn something of Saur history, society, and knowledge. Lodak told him that he would also like to know this, and so he studied the ancient books he had at hand, and that this was his task and his alone, except for help now from the young Hunar. Then he suddenly said quietly, "Maybe later, I will reveal some of what I've learned to you, Saammmm, but not right now." Sam was frustrated but persevered and found himself looking forward to spending time with Lodak daily.

III

Lodak came to the five one day and told them they were being invited to a grand banquet that would be held soon. They would need appropriate robes, and he had ordered their yellowsacks to get busy making them. Avar was the first to finish the one for Danielle and brought it by in the morning for Danielle to try on. It was covered with colored stones placed in swirl patterns that thrilled Danielle.

"Look at this, Lara. It's just so *belle et élégante*," Danielle said as she stood and allowed Avar to dress her.

Lara had been struggling to untangle her hair after a wash with Sencee's help. "You remind me of another French woman. I think it's Marie Antoinette."

"An appreciation of the fine skills of Avar does not mean I'm not an *égalitariste*. Besides, is there anything wrong in being an *élégant égalitaire?*"

"Ouch!" The tangled hair was fighting back. "Well, I would appreciate an elegant brush!"

"Unfortunately, these *espèce* do not have the necessity for such an implement to have been mothered into invention."

"Well, what are we going to do? Our hair isn't going to get any shorter." Lara frustratingly pulled at her long tresses as if to pull them out.

"La-ra," Sencee said, "you do not want your *hair*?"

"Not this long, not anymore."

"We thought you and Dan-el," Avar said, "were having a game to see how long—"

"A game?"

"And the males too, with face *hair*."

"Not a game, an amusement, possibly," Danielle said. "But one no longer amusing."

"We will be back," Sencee said. Come, Avar, come." They left quickly.

"Where are they going?" Lara asked the empty space the yellowsacks had vacated.

They had gone to their quarters, a dark, dank, dingy room off the human's quarters, which the humans had not been to nor would have been allowed to visit, and soon returned with several cutting tools.

"For making robes," Sencee explained.

They were essentially straight blades made from ceramic-like material embedded in wooden handles shaped to fit perfectly into their Saur's hands. There were two types, one fitted for a Downy and one for a Scale. But both would have been too large for either of the human women to have wielded with any precision.

"Ah! Cunie, Sencee, cunie! What a great idea! Danielle, why did we not think of this?"

"Ah, well, Lara. *Que Puis-je dire?* I suppose one can be a genius without always being smart."

"How much should I cut?" Sencee asked.

"A lot, Sencee, a lot."

Later that day, Guien, Nob, and Agfa became perfect barbers for the men, as Lara and Danielle, both now pixie-haired, looked on.

"Just trim the beards, though, guys," Sam said.

"Why?" John asked. "I would love to feel clean-shaven again."

"Because it is an extreme mark of your humanity," Sam said soberly.

"And what about us *femmes*? "

"Simple," John said, "don't shave your legs."

The levity was appreciated. However, the women had already done the deed.

"Strange thing, though," John said. "Here we are, four PhDs and a master's. And none of us thought of this."

Danielle gave Lara a knowing look.

///

Lodak was fascinated by the newly shorn five, and it led one day to a long conversation about hair between him and Sam in his study—the weirdness of it and the why of it. Sam did his best to explain the evolution of the human species, even referring to Cuz as a kind of "relative" of theirs, pointing out that his soft fur was much the same as their hair. That gave Lodak pause to wrestle with a thought or memory, and he stopped the conversation.

Then he leaped up and went to one case of cubbyholes full of long books and searched each one methodically until, "Ah, yes, these are the ones." He grabbed three of the long books and brought them to the table he and Sam had been sitting at. "These books say what you have been saying, I think about the—the—"

"Origin of your species?"

"Yes! But not just Downy. Also Scales. Cornar gave me these to read when I first started with him. It was too fantastic to believe. Many of these long books tell me things hard to believe. And yet other long books tell me things I know to be true."

"How?"

"I read one long book and said, 'That can't be right!' And I read another and said, 'Ah, of course, that is true.' But I don't know how I know."

"It's called the *sentiment of rationality*."

"It has a name? What does it mean?"

"It means that some things you learn will 'feel' true, and some won't. But that's just a feeling, an—an emotion. Do you understand? And it could be different for different readers. But to *know* what is true, not just feel it, takes personal observation and experiments."

"Experiments?"

"Well, it will take some time to explain that. But for now, Lodak, I would like to know where these long books came from, what you've learned from them, and what you are doing with what you've learned?"

"Ah, that will also take some time. And I'm not sure I should tell you."

"Why?"

"Danger, Saammmm, I don't want to put you—or me, for that matter—in danger."

"Danger?"

"Saammmm, most Saurs do not know these books exist."

"Yes, I had sort of gathered that. But we have a saying in Amerifrance—begin at the beginning. Where did they come from?"

"If I tell you, you will not tell Bert-ram?"

"Bert-ram? Why?"

"He has become the favorite of Savaan. I would not want Savaan to know."

"Keep it a secret?"

"A secret, yes, please."

"Well, I'll tell you a secret—I don't like Bert-ram. I wouldn't tell him the time of day if he asked."

"Could he not judge that by looking to the sun?"

"Okay…um… I wouldn't tell him if his robe was on fire. How's that?"

"Ahhhh. I see. I will trust you. It was traders that first brought long books to us. They had no idea what they were, but everyone knew all discoveries, especially from ruins, had to be brought to the Great Quan and stored away. At first, they were just curiosities. Until Cornar saw them. At the time, he was a young scribe of the Downy class, which had retained writing for record-keeping. The Great Quan and the Great Quans before him always must know the extent of what they have. It is their—passion—to see it all written down. Cornar's class was found in the mountains, living away from Anaraquan. I don't know when this was, but undoubtedly many generations ago. When he saw their marks on thin sheets that they made themselves, the Great Quan of the time was amused by such a useless activity. But then they explained what the marks meant and what they were for. They called them words frozen. They called them memory made solid. The Great Quan of the time was not stupid, as no Great Quan is, and he now saw the use. He brought all these Downies to the pyramidal building and put them to work, writing down what he had while teaching him to read their marks. These Downies proved their value repeatedly, and soon they were doing much for the Great Quan, especially in organizing his Saurs and the life they led, day by day.

"Cornar, as I said, was of this class, as am I. As a young scribe, he was tasked with listing these new ancient artifacts and these long books, and he recognized the writing within to be an older form of what he and other Downies used. It didn't take him long to start reading the books, and he found that they had answers to the many questions Downies had about the ancient past. He tracked down the traders and asked where they had found the long books. The traders told him from a set of ruins far to the north. He managed to get a private audience with the Great Quan and the Savaan and explained that he felt these long books were important. He asked permission to mount an expedition to this set of ruins to see what else could be found. Savaan was against it, but the Great Quan wanted more of them if they were important.

"So Cornar, but a lowly, young scribe, found himself leading the expedition with one of the traders. It was a long, arduous trip. Now, a trip of legend among Downies who serve the Great Quan. But its history is unknown to most Saurs. When they got to this set of ruins, Cornar decided that it had once been some great place of learning, for he found a trove of long books, papers, records, diagrams, and illustrations of many kinds. The information within all this was of history, of how things work, of how to build, and of how to destroy. And much about mysteries so hidden, we had no idea they were even there."

"What kind of mysteries?"

"That itself is a mystery that I'm working on. But I think it is of an invisible world that we do not know, yet it knows us. That is senseless, I know, but—"

"Not so senseless, Lodak. If you can teach me how to read these long books, maybe I can help unlock those mysteries."

Lodak looked deeply at Sam with questioning eyes.

"We have looked at such invisible mysteries in Amerifrance."

"I will consider doing so, but…"

"Well, for now, continue with the story."

"Cornar returned with this trove and secretly presented it to the Great Quan. He was pleased, put Cornar in charge of it all, and ordered him to catalog it."

"Catalog it?"

"This was all the Great Quan wanted. But Cornar devoted his life to studying the work, and he trained others to aid him. My father was one. I became one. But we had to suppress everything we learned from everyone except the Great Quan and Savaan. We discovered useful things. And the Great Quan was happy that we did, for he made use of the useful. But the history we found, the history of us—he said, 'This history is interesting, this history is amusing, but this history is meaningless to the people. All the people need to know is—the Great Quan.' So, I work, study, and learn only for the Great Quan."

"What was this history?'

"There had once been a great civilization. Of course, we knew this from the ruins. But we learned that it had lasted millions of years. Or, rather, there had been many such civilizations over that time. They were born. They grew. They flourished. Then they died. But they always left something behind to help build the next civilization. We found out that the last civilization lasted a hundred thousand years. And we learned how it ended a thousand years ago."

"War?"

"Of a sort. It was a war of ideas—of true things. Or rather, it was a war between those with ideas who wanted to know the true things and those afraid or indifferent to ideas and the true things. It was causing much upset in civilization, much pain, and flaunting of the false. Finally, those of ideas, those who saw no alternative to the truth, those—those like me, my class—they decided to leave."

"Where did they go?"

"It is almost too fantastic to say."

"But is it the truth?"

"Of course."

"And you are of the class unafraid of the truth."

"No, my fear is not of the truth. It is of other things."

"We are not talking about other things right now, but only of the truth. Where did they go?"

Lodak slowly patted his chest three times with an open hand, then took that hand and pointed straight up.

"To the stars, you mean," Sam stated without emotion.

"You are not surprised?"

"Well…"

"This heightens my idea that you and Dan-el and La-ra and Jaa-on and Bert-ram are from the stars. That Amerifrance is not across a great body of water but across the sky."

Sam smiled but decided not to confirm or deny. He said instead, "Lodak, where does the artificial light come from? The truth, please;

not what the Great Quan wants all to believe. The truth."

///

"Hydroelectric. The Great Quan's light is powered by hydroelectricity."

Sam was sitting down to dinner with John, Lara, and Danielle.

Bertram was late, as he had been recently, or was possibly having dinner with Savaan.

Sam had explained to the other three what he had learned from Lodak and the necessity of keeping this from Bertram.

"Hydroelectricity? You're kidding. That's awfully sophisticated," John said.

"The old civilizations existed for a million years longer than any of ours. The last one was around for a hundred thousand years. For them, this was primitive technology. Our Saurs just found it. They don't understand it. Lodak doesn't really understand it. But he showed me some diagrams, and it was easy to see that it was hydroelectric. Look, I told you about the expedition to this ruined university—or whatever it was. Besides the long books and documents and stuff, they found this hydroelectric generator. It was in a vacuum-sealed clean room of some sort. So, maybe it wasn't a university but a museum. Or a museum in a university. Doesn't matter; the important thing is it was at least a thousand years old, maybe much older, and in perfect working condition. And there were instructions on how to use it. I think it was all a display. In any case, Cornar and his people packed it all up, brought it back, and managed to demonstrate it for the Great Quan. He saw its value to him immediately."

"So, it's this generator—" John began.

"That powers the lights that shine on the city's outside walls and the spotlights on the Great Quan." Sam finished the thought.

"And the light in Lodak's study?" Lara asked.

"Of course. And it's hidden in a fake barge house on the river, where the water to power comes from."

"But what about the Great Quan's tent on the hunt?" Danielle asked.

"Ah, Danielle, that's the exciting stuff. Based on the plans, Cornar was able to construct a portable generator. I don't know how, but he did. It's built into the back of the tent. You'll remember there was a creek behind the tent. How it generated so much electricity from a slow-moving creek, I don't know. I suspect it may be the material the generator is made from. Something that has very little resistance, so it doesn't take much to spin the small turbines."

"So," John said," the Great Quan has access to a source of unlimited energy that could benefit all the people, which could take them, literally, out of a dark age, and he only uses it for his self-aggrandizement."

"Whose self-aggrandizement?" Bertram had entered at the end of John's statement. "Sam's, I assume?"

Although all four felt caught, they did not show it.

"Bertram—cut the crap!" John faked his irritation beautifully. "We're talking about the artificial light. We obviously don't believe it comes somehow magically from the Great Quan, so there must be a power source he has access to. But no one knows what it is."

"Even Lodak believes it's some magic from the Great Quan," Sam said.

"But I was just pointing out that, intrigued by this mystery as we might be, the real shame is that whatever the power source is, he could be using it to make life better for everyone and, instead, he uses it—as I said—just to illuminate his magnificence."

"Probably a smart move," Bertram said with an unfortunate lack of irony.

"*Quelle?*"

"No matter what the power source is, most Saurs are not going to understand it, much less have the smarts to exploit it."

"But where do you think it came from?" Lara asked Bertram.

"I don't know. Probably from that ruined city. Somebody found it, brought it to the Great Quan, and he saw how it could be used to enhance and solidify his power."

Lara frowned. "Yeah, his power to oppress."

"Lara, your naiveté is exhausting. In a society as primitive as this, it is the Strong Man who holds everything together. Without the Great Quan, you would have chaos. Is that what you would prefer for these people? Right, Sam?"

"Quite frankly, I don't prefer anything for these people. I prefer to reverse what we have done."

"Well, first, don't include me in that *we*. And, second, don't you think it's about time you accepted reality as it is now and gave some thanks for how privileged we are? For Christ's sake, we could have been eaten by a dinosaur. Instead, we are the honored guest of the Great Quan and treated rather well."

"Yes," Sam said, "it is about *time*. The time we altered. And now there is obviously a source of power we can use to restart the collider and correct that. Our privileged positions as honored guests—your new-found friendship with Savaan—gives us the potential to persuade them to let us have that power."

"You must be—"

"Look, all we have to do is tell them that we are explorers from the stars—this is what Lodak thinks anyway—and that—I don't know—we got separated from our rocket or something, and we're lost here. But, anyway, in our explorations, we found this other ruin, and it's full of wonderful 'magic' for the Great Quan. The 'other ruin' is of course, The Dark Lady. It just needs the power to fire it up. Then we get in there, figure out how to reverse what we did, reverse it, and get back to our reality."

"You're mad!"

"I suppose," John said, "it could potentially work, but—"

"Let's not kid ourselves," Bertram interrupted. "We wouldn't be 'getting back' to our reality like we just hopped on a plane and flew home. We would be re-creating our reality and thereby destroying this reality."

"What reality?" Sam rose up, raised his voice, and strode to Bertram to stand face to face. "A despotic dictatorship?"

"But there are still people here," Lara stood up as well. They were living, breathing people whom we had gotten to know."

"They're not people, they're Saurs, and they should never have existed. This reality should never have existed. We would just be putting things right."

"Sam, *mon amie*, I don't think you want to argue *existence* with me. But when universes and realities can be changed at the push of a button, does it really matter whose reality is real? Doesn't it just matter which reality exists at the moment? We don't know if we can recapture our reality. Maybe by reversing our experiment, we would create a different reality; different from ours and this one."

"Yeah, one where we get eaten," Bertram added.

"Sam," Danielle continued, "all we truly know is that this reality exists, and we are now a part of it. And that to do anything consciously to destroy it is *génocide*."

"But our world, our reality, everyone we know, the history of our civilization, the glory of it—"

"And the shame of it, the pain and death and destruction," Bertram enumerated.

"Yes, that too! We also wiped out all of that. We have a responsibility to bring it back."

"And we have no responsibility to these people, Sam?" Lara was louder, stronger, more assured than she had ever been. "I mean, if you think about it, we are their gods. We are their creators."

"Oh, shit! Don't tell Sam that. That'll just give him a rationale for destroying them. What a god creates, a god can destroy," Bertram said. "I long entertained the theory that you had a god complex, Sam. Now we can put it to the test."

The sudden confederation of Lara and Bertram angered Sam and unbalanced him with its surreality. "Guys—Don't you get it? *We don't belong here.* Lara, you'll never see your parents again. Or your little brother. John, I'm convinced you're in line for a Nobel Prize. Do you not want to go to Stockholm? Danielle—never to see Paris again?"

"Such emotional claptrap!" Bertram said. "What this is really all about is you want to do the experiment again. You want to find out what you did wrong. You can't stand the fact—the undeniable fact— that your so-called genius created this mess, that your so-called *genius* was wrong."

"And you just want to get close to power so raw and undiluted that—"

"Both of you, shut up!" John, the professor, teacher, mentor, and friend, called on all the authority and familiarity those positions gave him to stop the two. "We have a dilemma that must be discussed, not argued over! You know, like scientists, not like ignorant knee-jerkers."

"But—"

"Don't make my 'shut-up' a waste of breath, Sam."

Sam said no more.

"Bertram's point is that this is now reality. It is what it is; let's deal with it and make the best of it. Sam's point, as he once said, is that he's a *Homo sapiens* chauvinist, that if there is even the slightest chance that we can change this reality back to our reality, to *Homo sapiens* reality, aren't we obligated to do so? Well, I'm a *Homo sapiens* chauvinist as well. I have never been one to take the facile position that our species is a nasty virus, some scourge upon some perfect, natural Garden of

Eden earth. Not that our young species isn't ungainly on occasion, like any adolescent—no, pre-adolescent—no, toddler! But we can also be bright, charming, creative, and curious. Which are all functions of what? Rational, conscious, sentient intelligence. Possibly a very rare, thus precious, phenomenon in our, or *this*, or *any* universe.

"Now, as much as a *Homo sapiens* chauvinist as I am, I am no less of a pragmatist than Bertram. Sam, your plan, your scheme to somehow get power to the Dark Lady and get her to dance to your tune, is very much a long shot. Quell your emotions on this and think about it, and you'll agree. We don't know if it's possible. But we know that we are here, now, in this universe, in a world and society, despite being ages and ages older than ours, which is primitive. So very primitive in its intelligence, emotions, rationality, curiosity, and—can I say it?—humanity. So, if we are going to have to live among them, what good can we be to them? Maybe our chauvinism and loyalty shouldn't be to our species but to knowledge, to knowing. After all, what purpose do we fragile creatures—and in this world, *very* fragile creatures—have, in this or any other universe? None of us are religious, so none of us can call on comfort food fairy tales for a purpose. But can we call on what we know? Biology tells us that we, like all living organisms, strive to survive. Our history tells us that we are happiest when we not only survive but thrive as well. Our brains, our minds—if there is a difference—ask us to seek out and feed them with knowledge. So, as conscious, sentient, aware, rational biological units, what purpose could we have but to survive, thrive, and know? You said as much yourself a while back, Sam. What matters if we have hair, or down, or scales?

"We are now living in a world, or at least in this land of Where the Great Quan Rules, that does not value curiosity, knowledge, and reason. And a dark, mean, violent world it is because of it. The Saurs once did value them, as evidenced by their ruined past. If we must be here for the rest of our lives, can we not dedicate ourselves to serving knowledge and doing our best to help enlighten these people? Yes, Sam, *people*. Conscious, sentient, if not quite rational people. And Bertram, can we do that for their benefit and not just ours? And now, I'm going to bed. Dorm room bull sessions always wore me out."

The four John left behind said nothing. What could be said? But emotions were being felt. A range of them. Some may have been ennobling. Some mixed. Some possibly bordered on anger or disappointment. All spurred thought.

///

The next day, John and Lara were walking along a street they had not previously explored when suddenly Sencee and Nob, who were accompanying them, tried to stop them from turning a corner.

"Why?" John asked. "Won't this street take us directly to where we are going?"

"Yes, Jaa-on," Nob said. "But we forgot what day it was."

"What does the day have to do with it?" Lara asked as she pushed forward around the corner, then abruptly stopped.

A commercial activity was taking place down the street on what was obviously a temporary raised platform. An energetic salesman addressed a receptive crowd of well-robed Scales and Downies.

Lara turned quickly, upset, back to the intersecting street. "Let's go around the other way."

"No, that'll take us way out of our way," John said as he moved forward, around the corner, and faced a yellowsack market. Lara, Sencee, and Nob followed. Now John knew why Nob and Lara wanted to avoid this. But he said, "Come on, we'll be past it in a minute."

As they got closer, Nob and Sencee protecting their smaller masters, they could not help but be captured by the salesmanship of the energetic yellowsack merchant, a Scale of no great bulk but rather tall and wiry.

"Okay, so what we have next to offer is a pair, a pair, a mother and child. The mother, I grant you, is not much to look at, not much to look at. If I tried, I couldn't fool you about that— so why try? But look at this child! We have had our physical assessors look over this child, and they say, they say that the child will grow into full maturity, full maturity. This is an investment you're making, not just a purchase, an investment."

The yellowsack mother and child on display, off to the side, were Scales, but a Downy woman first spoke up. "I'll take the child, but I have no use for the mother."

"Cannot do that, cannot do that! I cannot break up a pair."

"But I don't want the mother; I want the child."

"And you'll want a discount, a discount for taking only one. Cannot, cannot do it."

"No, I'll pay full price. Just give me the child and throw the female away."

"All right! Who am I to argue with a customer? Bring the child."

Two bulky and muscular market Saurs approached the yellowsack mother and child standing on display and began to separate them. It was not easy. The screaming child clung tightly to his mother, and the wailing mother held tightly onto her son. But the market Saurs, after laying a few blows on both mother and child, completed the task.

One market Saur dragged the frightened child to the front of the platform, and the other held the crying, screaming, hysterical mother. As the merchant admonished the child to stop crying and stand up tall to be presented to his new mistress, the other market Saur began to beat the mother. To quiet her? No, to kill her. He beat her and slammed and pounded. Raw, red flesh was exposed. Her groans and cries grew weaker with each hammer-like slam. It was vicious and well-loved by the customers.

John had stopped. He could not have refused to witness the atrocity, and he would not let it pass.

"Stop! Stop this!" his soft, human voice yelled out, heard by no one. But he got everyone's attention when he pushed through the crowd, sliding and slipping between big Scale and Downy bulks, got to the front, and climbed up onto the platform.

"Stop this! Leave her alone! I'll buy them, I'm sure—"

Without thought or hesitation, the market Saur who had delivered the boy pulled out a long knife and ran it through John's stomach, pulled it out, then ran it through John's chest. And then through his stomach again—and again—and again.

Lara screamed.

Nob jumped up onto the platform and tried to stop the murderous Saur. The Saur brushed Nob off, let John's body collapse, then reached out, grabbed Nob, and without hesitation, slit his throat. The loyal yellowsack's body seemed to fold into itself to hang from the Saur's hand. The Saur promptly disposed himself of the encumbrance, tossing Nob on top of John's corpse, where the yellowsack's life quickly drained away.

Sencee grabbed Lara, covered her, and quickly spirited her off.

STEVEN PAUL LEIVA

EIGHTEEN

THE BLACKCLADS

"Saammmm! Saammmm!" Guien pleaded.

"Sam!" Lara yelled.

Sam ran down a dark corridor, hot with anger, his mind clouded with confusion, his chest bellowing breaths in and out, his stomach sick.

Guien ran behind him, trying to keep up. Despite having longer legs, Downy legs were not made for speed. He held up a torch, desperate to light Sam's way. "Saammmm! Saammmm!"

Lara followed behind Guien, streaming tears, fear of harm wanting to hold her back, yet fear for Sam driving her on. "Sam!"

Sencee followed them all in a panic, but she could not leave her Lara.

They all shot through a door connecting the dark corridor to a sunlit common room full of elite Saurs milling about, waiting to see Savaan. As unusual sights tend to do, this sprinting parade of human/yellowsack/human/yellowsack caught the Saurs by surprise, turned their heads, interrupted their conversations, and offended their well-tuned sensibilities of proper behavior. Nevertheless, as a mass, they parted into two groups, creating a path for Sam and the others that led to the antechamber to Savaan's office. There was a Downy official, the first stop to an audience with Savaan, who was patiently trying to explain something to a Scale applicant. Both were ignored as Sam, followed by the others, bolted through, leaving the official no time to respond.

As Savaan administered with a "my door is always open" policy, there was no door to impede Sam's progress. He rushed into Savaan's large, ornate room and abruptly stopped when he saw Savaan at a desk talking with Bertram.

Savaan looked up, unsurprised, and gave Sam a look of some concern. "Saammmm, I regret—"

"You regret? They murdered him in broad daylight, in the middle of the street, and nothing is being done about it!"

"What can be done?" Savaan sincerely asked, spreading his arms, his open hands palms up, which struck Sam as a far too human gesture.

"Arrest them, damn it! They murdered him just because he was trying to help a woman."

"A woman?" Savaan questioned, now perplexed. "My understanding is that it was a yellowsack."

Bertram stepped forward, coming up to Sam, who Lara had joined. Guien and Sencee stood way back, uncomfortable and apprehensive.

"Sam, I warned John. I warned you all. This is not our society, our culture. We have no right to judge."

"You are so full of piss and shit, Bert! They slaughtered John! Don't you get it? Have you seen John's body?"

"No, when I heard, I came directly here."

"To do what? To distance yourself from John?"

"No, of course not, I—"

"Bert-ram came to explain to me how you people have a different attitude toward the yellowsacks, based on your own culture. It was quite illuminating. And it explains the strange morphology your yellowsacks have taken on. We have been wondering about that. Bertram has done you well by his clear explanation. I see no reason why this should cause the rest of you any inconvenience."

"But what are you going to do about the murderers?"

Lara stepped slightly forward, crying tears, crying in anguish, crying out, "He was only trying to—"

"Lara—Sam—let's go home."

Sam laughed a harsh, strained laugh. "Home? You mean that place where we eat and sleep in this reality you want to save?"

"You're distraught."

"Distraught!? I'm fucking angry is what I am!"

"Saammmm, you are honored guests of the Great Quan, who values you greatly. But it is not the place of a guest to question his host."

"You smug son-of-a-bitch!"

Sam pushed Bertram aside, jumped onto Savaan's desk, and then leaped onto the powerful eight-foot Downy, trying to get his hands around Savaan's neck. Sam's momentum, combined with Savaan's reflex to pull away, pushed his chair back and over. They landed with a slam on the floor. Sam held on like a bronco buster and, failing to get his hands around the Downy's thick neck, began to punch at his face.

"Sam!" Bertram yelled as he ran over and tried his best to pull Sam off, his best being utterly inadequate to the task.

Scale guards rushed into the room, three of them grabbing Lara, Guien, and Sencee and locking painful grips on them; a fourth quickly grabbed Sam and extricated him from the precious person of Savaan. He held Sam up high, letting his legs flail in protest.

Savaan stood up, self-righteous white heat in his eyes. No one had ever attacked him before; no one would have dared.

"Incarcerate them!" Savaan ordered the guards, gesturing to Sam and Lara. "Them and their *fat* yellowsacks!"

The guards pushed and dragged and carried the four out of the room, leaving Savaan and Bertram—the former still seething, the latter making no protest at all.

///

It was like a dungeon in an old movie. Which should not have been surprising, but somehow Sam and Lara were depressed by that fact. It was a square space, illuminated only barely by two torches on the wall outside the cell. There were bars made of the porcelain-like material they had often seen, but they were horizontal, not vertical. It was dank, a companion to the dark, and it seemed as if the moist, humid, stale air seeped into their pores while it chilled them. The walls were stone, rough, ugly stone with many blunt-to-sharp protrusions. There was no furniture, and the floors were hard, compacted dirt.

Sam and Lara sat on the floor, despondent, their backs against a wall. It was not comfortable. The protrusions poked. They were no longer in their finely tailored robes but in rough-hewed, oversized yellowsack garments.

Sencee and Guien stood in the middle of the cell, huddling together, scared. But they were also worried about Sam and Lara, worried that their human kindness would kill them.

"Ow!" Sam had made a slight movement, and the wall made a sharp point.

Guien immediately pulled his yellowsack up over his head, leaving himself naked, and folded it into a cushion.

"Here, Saammmm, for your back."

Sam looked up at the naked Guien. "It's cold in here, Guien. Put it back on."

"It gives me little protection."

"Still—it's something."

"But—"

"Put it back on!" Sam said too sharply.

"Sam, don't." Lara put her hand on his arm. The touch was welcomed, Lara's warmth coming through despite her cold flesh.

Heeding the admonition, Sam looked over to Guien, who had backed away. "Guien—I'm sorry."

"You were hurting your back."

"I know, but—"

"I've got an idea," Lara said, standing up. "Sencee, come here and sit."

Sencee seemed reluctant.

"Sit. Here, by me."

Sencee came over and sat, her Scale back against the wall.

"No, turn sideways."

Sencee did, and then Lara sat behind her and leaned her back against Sencee's. Sencee bent her back slightly to recline Lara's back.

Sam and Guien were impressed and positioned themselves in the same way.

"Comfy?" Lara asked.

"Sure," Sam said. "Lucky for you, Scales did not evolve from the stegosaurus."

Suddenly, the cell's bars slid to one side, creating an opening. Danielle and Avar were tossed in roughly. Avar kept her footing, but Danielle fell to the ground.

"*Merde!*"

As Avar quickly went to Danielle and picked her up, everyone could see that she, too, had been put into a yellowsack garment. But as she recovered herself, brushing dust from the rough, yellow material, they could also see that she had altered it by tying a cord around the waist, taking it from a formless sack to something that honored her attractive female form.

"What the hell?" Lara asked, getting more comfortable with anger. "Are you so French that you *have* to be fashionable?"

"Ah, *ma chérie*, this is not fashion, *c'est un défi!*"

"Oh. Well, I guess that's okay then."

Sam stood up and walked over to Danielle. "I'm sorry," he said.

"*Pas de regrets,* Sam. "They took John's body away. I asked if I could bury him, but they just took him away."

"They will send him to Varneerah," Guien said.

"Where?" Lara asked.

"It is where we all go after we die."

"Oh." Lara, Sam, and Danielle dismissed the information as nothing but ancient Saur mythology.

"I suppose it's obvious, but what's happening out there?" Sam wanted to know.

"Well, we are no longer *invités honorés* of the Great Quan, that's *pour sûr.* They cleared out our rooms, took everything away, all our stuff and clothes. We managed, though, to sneak Cuz out."

Avar reached into a bag she was carrying and pulled the little creature out, holding it in her big palm.

"It was *stupide,* I know, but I felt John would have… Well, you know, he was so *sentimental.*"

"He would have been so grateful." Lara went to Avar, took Cuz, and held him close to her face.

"And what about Bertram?" Sam asked.

"He swears that he's trying to help us," Danielle answered.

"Well," Sam said, not hiding his cynicism, "I guess it's good to have a man on the inside."

///

The following became a well-told tale.

Late that night, two prison guards, both Scales, were at their station. One was on the verge of sleep, and the other was eating a piece of cold meat under the weak light of a torch in the wall. This was a lousy duty. The meat-eating guard longed for years to pass, as seniority would find him more pleasant duties.

Lodak walked in, resplendent in his official robe, surprising the chewing guard, whose disturbed exclamation woke the sleeping guard.

"Too late for visitors, scholar," The guard said after he swallowed.

"Not for a scholar with permission from the Great Quan."

Lodak handed over a small document with a triangular blotch on it. The guards looked at the document, and both were impressed.

"This is only the second time I have seen the Great Quan's seal," the eating guard said.

"Which should indicate to you how important my visit is."

"Yes, it does that. And I am honored to comply." He turned to the sleepy guard and said, "Bring them up."

The sleepy guard yawned but tried to stifle it. "Yes, yes, of course, right away." He left to comply.

"Tell me, scholar, after tomorrow, will you dissect the humans?"

"You know that dissection is not allowed."

"On us, yes, of course. But on them? They are not Saur."

"That's an interesting point of view. Do you think they should not be sent to the vortex? Do you think they should not go to Varneerah?"

"Varneerah is not for them."

"Only for us?"

"Of course."

"Assuming it is not all a myth."

The guard shook his head in arrogant amusement. "You scholars, questioning everything. Varneerah is no myth, my friend."

"And you look forward to going there?"

"Of course!"

"Have a pleasant journey." Lodak pulled a short sword from his robe and thrust it up into the guard's heart.

As the dead Scale fell to the ground, five Saurs—three Downy and two Scales—entered. They were dressed not in robes but rather were clad in black: black pullover long-sleeve shirts and tight black pants. One of them threw a black bundle at Lodak, who caught it, placed it on the guard's desk, then shed off his robe and quickly put on the black clothes.

The door the other guard had left by, now opened. Sam, Lara, and Danielle entered, followed by the sleepy guard, who was quickly jumped on and dispatched.

The humans were confused and questioning.

"Quiet!" Lodak said to them. "No discussion. We leave now."

"Wait a minute, Lodak," Sam grabbed him by the arm. "What are you doing?"

"Does it take a scholar to see?"

"Look, you can talk to the Great Quan, we can negotiate—"

"Sam," Danielle said, "I don't think—"

Sam turned to Danielle. "We can't leave. We need to be here, where the power is."

"That power killed John," Lara reminded Sam.

"The *hydro*power. And I need Lodak. We can't let him—"

"You are to be executed in the morning," The Downy scholar said, as a matter of most urgent fact.

"Surely, we can—"

"There is no appeal, Saammmm. You attacked Savaan, the Downy who sits at the right hand of the Great Quan. To let you live would diminish him. He will not allow himself to be diminished."

Danielle, adamant, looked deeply into Sam's eyes and said, "Wherever they are taking us, we are going."

"Give them the clothes," Lodak said to his men.

Several of them brought three bundles of clothes to the humans.

"They will fit," Lodak said. "I had them made a long time ago."

"You had them—"

"Sam," Lara said, taking off her yellowsack, unconcerned over her temporary nakedness. "Shut up and dress."

Once the humans were all in black, Lodak said, "Let's go."

"Wait!" Lara stopped them. "Sencee! And Avar and Guien!"

"What?"

"Our yellowsacks."

"We cannot take them."

"We must."

"Absurd!"

"Honor Jaa-on's death!" Lara said.

Lodak looked to the others. Danielle gave him a hard stare. Sam, still stunned over his own acquiescence, indicated that Lodak needed to do the same.

Lodak turned to two of the blackclads. "Get them. Bring them to the barge." He turned to the others. "Now, quickly but quietly, we must leave.

///

Lodak led them down a myriad of dark corridors, negotiating them—turns to the right, turns to the left—with no hesitation until he came to a door and slowly opened it. He brought his party, the three humans and several blackclads, out onto the narrow side street by which the humans had first entered the Pyramidal building. Waiting there for them were several more blackclads and a caravan of sleds and small wagons. The wagons, which were lined up behind the sleds, were loaded with stuff, packed haphazardly. The sleds were much like those used in the Arctic, except these were on small wheels and were pulled, not by dogs, but by what the humans could only consider micro-dinosaurs; about three feet long from snout to the end of their tails, running on two legs, their little arms (that Lara could not help but see as cute), hanging down. Six micro-dinosaurs, in three pairs, were hitched side-by-side to each sled.

Sam, Lara, and Danielle were each directed to separate sleds. Their drivers helped them on and covered them, jumping onto the backs of the sleds. Lodak and the blackclads got onto their own sleds, and then they were off.

It was a fast, wild ride through narrow streets and alleys, all lit in a sequence of blackclad held torches, suddenly appearing out of the dark before them to light their way, until the caravan reached the next suddenly-appearing blackclad with a torch, the one now behind disappearing quickly.

They stopped by the city wall. Several of the blackclads jumped to the wall, pushing together at a certain spot, and that section of the wall opened. The sleds and wagons were driven through, and then they were outside Quannak in the golden illumination of its reflective exterior surface. But this was a side of the city far away from the main gate and the main road, so no one was looking. Close to the wall was an overgrowth of tall, thick bushes. Several blackclads ran to one bush and easily moved it aside, revealing a descending pathway just wide enough for the sleds and small wagons.

The sleds headed down the great hill, in twists and turns, through a tunnel of closely-packed vegetation, faster than what was comfortable for Lara, but which reminded Danielle and Sam of their teenage days, riding massive roller coasters on two continents, on an Earth that no longer existed.

They emerged out of the forest of bushes that covered this side of the hill and stopped before a tributary of the great river. There two flatboat barges half the size of the one that had brought them to the city, floated just offshore, tied down to posts stuck into the ground. Each barge was connected to the land by a plank, which blackclads were using to load stuff (obviously looted from the city) onto the barges. Five small, nearly empty wagons stood nearby.

Sam, Lara, and Danielle were rushed to one of the barges, followed by Lodak. Once on board, once breaths were caught, Sam turned to Lodak, many questions in mind.

"Lodak?"

"There is much I haven't told you, Saammmm."

"Obviously."

"No time now. Sleep is required."

"With the adrenaline rush we just had?"

"Look!" Lara, who had been keeping an eye on the path, called out when a small wagon appeared.

On it stood Sencee, Avar, and Guien, in and among and holding onto a bunch of stuff. When the wagons stopped, they jumped off and were taken to the vessel with the humans. The reunion was quick and quiet. The yellowsacks were confused but grateful for the affectionate reception they received from Danielle and Lara.

blackclads rapidly unloaded the wagon and loaded their contents onto the second barge, tying everything down.

"What are they loading, Lodak?"

"Food, long books, machines from the ruins that I have been storing, Saammmm."

"Ah."

"And scrap material, and medical supplies, all of which we obtained through barter, bribery, or theft."

"You are more than a scholar, Lodak."

"This activity makes me less than a scholar. But it is necessary."

"Where are we going?"

"This tributary will take us to a point in the great river, out of sight from Quannak."

"And then to where?"

"No more questions. Now to sleep. You will need restful sleep."

"Why?"

"If I told you that—you would not sleep."

Lodak pointed to sleeping cushions tucked among tied-down crates. The humans and their yellowsack friends dutifully went to them, laid down, and prepared to sleep.

NINETEEN

THE VORTEX

Lara had always been an early riser. This proclivity established itself when she was but eighteen months old, and it seemed so unusual to her parents that they considered renaming her Dawn. But she always woke up refreshed, bright, and mentally active. This habit had never left her, and so she never had the life advantage of excusing herself by claiming she "wasn't a morning person." The morning hours—quiet, gentle, cool, or snugly warm if the weather was deeply cold—were when she did her homework, read voraciously, played with her science kits, wrote in her diary, daydreamed, composed school themes, wrote her master's dissertation. Changing universes had not altered this at all. She was the first one to rise the next morning.

Lara got up from the sleeping cushion and saw that the two blackclad barges were now moving with the flow of the great river, which was wide and, she assumed, deep. The barge was in the control of just two of the blackclads, one at a tiller, one who seemed to be a lookout. They greeted her by touching their open right hands to their chests. She looked toward the banks of the river and saw that they were passing grass-covered flatlands punctuated by widely spaced trees. Creatures flew overhead, both feathered and scaled. She took a deep breath of cool air. Nothing at all, at this moment, seemed wrong with this world, this universe.

"AHHHHHHH! AWAKE! AWAKE!" The lookout screamed.

Immediately, blackclads were on their feet, scrambling to assigned places after gathering weapons. One grabbed Lara picked her up, and carried her back to the sleeping cushions, where Sam and Danielle were rousing themselves.

"Please," the blackclad said. "All of you, stay here behind these crates and stay down."

But they did not. They located Lodak at the stern of the barge and ran to him. He was fully in charge and issuing orders to others.

"What's happening?" Sam cried out.

"It's the Great Quan's forces." He pointed to a huge barge moving faster than might be expected.

"How is it...?" Danielle asked.

"Look in front of it. See something just out of the water?"

They spotted it. It looked like a small boat with a Scale soldier riding on it.

"That is a river-runner. You cannot see most of it."

"You mean that little boat?"

"It's not a boat. It's a head. The river-runner is a giant swimming creature with a neck longer than its body. It has powerful flippers and can swim very fast. It is hitched to the barge, pulling it faster than the river flows. It will catch up to us soon. Look to its sides. Two more river-runners with riders. They have learned how to control these creatures."

"What are you going to do?"

"Fight them off as long as possible. You all should get behind the crates in front of your sleeping cushions and cover yourself to diminish exposure."

"Can we not fight?" Danielle asked.

"Have you been trained to?"

"No."

"Then how can you ask the question? Do not be a burden to our efforts. Go now"

Sencee and Avar pulled at Lara and Danielle, dragging them back.

"Guien, you too, go back."

"But, Saammmm..."

"Please. Go. Protect the others."

Guien left, and Lodak turned to Sam. "Is your life not worth saving?"

"You look outnumbered. You are going to be outrun."

Lodak was calm and unconcerned. "This is not unexpected."

"What? Then maybe you have a secret weapon?"

"It is no secret. It is just that too few people use it."

Shouts and warnings suddenly filled the air. Pointed fingers directed their attention to one of the river-runners, moving fast, gaining on the barge behind them. The blackclads on that barge began a barrage of arrows, aiming for the river-runner's head, but the rider kept the creature's long neck weaving while it continued gaining on them. Not one arrow hit its mark.

Soon, the river-runner was almost upon the barge.

"Once the creature gets close enough, it will be easier to hit," Sam told Lodak. "They should be safe, right?"

"Unfortunately, no," Lodak said, already grieving.

The creature stopped weaving its long neck and head. Skimming the surface of the water now, it seemed the perfect target. But before advantage could be taken, the head rose slightly, then, with the rider holding on, dove beneath the surface and disappeared.

There was a horrible moment of calm. Then, the creature (forty feet long, at least) surfaced its head and rider well ahead of the barge. The hump of its body came up under the barge and lifted it, taking it out of the water. Then the barge, with its blackclads screaming, slid off the side of the creature's body and fell back into the river, capsized and broken. As the Great Quan's forces passed the wreckage, they picked off the swimming blackclads with arrows and spears.

All were lost.

The Great Quan's barge was close enough now that Lodak and Sam could make out Savaan standing at the bow. And with him, standing on a crate to come up to Savaan's eye level, was Bertram.

"SAM!" Bertram yelled, pointing to the blackclads surrounding Sam. "THEY ARE CRIMINALS AND TRAITORS."

"POINT THAT FINGER BACK AT YOURSELF, YOU SON-OF-A-BITCH!"

"I'M TRYING TO SAVE YOUR LIVES!"

"GO TO HELL!"

Savaan turned to his soldiers and issued an order. Arrows began to fly.

Lodak issued the same order to his troops, then yelled to a blackclad standing at the barge's bow, "How close are we?"

"Now! It's coming up now!"

Lodak ran to the bow, followed by Sam, dodging arrows and spears. Once there, Lodak pointed ahead. "Look!"

Sam looked and saw the river forking ahead, with the main body flowing off to the left and a narrow tributary branching to the right.

Lodak turned around. "Follow the main river!" he shouted to the blackclad on the tiller.

The blackclad barge moved in that direction, but the two river-runners sped ahead and passed them, going beyond them, to turn around and cut off their path to the main river.

Lodak smiled. "Good."

"Good?" Sam asked with confused concern.

"Make for the tributary. Now! Now!" Lodak ordered.

The blackclad worked the tiller. The barge groaned as it tried to change course, but soon, it caught the flow heading into the tributary.

"SAM, YOU FOOL! YOU'LL DIE!" Bertram yelled from his barge, which had stopped at the mouth of the tributary.

"Why aren't they following?" Sam asked Lodak.

"Because there is only one place this tributary takes us. To the vortex."

"The vortex? That does not sound good, Lodak."

"It is the passageway to Varneerah, the resting place for all Saurs. We do not bury our dead. We set them adrift on rafts down this tributary. The vortex takes them in its arms and carries them to Varneerah. Jaa-on has preceded us."

Lodak pointed ahead again.

In the distance, Sam saw agitated, swirling waters. "Lodak, this is hardly a solution."

"No time for conversation, Saammmm. Only time to hang on."

Lodak grabbed one of Sam's hands and directed it to a loop of thick rope attached to the inside of the barge.

"You'll need to use both hands," Lodak said as he grabbed another loop with one hand.

Sam looked around. All the blackclads were now hanging onto loops, attached down the length of the barge. As were Avar, Sencee, and Guien. Even Lara and Danielle were clinging onto loops with both hands as the barge began to move faster and faster, having been captured by the quick-flowing waters streaming toward the vortex.

///

And what about Bertram? What was he feeling at the loss of all his human companions? Can we suppose?

"I am sorry, Bert-Ram," Savaan may well have said to him as they stood on the big barge, watching the smaller one diminish in the distance. "You must be upset. I know the Great Quan will be. He will cry over this. He is quite emotional, you know."

But would Bertram have been crying?

"This outcome was inevitable." It is probably safe to assume Bertram assured Savaan.

"From what you tell me, yes, I believe you are right. You will, of course, reveal to no one the existence of organized traitors."

"Who would I tell? I am alone now."

"No, Bert-ram, you are family now—a child of the Great Quan. You will be his only solace."

"An overstatement, I'm sure, Savaan. But if I can serve..."

TWENTY

VARNEERAH

Sam hunkered down, held on tight to the rope handle, and squeezed his eyes shut. His emotions flowed like the agitated tributary, mixing fear, apprehension, panic, resignation, and—curiosity. *Where the hell were they going?* Hopefully, it wasn't a Saur version of hell.

He couldn't help himself; he opened his eyes and rose enough to look ahead. There was the vortex, getting closer and closer. And there, beyond, was a magnificent mountain range. *Who the hell cared that it was magnificent?* But Sam guessed you couldn't cut off impressions, even if impressions were about to be permanently cut off.

He hunkered down again and looked to Lodak, who was holding on tight but smiling and seemed, although alert, calm. *What the hell?* Or, rather, *what the heaven?* Did Lodak think they were going to end up in—

The barge suddenly tilted forward.

This is it! Sam thought. *We're going in!* He took a deep breath, held it, and shut his eyes again. *We're going down!*

And down they went, at a thrilling but hardly dangerous forty-five-degree angle as the tributary flowed underground. All now was speed and the amplified sound of rushing water. And then—a deep dark.

It's a water slide, Sam thought. *It's a goddamn water slide!*

And it was. A natural water slide through a tunnel with a few twists and turns, which probably turned a few stomachs and twisted a few faces. Besides the surrounding black, it was suddenly cold.

The cold attacked Sam's face and hands and crept through his blackclad clothes. He tried to talk to Lodak, but the roar of the rushing water, echoing off the tunnel walls, made it impossible.

Then, the barge tilted up a little, and a welcome light came from up ahead. Sam looked. There was an opening before them. A golden light was streaming through. But an opening into what? Sam wondered as the opening became more extensive the closer they came. Lodak wrapped one arm around Sam and held him close to the barge's deck.

Then, they were flying out of a grand opening in the side of the wall of a grand cavern, flying over a lake that filled the bottom of the cavern. Flying—and falling.

They smacked the lake's surface, and the barge skipped across it once, twice, and a third time. The collective grunts of Saurs and humans echoed in the cavern at each skip. The barge finally came to a rocking rest on the water it had disturbed and shook those holding onto the rope handles, causing not a few bumps and bruises.

Soon, calm returned, and Saurs and humans got up onto their feet. The blackclads moved to various stations to perform various tasks, several of them retrieving long poles that they put into the water, touched the bottom with, and used to push the barge toward the end of the grand cavern. A large opening let in intense daylight while letting out water, which flowed into a continuation of the river.

"Is this Varneerah?" Sam asked Lodak.

"Yes. But you are not dead."

"The secret weapon?"

"Knowledge, Saammmm. The knowledge that this is just a geological formation and not the mythic resting place of all Saurs."

III

Danielle and Lara joined Sam and Lodak at the bow just as the barge emerged from the cavern. Behind them were foothills before a mountain range. Sam assumed this was the other side of the mountain range he had seen before entering the vortex. But they had descended for a long time; they must now be at a much lower level than Anaraquan. Ahead, far in the distance, was another mountain range. And just before them was a verdant valley that the river they were now on was taking them through.

The river began to bend, and around the bend, they saw a village bustling with Saurs, both Downies and Scales. They all wore garments much like the blackclads but of various hues, none bright, in the beige to brown range. And none were adorned with colored stones or nuggets of gold. Yellow garments were seen nowhere.

When the Saurs on shore spotted the barge, shouts of greeting went up, and many started to move toward a dock extending out onto the river. The village's buildings were essentially huts made of natural materials. Most were round with conical roofs and only one level. They were laid out in a sensible grid pattern. In the middle of the village was a large, round structure with a dome roof. There were workers in the fields, but they were far from the emaciated yellowsacks of Anaraquan. These were robust and vibrant. And there was a blessed lack of overseers.

"This," Lodak said, "is the real Varneerah." His pride, his relief, his sense of homecoming was palpable.

The barge was guided with the long poles to the dock and tied up. A plank was laid.

"Come," Lodak said to the humans, taking them to the plank and leading them off the barge.

Many Saurs were standing on the dock. They were happy to see the barge's arrival. Some were happy to see the return of friends or relatives. Some were anxious to see what the barge contained. All were fascinated to see the humans.

The crowd of Saurs parted as Lodak and the humans walked down the dock.

"Lodak," a female Scale reached out. "Harnack?"

"He was on the other barge, Cinsun. Destroyed by a river-runner."

"Oh." The female seemed immediately resigned to the fact presented. And yet, a sadness could be detected. "Perhaps his bones will come through."

"Perhaps."

When they reached the shore, they were greeted by an older Scale, maybe fourteen feet tall, the tallest Scale they had seen except for the Great Quan. He seemed very strong in body and, they soon discovered, very strong in voice.

"Lodak! Son of my old friend! It has been far too long since we have seen you."

"I know. Cornar would never give me leave. And after his death, my increased responsibilities…"

"Which have been of immeasurable help to us."

"Thank you."

Lodak turned to the humans. "Saammmm, La-ra, Dan-el, please meet Rodash, the organizer of Varneerah."

Rodash looked intently down on the humans, his eyes darting over every strange detail. "You are even more intriguing than the reports have indicated. Small, soft-looking, and yet magnificent in your way." He pointed to Sam. "You are the male. And these two are female."

"That is correct," Sam said.

"Ah! I was a scholar of creature morphology before I became the organizer of Varneerah. It is nice to see that I have not lost my knowledgeable instincts. Now! The journey to Varneerah is both energetic and energy-depleting. You will need sustenance! Lodak, take them to the dome. A morning meal has been laid out. Let them calm themselves and relax. Huts have been made ready for them. At the end of this day, we will meet in the dome and discuss what should be, what can be, and then decide what will be."

"Thank you, Rodash. Saammmm, everyone, follow me."

"What about Sencee? And Avar and Guien?" Lara spoke up.

"Yes, of course, them too. An absurd danger you put some through to get them here, but here they are now. They are welcome. They are yellowsacks no more. I will send for some new clothes."

Lodak ordered clothes and then called to have the three brought forward. Sencee had Cuz with her and handed him to Lara.

"All right. If we are all together, humans, Downies, Scales, and this little human relative, can we possibly now go to eat? I am hungry. And the food in Varneerah is excellent. It is all I thought about on our journey here."

"No wonder you were smiling," Sam said.

"What else would I smile about? Now, please, follow me."

Lodak led them through the village, followed by curious children fascinated by the strange humans and delighted with Cuz. Lara handed him over to one of the children, who held him out to share with the others. Cuz then found himself passed on and on, to child after child, petted, hugged, and cooed over. He seemed no worse for the wear when he was returned to Lara.

As they walked, Sam took in all he could about the village. There was a logic to the layout that he admired, and the huts, while all the same design, were individualized by decorations attached to their outside walls and by encircling plants of attractive leaves and flowers. And the paths between the huts, while dirt, were hard, compacted, and swept clean. There were rock-paved gutters along the sides for rain runoff.

Sam was disappointed to see smoke from fires—presumably for heating and cooking—rising from the tops of many huts and notice unlit torches at their doors.

As they approached the dome, Sam saw several large round

openings in its roof, which he assumed were the source of its daytime lighting. He was disturbed by that assumption. Each opening featured a round flap that was probably closed when it rained and at night in cold weather.

When they entered, they found the interior of the large structure to be one undivided space with dedicated areas. One area featured many tall cubbyhole cases filled with long books, rolled-up maps, and documents. There were tables and chairs for studying; indeed, several Saurs sat around the tables doing just that. An area was laid out for meetings, maybe presentations, with a raised platform and chairs arranged for an audience. Another area was set aside for lounging, with comfortable-looking seats, cushions, and couches. And there was a common dining area where Lodak took them, presenting a large table with plenty of potan, stoll, and hot and cold meats.

"Please, everyone, sit and eat. Ah, but first, here are the garments."

A male Downy came in with an armful of clothes and brought them to Avar, Sencee, and Guien, who took them gratefully. With no hesitation or shyness, they rid themselves of the horrid yellowsacks and donned their new clothes, although Avar had a problem dealing with pants legs.

It was a most satisfying meal. Good food, good feelings.

But at the end of it, Sam knew more was required. "Lodak, the food was delicious."

"More delicious than the food in Quannak?"

"*Oh, oui, beaucoup plus.*"

"What did she say?" Lodak asked Sam.

"She is speaking in her native language. Sometimes, she feels compelled to do that. But she said, *yes, very much so.* But now, Lodak, you must feed us with information."

141

STEVEN PAUL LEIVA

TWENTY-ONE

LODAK'S TALE

"My father discovered the truth about Varneerah. As I have told you, he was one of Cornar's first scholars. He was a very eager one. Since childhood, he had many questions about many things. He was thought to be quite strange in that and suffered a little ridicule and many admonitions. But when Cornar discovered the trove of long books, documents, and machines, he convinced the Great Quan that he could not study them all by himself, that if the Great Quan wanted to be informed of what they contained, he would need to train scholars. The Great Quan was reluctant; he did not like spreading this information. Still, he approved the training of a few—but only a few. My father was one of the few. This made him happy, as his peculiarness was now a virtue.

"But, after a few years, his happiness faded. He had learned much from Cornar but mostly from the long books. But he was disturbed by how much, how fiercely, Cornar did the Great Quan's bidding and 'safeguarded' what they had learned from everyone, except Savaan and the Great Quan. And even how Cornar kept any information he felt might upset the Great Quan—information on history, biology, geography, or origins—from the Great Quan himself. Cornar's motto was 'Always delight, never disturb the Great Quan.'

"Cornar himself delighted in most information, but only as a collector and, on occasion, as a way to keep the favor of the Great Quan. The artificial light you so love, Sam, is a good example. And how to fashion the material from the walls of ruined cities into sharper arrows and spears.

"My father's most important discovery was of the history of the divide between those who had written the histories—who had known for ages the details of life, rocks, plants, clouds, sky, and stars—and

143

those who did not want to see this information, who did not care, who only wanted comforts of both the body and the mind. When he presented it to Cornar, it was Cornar who was disturbed.

You see, Cornar was convinced that the benefits of scholarship were for the Great Quan and his scholars only. That all other Saurs did not need such information. That long-ago scholars were always willing to share information for the good of all, he thought strange. That most of the 'all' wanted no part of what they had to share—that he was not surprised by. But another portion of the 'all' relished the information, and he found this obscene. So, what my father discovered was never shared with the Great Quan.

"Later, when my father found the history of the final divide between the excitedly knowledgeable and the blissfully ignorant, with the blissfully ignorant in the growing majority, he knew it was useless to present it to Cornar, especially when he read about the plans of the scholars to abandon the ignorant and escape to the stars. He assumed this must have happened because now, a thousand years later, the blissfully ignorant are by far in the majority. So, he hid those long books from Cornar and kept the information to himself.

"This did not make him happy. *Was he no better than Cornar, hoarding such information?* It caused him great concern—great consternation. To relieve this—at least temporarily—he liked to go out barging. He had a small barge, just large enough to lay down a sleeping cushion and to store supplies. He would go out alone to be, as he put it, 'In my small head, in a vast landscape.' The problem was, he was never a very good bargeman. Often, he would leave the tiller alone and just let the barge drift off. I assume his mind did as well. One day, when he was drifting, the barge caught the flow into the tributary heading toward the vortex. He knew immediately he was in trouble. After all, he had attended many ceremonies launching the dead on their rafts down the tributary to Varneerah. This saddened him. I was young then, and he wanted to see me grow. But it exhilarated him as well. No living Saur had ever gone to Varneerah. *What would he see? What would he learn?* If he survived the trip, that is.

"He tied a rope to the tiller and tied the other end to himself, making himself as secure as possible. Then he held on, deeply frightened but determined never to close his eyes. He looked always ahead as the barge went faster, got closer, and was finally sucked into the vortex that took him underground. It was a violent trip. The barge was battered against the tunnel's walls, submerged a few times, and the darkness he thought was death itself. But then, he saw the light up ahead, which grew and grew, until the barge was shot out to land on the cavern lake.

"The impact shattered the barge, but my father managed to untie himself from the tiller, saving himself from drowning. He then swam for the cavern mouth and emerged into this land, verdant and lovely. Had my father not been a scholar, he might have thought this place was some sustaining afterlife. However, hunger and cold would have eventually dissuaded him from that pleasant but impractical notion. No, he immediately understood this was a hidden valley, unknown to the Great Quan and everyone in Anaraquan. My father managed to build himself a shelter. He foraged and hunted. He contemplated a future alone but free. It was ultimately an unappealing idea. The valley was so primitive. It allowed him to live but not to learn. At least, anything beyond fundamentals. He missed the long books. Then, he began to imagine what this hidden valley could mean to others like him, who felt that the Great Quan's suppression of information and oppression of the mind was too much to take. If only he could get them here. But that would mean…

My father became determined to find a path over the mountains and back to Quannak. It took him weeks to do it, but he did. He prepared for it. He made new clothes from the hides and skins of creatures, warm clothes, because he had read of the cold of mountain tops in the long books. He foraged, hunted, dried the food, and packed it up. Then, when he felt he was ready, he left. It was an arduous trek. His new clothes barely protected him. His food ran out. But he made it home, months after he had left.

"Against all law and custom, he did not tell the Great Quan of his discovery. He told a tale of getting lost down another tributary, his barge sinking, surviving in a wilderness beyond, and eventually finding his way home. He was greeted with surprise and amusement. No one had ever done such a thing. He was a well-known anomaly and a favorite of the Great Quan for a while. But soon, he was back as a scholar, working under Cornar. He started to tell the truth to others like him quietly. Not just scholars, but merchants, soldiers, dockworkers, craftsmen, builders, anyone he knew of, or had heard of, who was chafing under the way things were, who feared the Great Quan but abhorred their life even more. There were far more of them than even my father thought. My father sketched out a plan and prepared them to execute it.

"The next time he took a holiday, he organized a group to go with him, to have a relaxing time barging down the river. Rodash was one member of the group. I was another. He took us to Varneerah, the new Varneerah, not the one of myth, but the one of a new reality. Rodash and all the others stayed. My father and I returned, well prepared to move swiftly over the mountains.

"Little by little, over many years, Saurs went missing. And things went missing. A large conundrum Savaan and the Great Quan kept to themselves. So, this Varneerah was built slowly, organized by Rodash here, and supported by my father, who remained in Quannak to exploit his position. When my father died, I took on his role."

There was a moment of silence after Lodak had concluded his tale.

Then, Danielle spoke up. "So, Varneerah, this Varneerah, exists as a refuge from the Great Quan, to escape his oppression?"

"No. Varneerah exists to grow in information and gain knowledge and strength until the day comes when we can overthrow the Great Quan. It is the purpose of our lives. And tonight, when you meet with Rodash, he will ask you to join us."

"We would be honored to help," Lara volunteered quickly, surprising Sam.

"Uh, yes, honored, Lodak. But I'm not sure what we small humans can do."

"Saammmm, we have spent much time together. I knew you when you were smart enough to pretend you were dumb. I saw how quickly you, all of you, grasped our language. I have fielded from you questions of the most thoughtful sort. And I have seen how you have treated your yellowsacks. I think there are many ways for you to help. We cannot just overthrow the Great Quan. We must replace him with a manner of life that would make those who left for the stars be not ashamed to return."

TWENTY-TWO

PROPOSITIONS MADE

After their morning meal, the six new arrivals were escorted to the huts. Each was given their own, even Avar, Guien, and Sencee. But the three now-former yellowsacks protested. They wanted to stay together.

The blackclad who had escorted them understood. "Yes, I suppose we should have thought of that. I will find a family hut for you three."

However, Sam, Lara, and Danielle were grateful for their individual huts. The privacy was welcome—not just to be alone but also to be alone with their thoughts.

They did not think about much at first, though. There was a natural interest in exploring their huts, which, although small for Saurs, were roomy for humans. And they were laid out well, with the circular space broken up into three wedge rooms of different sizes—a general room for cooking, eating, and relaxing, with an oven built into the wall; a room for sleeping, with a small fireplace; and a functional room, to take care of natural biological functions. There was no bath. They assumed that would be communal, like in Quannak. Illumination came from windows and openings in the conical roofs, all with shutters. There were cubby-hole cases for plates and utensils, cooking implements, clothes, and other such stuff.

The huts took little time to explore, and being exhausted, Lara, Danielle, and Sam did not take long to lie down on the sleeping cushions in the sleeping rooms and fall into deep slumbers.

///

They slept most of the day and woke in the late afternoon. Lara and Danielle found that fresh clothes had been delivered to their huts. They were tunics and pants again, no robes, but not black. Lara's was beige, and Danielle's was light brown. The material was soft but looked durable. And they fit.

"Lodak must have brought our measurements with him," Lara said to Danielle when they got together. "Or memorized them."

"*Non bien sûr que non.* It was Avar and Sencee, they made them."

"What? Why? They're no longer our—our slaves."

"No, but now they are *nos amis,* who know us, who have the skills. A pragmatic thing, *non?*"

"Well...as long as they weren't forced."

Danielle smiled at Lara and realized that the young woman had become precious to her. "Come, we'd better get Sam."

They entered Sam's hut, went to the sleeping room, and found him lying on his cushion, hands behind his head, staring up.

"Sam, we have to go to the dome soon," Lara said.

"Okay."

"Did you get some sleep?" Danielle asked.

"Yeah, pretty much. Woke up about, I don't know, maybe half an hour ago. I've just been lying here, in the waning light. Just like I used to do when my mom made me take an afternoon nap. Never slept then. Enjoyed letting my mind wander too much."

"Is your mother still alive?"

"Nobody we knew is still alive, Lara," Sam said suddenly, harshly, and pointedly.

But Lara was not intimidated. "You know what I meant."

"Sorry. But I've been thinking of those gone. Dead and living. My mother died from a fall three years ago."

"I'm sorry," the women said together.

"She was a crazy woman. I don't mean awful crazy—fun crazy. Knew how to be silly, how to make us kids laugh. But then, I guess that never really happened—we never really laughed. Our brains are full of false memories now."

"Sam..."

Sam sat up, looking at the women. His face was set; determined. "Here's what I've been thinking about. You guys want to help Lodak and Rodash overthrow the Great Quan? Great, fine. I don't know what you think we can do, but—whatever. Especially if we succeed and get access to a generator from Quannak to power the Dark Lady and maybe set things right. But, of course, that could take years, most likely will. So, if we get to go back, we'll be quite old and—"

"*Oh, calme-toi, Sam!* Our world is dead to us! Don't you understand that? You so much have the head of a pig!"

"What?"

"She means you're pigheaded, Sam."

"*Mort, notre monde est mort.* Our world is—gone!"

Sam looked at Danielle, then extended his look to Lara. "But not forgotten."

Sam had said it so sadly that Danielle could not help but be moved. She got down on her knees before the sitting Sam. "Sam, I know but... Remember John, what he said. *Pour survivre, pour prospérer, pour savoir.* Ah, you know, I mean, to survive, to thrive, to know. *N'est-ce pas?* A purpose. A purpose to live for. Not just for us humans, but for—for Lodak, for Rodash. How about Guien? They are here now. They exist. They have memories that are not false. Don't they deserve to—"

"Yes. I've been thinking of that also. I didn't want to, but—"

"This is our world now, Sam," Lara said. She picked up Sam's fresh clothes and tossed them to him. "Our future is here and only here."

Sam looked to Lara. No longer his shy doctoral student, no longer naive about most things except science and math. Tougher now and yet, still...

Sam nodded, gathered up his new clothes, and stood, as did Danielle.

"*Et dans cet esprit, vous devrez imprégner Lara et moi.*"

"What?"

"Danielle and I have been talking. You're going to have to knock us both up."

"What!?"

"It's your duty. As a *Homo sapiens* chauvinist."

Lodak walked into the hut at that moment. "Saammmm?" And into the sleeping room. "Oh, here you all are. Good. It is time to meet with Rodash."

It must have been like walking into an altered climate. Lodak would have had no idea what this strange atmosphere was among the three humans. But he must have found it intriguing.

III

As twilight was setting, there was much activity in Varneerah. Torches were lit here and there to provide illumination. Saurs were bringing fresh food to the huts for preparation and cooking. Tables were set up and spaced between huts for communal dining. There was much chatter and even Saur laughter in two different tones—the light, almost twittering laugh of the Downies and the deep and breathy laugh of the Scales.

Sam, Danielle, and Lara enjoyed the mood and sense of well-being this activity created as Lodak led them to the dome. They were happy to see Avar, Guien, and Sencee integrated into one group's meal plans.

Several children ran up to Lara, wanting to hold Cuz.

"Would you like to care for him while I'm in the dome?"

The children made it clear that they would be happy to do this.

"Good. Be gentle. And feed him potan. He loves potan." She handed over Cuz, and the children ran off with him.

"You'll make a *bonne mère*, Lara. Right, Sam?"

Before Sam could answer, they entered the dome. It was empty except for Rodash, who sat at a study table by the cubby-hole cases of long books and documents. His head was low, close to a map he was intently studying in the meager light of the waning day.

"You need light, Rodash," Lodak said, announcing their arrival.

Startled, Rodash pulled his head up, then stood up.

"Oh! I did not see you. Come in! come in! I was looking over old maps of Anaraquan and planning strategies for when we can mount an offensive! Dreaming, possibly. But I like to think not."

Lodak moved to a section of the curved wall that featured a small pull rope. "And do you find it easier to dream in the dark?"

"Ah, well. I hadn't noticed how dark it had gotten."

"This should help." Lodak pulled on the rope, and immediately, they could hear a motor and the sound of movement from above. It was the hatches over the openings in the roof closing. Then, surrounding the now-closed circles, bright lights turned on, illuminating the whole interior of the dome.

"You have light! Artificial light!" Sam exclaimed with a strange joy that must have perplexed Rodash.

"Yes. A gift from Lodak. He is good at building things he does not understand."

"The plans were clear and easy to follow. Cornar found them in an old long book. How to build, how to operate. It was easy. Cornar built all the lights for the Great Quan. But he could not do it alone. I assisted. I learned how to do it, how to make it happen. Why it happens—that is still magic to me. Just not the Great Quan's magic."

"But, why only the dome, not—"

"These were made for the Great Quan's private space. Back-ups for what Cornar and I installed. They were put in storage. Cornar never went to storage. He was much too important for that."

"Well…" Sam looked up at each source of light. "Well…" He brought his arms up, then smiled and turned around as if he were twirling in a gentle rain—which he was—a gentle rain of photons.

Danielle and Lara found it disconcerting.

"Sam…?" Danielle quietly uttered.

Sam suddenly stopped, facing Rodash and Lodak. "That offensive you want to mount. It may not be so much a dream."

"Sam…?" Lara quietly uttered.

"Later," Sam said to the women. To Lodak and Rodash, he said, "Lodak was right about us. We do come from the stars. We are explorers of planets and civilizations. When we were exploring your planet, we came across—"

"Sam!" The women said in unison.

Sam turned to them, irritated over the interruption. "Surely, that discussion can wait." When he turned back to the Saurs, he found both the Downy and the Scale to have quizzical faces. "Well, um, you see, they want me to impregnate them."

"Really?" Lodak asked.

"Yes. As part of our commitment here, you know, putting down roots."

"A fine idea!" Rodash said with enthusiasm. "And necessary if you are staying here. But why are you staying here? Do you not want to return to your planet?"

"Well… no because our planet is very, very…hot and dry, and not at all pretty. So… we like your climate better."

"So, you must make more of you, or you will be the only yous," Rodash said. "Good! I do not like to think you will be the only humans I'll ever meet. You must do it, Saammmm. And soon!"

"I will, sure. I mean, I'm willing to make that sacrifice, but anyway, let me tell you that…we found this ancient ruin. Unlike any you've seen, it's intact. Most of it is underground, you see. And it's filled with technology that could give you—us—a real advantage against the Great Quan. It just needs power—a great deal of power."

///

The three males, one human, one Downy, and one Scale, fell with glee into a long night of conversation about the necessary battles of matter and mind to come and the difficulties thereof. There might be many dark outcomes. But the bright outcomes desired were worth the possibility of the dark ones.

"Look," Sam, to make a point, plagiarized John. "On my planet, we have but one purpose. To survive, to thrive, to know. Well, under the Great Quan, all survive; only his favored thrive, and no one knows. This wasn't always true, from what Lodak tells me. Your world was once filled with knowledge, even if everyone did not appreciate it."

"From the account in one long book," Lodak said, "it was not so much they did not appreciate it as they resented it."

"Resented it?"

"Resented it. As if its very existence insulted them."

"Ah. Because it did not strike their sentiments of rationality."

"What?" Rodash asked.

"A human feeling, Rodash, that Saammmm has told me about."

"Not just human, Lodak, it seems."

"Yes, Saammmm, so it seems."

Sam turned to Rodash. "Rodash, every mind, every sentient, cognizant mind, upon being presented with new information, the result of knowledge that someone has gathered, has a filter that accepts it as rational or rejects it. But it is primitive, this filter, and different in each, as each is different. Therefore, it is unreliable. Only through a systematic search for knowledge can it be risen above while ironically serving as a guide for that search. It is not a simple thing. But those who try are rewarded. And those who don't are...well, they're never unhappy because they find their sentiments comforting. And they become annoyed—"

"And insulted."

"Yes, and insulted when anyone upsets their sentiments. While that's okay, individual by individual, it is not okay for a civilized species. If a civilized species does not rise above its sentiments, it will not remain civilized for long."

"But our past civilizations lasted a long time, Saammmm. Or so, the long books say."

"Well, true. A good run, I suppose. But something happened. Or else the knowledgeable ones of the past civilization would not have abandoned this planet to those of only sentiment. Perhaps they lost their hold after being dominant for such a long time. Maybe the Saurs of sentiments outnumbered them, or they gained power or something. Maybe these things go in cycles."

"Cycles?"

"Turns. Maybe it was the sentiments' turn to dominate. I hate that idea. I hate it, but, well, you know, history... Anyway, your long books tell you that the knowledgeable ones had the knowledge to get out. So, they did. Leaving the sentiments to stew in their own juices, as we say on my planet. Do you see? But what you, who are knowledgeable and who want knowledge, desire now...is your turn."

Lara and Danielle had left long before this conversation to join the others for the evening meal. Food was sent into the dome for the three left behind, but little was touched. The conversation was sustenance enough: the conversation and several bottles of numb.

///

Very late in the evening, Sam asked about the ceramic-like building material from the ruined city he had seen used for weapons and wall hangings. Lodak was happy to answer his questions, pulling from cubbyholes three examples of the substance. One was a sheet torn off an ancient, ruined building. One was a smooth block form, heavy and hard. One was a sphere you could hold in your hand.

"The ancients just called it the medium. For years, we have found it in all the ruins in many different forms, as you can see." Lodak picked up the block, held it high over the table, and let it drop. It hit the table with a heavy bang. Then he picked up the sphere, held it high, and let it drop. It bounced, bounced, bounced, then rolled off the table. "But we could tell it was the same material. We always assumed it was not natural, that it was synthetic. But how to make it has been lost. Or, at least, we have never found a long book that told us how. So, we just used it for scrap building materials. Precious scrap, for the Great Quan hoards it and sells it dear."

"But Lodak—as brilliant as his father—found the key," Rodash said.

"It was luck. I was doing my task, going through long books and documents, trying to understand, looking for useful things for Cornar to present to the Great Quan, and found one on medium. It did not tell how to make it but did inform of its properties. It seems it had been designed to never become waste."

"What do you mean?" Sam asked.

"If you heat it, it melts at a certain point. Then, depending on how much more heat you apply, and when you stop and let it cool, it will become solid again in different forms, even a form different from what it was originally." Lodak picked up the block. "So, I could melt this—" Lodak leaned down, reached for, and picked up the sphere. "Into this. Depending on having molds or ways to shape it, you could melt down this scrap and make things as hard as this block, or soft and flexible like this sphere here, or the clothes you're wearing, or something as thin as skin. I made the generator for this dome from melted down scrap medium, as I did the conduit that moves the power from the generator to here."

"But, how do you know what temperature each different material needs to cool to?"

"Ah. That took many times of trying without success. Eventually, it became deep knowledge. Then I began training others in Quannak, and here, to achieve this same knowledge."

"So—with enough medium, you could make a larger generator, right? Because we're going to need a large one."

"Yes, Saammmm, I think I could. But we don't have that much medium. We can only steal a little at a time. It will take years to get enough."

"We don't have years, Lodak."

"Saammmm," Rodash said, smiling down at the diminutive human. "We have nothing but years. Civilizations have grown and died, one way or another, and never in a day. As long as each day, we make progress, we are patient."

"Well, sure, but..." Sam needed a good, convincing argument. And he had one. "You know, the Great Quan may swallow the myth of Varneerah, but I doubt if Bert-ram will. What if he convinces Savaan to investigate, and they find this place?"

The idea upset Rodash, frightened him. "It would be the end of us. We are not set up for defense."

"Exactly. The only thing between you and destruction is their ignorance of this place. Bert-Ram is not an ignorant human. He will figure it out, and I'm sure he will be happy to report it to Savaan and the Great Quan. We need to get creative. We need to find a way to get a lot of medium."

"We could raid a caravan!" Rodash said.

"Rodash!" Lodak said.

"I've wanted to for years. Sneak-thieving should not be our way. Huge caravans are coming from the hinterland ruins, bringing masses of medium to the Great Quan. We've got spies who can tell us the route. We lay in wait, we pounce, we take."

"But Rodash, they are accompanied by many of the Great Quan's soldiers. We will suffer much loss of life, even if we succeed. Which you cannot guarantee."

"Well, Lodak," Sam said. "You can lose your life actively or passively. Which would you prefer?"

"Small in body, but large in wisdom, that's you, Saammmm. Lodak, listen to his tiny voice, listen carefully. What would those who went to the stars think of us if we did not act on this knowledge?"

///

Sam left the dome with a flaming torch to light his way. He was deeply satisfied, with equations dancing in his head, leaving little room for thoughts of consequences. But he had hope again, instead of despair, and some of the confidence that had been his constant companion through most of his life—his life in his universe. His universe that fit him well fit him like comfy clothes. Indeed, as he walked to his hut, he felt already clothed in his universe, too arrogant to realize that it was the finely tailored—with skill, and possibly a form of love—tunic and pants made for him by Guien, out of one form of medium.

Sam entered his hut and went directly to the sleeping room. He lit the small fireplace with the torch, then extinguished it in a small bucket of loose sand placed there for that purpose.

"Well, are you boys done?" It was Lara, on the sleeping cushion, a thin covering blanketing her.

"Oh! Sorry. I was sure this was my hut."

"It is your hut."

"It is?"

"Danielle and I played rock/paper/scissors. I get the first night."

"You're kidding?"

"No."

"But we have a plan now. We're going to raid a caravan, get this medium stuff—it's great—build a huge generator, power up the Dark Lady, and go home."

"When I was a kid, I remember how my brother was going to dig a

155

tunnel under the street to his best friend's house."

"Lara, we have to make the attempt."

"My and Danielle's point exactly."

"Look, I'm—I'm practically a warlord now. I must preserve my strength."

"Is it because you find me unattractive?" Lara removed the thin blanket. Danielle had been right—she had nothing to be shy about.

"No, of course not. It's just—"

"And Danielle—I know she's a little older but—"

"You're both attractive; that's not the issue. And it's not that I'm not—"

"Sam. Tonight make love. Tomorrow, make war."

"You—you used to be so shy."

"I used to not live among dinosaurs. And I don't want to become one myself. I mean—"

"Yes. I understand."

"I'll be gentle."

"Well—I guess that's all I can ask."

TWENTY-THREE

MERDE ET PISSE

The residents of Varneerah had no substantial objections to the plans developed by Lodak, Rodash, and Sam. However, they did express concerns, anxieties, and apprehensions in a mass meeting in the dome. But the single, simple fact that their hidden valley might soon be no more overcame all and set them on a course to meet the inevitable head-on rather than wait for it to come to them.

Among the residents of Varneerah were several ex-soldiers of the Great Quan, and they were tasked with training every able-bodied Saur—Scale and Downy; male and female —who were willing to join the blackclads. Of those, Saurs whose potential skills were more mechanical than military, some were taught by Lodak the craft of making the molds that would be needed for all the various functional parts and things that could be made with medium. Others, he trained in the art of heating and cooling medium. Then, he brought the two groups together for their first assignment—making superior bows, arrows, and spears, including a custom-made set for Danielle and Sam.

Rodash was skeptical over the inclusion of Sam and Danielle into the blackclads, but Danielle said that she wouldn't miss it for the world.

"Well, that's fine," Sam said to her privately. "You don't have to miss it for the world, but why can't I miss it for the world?"

"What world are you talking about, Sam? Theirs or ours?"

"I hate witty French women."

"Besides…Lara tells me you now consider yourself a warlord."

"Sure. A lord, not a soldier."

"Ah, come on, Sam, it will be fun."

"Fun? Danielle, this is serious stuff."

"Sam, *vous êtes un scientifique et je suis un philosophe.* Serious stuff is fun for us."

Once the training started, Sam did find it fun, which was amusing

157

but also a bit disconcerting. He had not known he had the capacity for violent solutions to intractable problems rather than thoughtful ones. But he should not have been surprised. He was, after all, a not-too-long-distanced descendant of his ancestors.

"Saammmm, Dan-el, how goes the training?"

Rodash came up to them in their corner of the training field. They had been segregated from the other blackclads not only to avoid getting underfoot of the larger Saurs but also for some special training designed for their size.

"Good," Sam said. "Actually, it's fun. No, that's frivolous, isn't it? Exhilarating, I guess."

"La-ra has not joined you?"

"No, she's continuing her reading lessons. She's getting quite good at it. Besides, she's a lover, not a fighter."

"I'm both!" Danielle said with a smile as she let loose a spear, which hit its intended twelve-foot-tall Quan soldier dummy target in the neck.

"Impressive," Rodash said but then with concern, "You do realize, Dan-el, that one day soon, that will not be a target but an individual of flesh and blood, loves and hates."

"*Oui*, I think about it every day, Rodash. But I also think of the great potential to build a new civilization here—once certain impediments are removed." She threw another spear, and it pierced the dummy's heart.

"Ah, removal, yes, that is—" At the sound of a whistle, Rodash ducked, avoiding a flying reptile about the size of a large hawk, which had swooped down by them. Its claws held something about the size of a tennis ball.

There was another whistle, different in tone and length than the first. The creature slightly adjusted its direction and headed to the dummy. Then, another whistle sounded, distinct from the first two, and the flying reptile released the object, a seedpod, just shy of the dummy. Momentum, though, took the pod forward as it fell. It smashed into the head of the dummy, bursting open and covering it with a cloud of fine purple dust.

Rodash raised himself to his full height, turned, and spied a young male Downy about a hundred feet behind them. "Back to your field," he yelled with all appropriate anger at the boy.

The boy whistled again, and the winged reptile flew to him, landing on his outstretched arm. The boy turned and ran.

"No, wait!" Danielle shouted, surprising Rodash and Sam and stopping the boy. "Can we see him do that again?"

"It's just a children's game, Dan-el. He should not have been playing it this close to the training field."

"Well, it may be a good thing he was. Please call him over. I want to see how he does it."

Rodash called the boy forward. He came with the creature on his arm and a bag of seedpods.

"Neemak, show Dan-el how good you are."

The boy was happy to no longer be in trouble and was glad to perform for the funny-looking little humans.

"He captured the dornish himself or possibly robbed it from its nest and raised it. In any case, he raised and trained it. First, he will let the dornish go, and it will soar above him in circles."

The boy did so, giving them a good view of the reptile in flight. Its wingspan was about six feet, and its body, from nose to the end of a long skinny tail, was just a little less than that. At the end of the tail was a flat, diamond-shaped flap of skin that Sam assumed aided in stabilizing its flight. The dornish's head reminded him of a puffin's head, which would have made it cute if not for the large fangs in its mouth.

The boy took another seedpod out of his bag, holding it up high in the palm of his hand. When he whistled, the dornish immediately dove and snatched it away, holding it in the claws of its feet. The boy then pointed in the direction of the target. He watched its flight intensely and seemed deeply aware of the surrounding conditions. He whistled again to adjust the creature's flight path, then again, and the seedpod was let loose. It fell, striking the target directly once again.

It was an awe-inspiring demonstration of skills.

"A children's game?" Danielle asked.

"Yes," Rodash said. "Just a simple children's game."

Danielle pointed to Sam's bow and arrows. "So is this—until your target is flesh and blood."

"Ah, I see what you see, Dan-el. But dornishes cannot carry anything much heavier. It would not even knock out a soldier. So, what would it do? Cover him in purple? Blind him, maybe?"

"What if the seedpod was filled with something that could— could…I'm not sure you have a word for it."

Sam, who now got it, looked at Rodash and said, "Let us work on something. Then we'll show you."

"Of course, it will take a lot of *merde et pisse.*"

"Of what?" Rodash was confused.

"Shit and piss, Rodash, it's going to take a lot of shit and piss," Sam translated.

///

A week later, Sam and Danielle were ready for a demonstration after learning how to hollow out the seedpods without breaking them, applying some basic chemistry, and rigging a simple fuse.

All the blackclads gathered on the training field. A target was set up. The boy and his dornish came forth with Sam. The boy sent the dornish flying. He held the modified seedpod in his hand. Sam had trained him to light the fuse with a small pot of embers. He whistled, lit the fuse, and handed the seedpod off to the dornish. Then he guided him through whistles until his final whistle sent the seedpod down towards the target, which it hit with an explosion of sound and a scattering of the dummy target that was startling to all, even Sam and Danielle.

There was a moment of quiet and stillness.

Then Rodash came up to Sam and Danielle. "What do you call this—"

"Gunpowder, Rodash. That's what it's called. Easy to make if you know how."

"Make a lot, Saammmm and Dan-el. Make a lot."

TWENTY-FOUR

PILLOW TALK

They made a lot while training continued, and a plan of attack was developed. When Rodash received the intelligence of when a large caravan containing a massive amount of scrap medium would be on the move and by what route, a date was set for the raid.

The night before was one of Danielle's nights with Sam. It had been a more than satisfying night in the generation of pleasure, tension release, and cozy post-coitus relaxation. How effective it was in continuing the *Homo sapiens* species only time would tell. Or so Sam thought.

After some quiet moments, Sam said, "You know, Danielle, if perpetuating our species is so important to you, then you shouldn't come on the raid tomorrow."

"*Pourquoi?*"

"Because it's likely to be dangerous. You could get killed. And then we would be down one potential mother."

"La vie est pleine de risques, mon cher"

"So, why do you want to go?"

"To protect you and make sure *you* are not killed."

"Well, *my* not going would assure that, don't you think?"

"But you must go. You are committed."

"And you and Lara have committed me to father the future of humanity. There's a bit of a conflict there, don't you think?"

"Ah, conflicts. Contradictions. *La condition humaine.* It is absurd."

"Still…"

"Don't worry about me. I am expendable. I had my tubes tied two years ago."

"What? Why then—"

"I could not let Lara have all the fun."

"Well, that's just—"

"Yes, I know, Sam. *Je suis un animal.* But I am also more experienced. I've been able to instruct Lara on how best to pleasure you."

"Jeez, it's a damn conspiracy. I feel so used."

"If that is the only thing you are feeling, then you are an *imbécile.*"

"No, no, I'm feeling all the good things I should feel. But you and Lara—you guys aren't having any problems with jealousy, are you?"

"*Je suis Français,* Sam. We do not feel jealousy; we only use it to our advantage. In this case, there is no advantage."

"And Lara?"

Ah, well, Lara *est un Américain.* It could be volatile. But she is also, *un scientifique pragmatique, n'est-ce pas?* I think she sees the larger purpose here."

"Well, sure, but what's this all going to mean if we get back to our world?"

Danielle sighed a sigh that it seems only the French can sigh. "Sam, is it really even worth trying? We could destroy them—people who have become our comrades. We could possibly destroy everything. Their world. Our world. You don't know. And what if we do get back to our world? Where is it going? We are so prone, people like you and me, to lose ourselves in grand questions, in deep theories, that we often let the world slide past us. Well, our world seems to be having *une régression*, a…how you say, falling back. If we get back, what can we do about it? Will it be too much for us? Will we be marginalized? But here, right now, Sam, we are participating in something that could be glorious! How often do you get the chance to help make a new civilization? Wouldn't you rather be in on the birth of a new civilization than an observer of the death of an old one? Why not *just* raid the caravan and acquire the medium, so we can build the things that will help them overthrow the Great Quan?"

"You think this is easy for me?"

"I think you are obsessed with an idea. An obsession has nothing to do with easy."

"I…I can't explain it."

"To whom? To me? Or to yourself?"

Irritating questions, which Sam was too tired to think about, much less answer. "Are you going to sleep here tonight? Or are you going back to your own hut? Because we need sleep. Tomorrow is—"

"Yes, I know," Danielle said, getting up off the sleeping cushion and starting to dress. Tomorrow will tell us a lot. We will succeed or we will not. We will live or we will die."

"Do you have a preference?"

"Well, you die in only one way, but you can live in many ways. *La condition humaine.* It is absurd."

STEVEN PAUL LEIVA

TWENTY-FIVE

THE RAID

At dawn the next day, the new—and, it was hoped, well-trained—blackclad army mustered, was inspected, and then marched out of Varneerah. Rodash and Lodak were in the lead. Danielle and Sam rode in a special cart, followed by another special cart containing a good supply of the altered seedpods. A small contingent of the blackclads marched with dornishes on their shoulders. Avar, Sencee, and Guien marched in the ranks.

The only sounds were of feet hitting the ground and the rustle of clothes and armaments. There were no marching songs from the blackclads or *hoorahs* from the gathered villagers seeing them off. Not that such bucking-up vocal expressions might not have been emotionally satisfying, but these Saurs just did not have the tradition of them. There were goodbye waves from the villagers, Lara among them. She held Cuz, feeling sad, anxious, and worried. She was not alone in that.

When the marching line of blackclads was finally out of sight, the crowd of villagers broke up, and the Saurs went about their normal daily routines. Lara went to the dome to continue her reading lessons, putting Cuz in the hands of some children. Before she got to the lessons, sitting at a study table by the cubby holes of long books, she started to cry. A female Scale and a male Downy both came over to her and sat at the table. Lara looked up at their large eyes and found solace there.

///

Deep in a thick forest, moving along a narrow path that would eventually take them to Quannak, a long caravan moved at a casual and comfortable pace. It consisted of many wagons filled with scrap medium. They were being driven by yellowsacks shackled to the seats they sat on. The beasts of burden that were hitched to each wagon were unrelenting in their slow march as if walking along this path was the sole purpose of their lives. In between every group of three wagons was a small cohort of soldiers of the Great Quan, just as unrelenting in their march forward and seemingly just as dumb to any other purpose.

Trailing behind the wagons and soldiers were about fifty yellowsacks, chained together, heads bowed, not so much in submission as in the hope of avoiding the massive droppings of the beasts of burden. After all, life for them was shitty enough. They were guarded by two soldiers, one on either side of the caravan, riding high on suunars.

The captain of these soldiers, accompanied by several other officers, was at the head of the caravan, riding on a magnificent suunar. His attitude of arrogance should not be surprising; it came with the rank.

The wind in the trees produced a steady sound. There was the occasional rustle of ground creatures skittering unseen, just inside the forest, following the caravan, hoping for cast-offs of something they might eat. There was the occasional howl of some large creature deep in the forest, most likely looking to mate. And then came a shrill whistle from somewhere nearby.

The captain cocked his head. It was an unusual sound in the forest, but—

A second whistle.

Odd.

A third.

Then something fell about twenty-five feet in front of the captain, and the ground exploded before him. The captain pulled on the reins of the suunar to stop it, but it would have stopped on its own. Then, the whole of the caravan stopped, but not without bumps, some trips, and a few falls.

When the cloud of dust from the greatly disrupted ground dissipated before the captain, Rodash was revealed, standing in the center of the path.

"Greetings, Captain of the Great Quan. Amazing, isn't it? The next one lands on your head, if you and your soldiers do not drop your armaments, turn around, and run away. Leave the wagons, though.

And the yellowsacks."

But the captain's attitude of arrogance would not allow him to back down. He grabbed a spear from a holster strapped to the side of the suunar, lifted it into the perfect throwing position, and let it fly toward Rodash.

Rodash watched the spear's flight, calculating the point of its eventual landfall, which was exactly where he was standing, then he stepped to one side. The spear came down, swift and heavy, deep into the ground to Rodash's left.

Rodash, smiling at the captain, held up his right hand and whistled. The seedpod with the lit fuse that he balanced on his palm was suddenly snatched away by a swiftly flying dornish, which flew toward the captain. The captain was perplexed but strangely fascinated. Rodash whistled again to adjust the dornish's flight and then again. The dornish released the seedpod.

The seedpod landed in the lap of the captain and exploded, tearing him asunder, sending flesh, bone, and blood up and out, and finally down, and rending the neck of the suunar, separating the head from the body, the body collapsing to the ground in a heap, the head following a second later, making one short bounce as it landed.

Immediately, a barrage of arrows and spears came flying out of the forest on the caravan's left side, cutting down dozens of the Great Quan's soldiers. Those left standing sent their own barrage into the forest, not knowing who they were hoping to kill.

The yellowsack wagon drivers jumped off their seats, looking for what little cover they could find, crouching behind scrap medium. Being shackled to the seats, they could not run to escape. The mass of shackled-together yellowsacks in the rear could only squat in unison, hoping to make themselves as small of targets as possible. But not one arrow, not one spear, headed their way. They seemed oddly safe in the center of chaos. They were probably the first ones to hear the whistles.

One after another after another, the whistles came, each with different lengths and tones, making for weird music in the air. Then came the percussions. Seedpods rained. Explosions flowered. Flesh and bone flew. Blood spurted and flowed.

Then the strange music suddenly stopped.

The still-standing, still-living soldiers of the Great Quan froze in their field of dead comrades, unable or unwilling to move.

An under-captain, now in command, rode up the line on his suunar, yelling. "What are you doing, you idiots! Into the forest! Engage the killers of your brothers!"

Happy to have had all decisions taken from them, the soldiers poured into the thick forest on the left side of the caravan, led by the under-captain and the only other officer left alive and mounted on his suunar.

From the right of the caravan, a dozen blackclads ran to the yellowsacks, hacked off their shackles, and moved them quickly back into the forest, not forgetting those who had been driving the wagons.

In the thick of the forest, the soldiers of the Great Quan found nothing, their attackers having fled. But they still moved forward, looking, looking, cautious in their boldness, bold in their cautiousness.

An arrow, smaller than any other shot that day, flew down from above, pierced the right eye of a soldier, and stuck into his immediately useless brain. His body fell like a sack dumped on the ground.

A spear, the size of a normal 'Saur arrow, flew into the soldiers and through the throat of the under-captain's suunar. The beast moaned, groaned, and wailed as it tossed the under-captain off. The suunar shook loose the spear, then, crazy with pain and confusion, ran away to be alone.

The under-captain, unhurt, got up and saw the small spear on the ground. He picked it up, looked at it, found he hated it, and broke it in two. He looked ahead and saw Sam and Danielle up in separate trees, dressed in black, standing in the crooks of large, round limbs, each with a bow and a basket of small spears and arrows.

"Attack!" the under-captain yelled at his men.

But before they could move, blackclads came out of hiding from all directions and engaged the soldiers of the Great Quan in a melee of flashing swords, thrown spears, shot arrows, flying fists, and stomping feet.

Sam and Danielle continued their efforts from above, adrenaline causing exhilaration and carelessness. Soon, Danielle found herself falling out of her tree after too aggressively tossing a spear. The under-captain saw this and, sword in hand and hate in his head, rushed toward Danielle, who was just recovering herself, unaware of what was coming. But an arrow from Sam sliced into the under-captain's shoulder, which stopped him for a moment. Sam shot another arrow, which pierced the under-captain's side and dropped him to the ground, alive but no longer dangerous.

Danielle stood up, ready to climb back into the tree, when she saw that Lodak was about to be attacked from the rear. She picked up one of her spears from the ground and flung it, hitting the attacker in the neck and killing him instantly. Lodak turned and, seeing Danielle, gave her an open-handed, chest-slapping salute. Pleased, Danielle let out a warrior's cry.

It was such a ludicrous thing, seeing Danielle trilling with blood lust, that Sam couldn't help but laugh. Unfortunately, this took his mind away from balancing, and he fell out of his tree backward, finding himself stunned and splayed on the ground at the feet of a soldier of the Great Quan. The soldier took a militant delight in this gift from above and was preparing to skewer Sam when he was grabbed from behind by Rodash, who lifted the soldier and squeezed the life out of him, tossing him aside with glee. Sam looked up from the ground at the giant Scale, and it seemed to him that all strength and good purpose and life force resided in this one body, and he was damn grateful to have benefited from—

The spear came from behind and seemed to spring out of Rodash's chest, blood-covered and angry. Rodash collapsed, falling as a meteor might, slamming into the ground, quaking the immediate area.

It was the last death of the afternoon.

A call went up. What few soldiers of the Great Quan left were in retreat. They gathered up their wounded, including the under-captain, leaving the field to the victors and the dead.

The forest was suddenly quiet. Sam still lay on the ground, his mouth open with horror, as he stared into the dead eyes in the huge head of Rodash, which was resting but inches away.

Danielle came to Sam and helped him up. Blackclads came from all directions to surround the body of Rodash; their heads bowed in sadness and grief, and disbelief. Lodak openly wept.

///

The caravan, now in control of the blackclads, moved down the path, avoiding the turn-off that would lead to Quannak, and continued on to the end of the forest and onto a plain of harsh terrain. The medium from several of the wagons had been distributed among other wagons, and the now-emptied wagons were being used to carry their dead and wounded, and any of the yellowsacks too weak to continue walking.

Lodak walked beside the first wagon, which was carrying the body of Rodash. Danielle and Sam walked behind Lodak.

They were not heading to the path through the mountains but to another tributary of the great river. When they arrived, they found comrades who had been sent there to build many simple barges. The two groups of blackclads greeted each other with relief, enthusiasm, and joy, all dulled by the presence of their slain organizer. But they had little time for sorrow. The medium was quickly loaded onto the barges, as were blackclads and yellowsacks. Then, they launched from the shore to make their way to the great river and, eventually, to the vortex and Varneerah with their treasure.

On the way, as they journeyed along a particularly lovely stretch of the river that seemed to call into question their recent reality of bloodlust and deathblows, Danielle turned to Sam and said: "I'm thinking of Bertram."

"Why?"

"I'm wondering—"

"Not about his welfare, I hope."

"No. But his impact on ours."

"Meaning?"

"It would have been better if we had managed to kill all of the Great Quan's soldiers."

"You know, I think you're liking this warrior stuff a bit too much."

"*Tu me comprends mal.*"

"Ah. *C'est possible.*"

"If the soldiers who escaped return to Quannak and report what they experienced, and if Bertram hears the report, he will know what we did."

"Yes?"

"I mean, not just the raid, but our *petites bombes.*"

"You French can make the worst things sound good. They were not *petites bombes*; they were death-dealing grenades, weapons of destruction."

"*Exactement.* And Bertram will know how to make them, just as we did."

"Oh. I see. So, we've possibly started an arms race."

"Yes. But unavoidable, I think."

"Unless we had killed all of their soldiers."

"*Cette vérité est également inévitable. Excusez-moi*, what I mean is—"

"Yeah. I think I get it."

"Dan-el, Saammmm, prepare." Lodak had come up to them. "The vortex is just ahead."

STEVEN PAUL LEIVA

TWENTY-SIX

EQUIPMENT AND EQUATIONS

Upon seeing Danielle and Sam standing on the barge, in the lead of the blackclad convoy, Lara's relief was so intense that she began to shake uncontrollably. Aneeda, the Downy scholar who had been helping Lara with her reading lessons, grew quite concerned and held her as gently as possible. It was the right thing to have done, and Lara, the size of a child in Aneeda's arms, received the comfort she needed to recover.

By the time Danielle and Sam were off the barge, Lara was all smiles and greeted them with great enthusiasm and tight hugs.

The shock of the deaths, especially Rodash's, spread quickly throughout the village, but the need to celebrate the victory was commanding and, within an hour, great tales of danger and derring-do, of successful strategies and searing fear, of the awfulness of exploded bodies and the awesomeness of success overtook their emotions and spent them by night's end.

The next day, shock and grief, celebrations and satisfaction were put aside as everyone got to work. All the captured medium was received into an outdoor factory of large pots suspended over fire pits. A supervisor trained by Lodak gave the masters of each pot specific instructions as to the kind and quality of medium they would be converting the scrap into.

Lodak and Sam went over their redrawn plans for the hydroelectric generator based on the ones found in an ancient, ruined city and adapted to the river by the Dark Lady, as Sam could best remember it.

Molds were designed and made.

Lara took charge of the rescued yellowsacks and found it difficult to convince them they were no longer slaves. She brought Avar, Guien, and Sencee, ex-yellowsacks, now veteran warriors, to talk to them.

They were brilliant at it, and soon Lara was back to her studies of the written Saur language.

Soon, masters poured molten medium of various degrees of temperature into molds. Parts for the generator and other valuable things, as well as more armaments and material equivalents of wire, rubber, and cloth, were being made, crafted, refined, and stockpiled.

III

Lara had always been known as a quick study. This gave her no end of pleasure—and no end of grief—while she progressed through lower education. She was a teacher's pet, a nerd, and a know-it-all, and so was disliked by peers who had gotten it into their heads that her existence was a personal slight against them and an effort to diminish their existence. Unfortunately, these peers were the ones who mattered in the horrible social microcosms that were middle school and high school. And so, she was often hormonally miserable while intellectually stimulated.

But once she was in higher education, her natural ability to read, study, analyze, memorize, learn, and understand with zeal and accuracy gave her excellent advantages and exciting opportunities, such as being mentored by Sam Reynolds while pursuing her doctorate in physics.

This ability, which had yet to be called upon during their journey to Where the Great Quan Rules, found revival when she set about to learn to read the Saur language. She became competent with it quickly. Mastery would take just a little while longer. And she looked forward to that, as she was finding much to interest her in the long books. Not only the history of Saurs and their several civilizations, technology, and social structures, but she also found what she assumed was Saur literature. Tales from when the Saurs were still primitive—the several times they were primitive, in fact—and novels, stories of the way the Saurs lived now, during many *nows* that were no longer primitive. Stories that revealed complex minds in confusion, pain, and conflict but also experiencing pleasure, exhilaration, and what Lara could only translate as love.

She was still at it late one evening, in the scholar's area of the dome, when Sam came in. She did not notice his arrival, as her nose was deeply stuck in a long book. Sam came up to her table and watched her do nothing but breathe and read, and he wondered what was going on that he couldn't see.

"Hi," Sam said quietly.

Yanked away from a story about a sibling rivalry on the moon, she raised her head and noticed Sam—then looked at him closely. "I think you need to trim your beard. It's getting raggedy again."

"I've been a bit busy."

"Sure."

"You've been busy too." Sam indicated the pile of long books by her elbows. "I thought this was our night."

"For what?"

"You know. Your and Danielle's procreation project?"

"Oh, of course, sure. What time is it?"

"Long past the evening meal. Aren't you hungry?"

"There were some left-overs on the dining table. Cuz brought some over for me."

"Cuz did?"

"Smart little relative we've got there."

"Well, shall we?"

Rather than answer, Lara looked down upon the long books spread out on the table before her. "This is a hell of a world, Sam. Millions of years old. A multitude of civilizations. Glory and shame, triumphs and disasters. Vast intelligence. Deep stupidity."

"Sounds a lot like our world."

"Yes, but they've been doing it for a much longer time."

Sam sat down at the table. "Have they? Or have they only been doing it since we threw the switch in the Dark Lady?"

Lara had heard it before and was exhausted by it. "Sam, haven't you ever heard about living in the moment?"

"It's the lost moments—our lost moments—that I'm concerned with."

"Is it? Or is it your lost experiment?"

"Why is it I'm the only one who's horrified over being a destroyer of worlds?"

"Why is it you're the only one who isn't amazed at possibly being the creator of a world? And why are you not horrified about potentially being the destroyer of *it*?"

"So, you've gone completely native."

Lara stood up swiftly, angry and upset. "No, Sam. I'm just trying to stay human." As aggressively as she could, Lara stomped out of the dome, leaving Sam alone.

III

Lara stomped at Danielle's hut. "He's determined, he's just so damn determined!"

"I know, *ma chérie*. Push against him and he just becomes more stubborn. You should stop arguing with him."

"We've got to tell Lodak. We've got to tell him that it's all a sham, that we aren't aliens from another planet, that—"

"But we *are* aliens from another planet. We just didn't get here in a spaceship."

"You know what I mean."

"*Oui. Je l'ai considéré.* But Sam has given them hope. And that hope has made them a force. That is a good thing."

"Not so good if we destroy their world."

"Do you really think we will? *Quelles sont les chances?* Not good, I think. So, we go. We bring power to the Dark Lady. Sam tries to figure out what went wrong. Assuming he can do that. Then he must figure out how to reverse it. Do you think he can? Sam is brilliant, but his brilliance is like, how you say, *feux d'artifice.*"

"Fireworks?"

"*Oui*, fireworks. Big, bright, bursting booms of inspiration, *c'est Sam.* But he has always needed a *collaborateur* to keep him on track, grounded, focused. That was John. *John est mort.* So, we go to the Dark Lady and make a request of her and she refuses. Sam will have to accept that this is now his world. And his revolution. Knowing Sam, he will throw himself into it *avec vigueur et force.* All will be well. We will get out of the Dark Lady anything that can help. Lodak will be pleased. And you will be able to stock up on *votre délicieux Spam.*"

Lara had to smile at that, but it was short-lived. "Sam will be so sad. I don't think he will accept it. I think it will destroy him."

The pain, the anticipated regret threaded throughout Lara's last words, brought Danielle to a certain light. "*Oh, je vois. Vous êtes amoureux de Sam.*"

"In love with Sam? Me? No, I just..."

"Then you must help him. *You* must become his *collaborateur.*"

"But then, maybe we'll destroy this world"

"*Ma chérie,* we don't really know what happened. All we know is it wasn't *voyage dans le temps.* Lara, I know it has been a while, but you have stopped thinking like a physicist. Something on the quantum level caused this. Possibly in the dark quantum. Maybe something on the quantum level can solve it—without destroying any world. All you need is a *théorie viable*. All you need *est un papier et un crayon.*"

Lara laughed.

"*Quelle?*"

"In English, a crayon is only for children."

"Well, compared to the age of the 'Scales, we are but children. Let us just hope *tu es un enfant prodige.*

III

Lara was not seen around the village for days. She was in her hut *avec du papier et un crayon.* Her personal world shrunk to just that. If Danielle had not brought food, she might have starved. Cuz, too, for he would not leave her side. He was a living presence she could talk to, so she could hear her own thoughts out loud and try to unjumble them.

Because of her prodigious memory, she could recall all the steps that led to Sam's theory and the design of the experiment. She wrote it all down, surrounding herself with equations. But all that was only a base for further equations, equations to try to figure out what happened and how it might be reversed or...

She made some progress in those directions, but it was halting and filled with U-turns. She so wished she had access to current peer-reviewed papers in the field, no matter how wild. Indeed, she felt she needed something wild. But if they even existed, they only existed in her own universe, assuming her own universe still existed.

Or did they? Lara jumped to her feet and ran out of her hut.

III

It was very late at night, but Lodak was in the dome alone, resting his head on a laid-out map.

"Lodak!" Lara said with no gentleness but with plenty of urgency.

Lodak, startled, raised his head, focused his eyes, and saw Lara. "La-ra, hello. Is there something you want?"

"Yes, much, if you have it."

"If I have it, you will have it."

"In your studies of the ancients, have you ever found any speculations by them on the nature of—of everything? I mean, here, the stars, everything in between. On how it was all formed, what's it made of, what the forces are that hold it together. Possibly, whether there might be—"

"Yes, there are many long books, but they are not easy to understand. Cornar hated them, saying they gave him a headache. He never missed them when we stole them."

"Do you mind if I take a crack at them?"

"No, of course not." Lodak rose and retrieved quite a few of the long books from cubby holes and brought them to Lara. "I would be pleased to have you read them."

"Thank you," Lara said as she reached out to take the long books from Lodak. "I'll take them to my hut to study."

But Lodak did not hand them over. It was obvious that they would be too much for the diminutive human to handle.

"I must return to my hut to rest. Yours is on my way. I will carry them for you."

"Thank you, Lodak. They do seem a bit bulky for me."

"And, please, if you find understanding, you will share?"

"If there is a benefit in these long books, Lodak, I absolutely promise that you will share in it."

TWENTY-SEVEN

HOT AIR AND HIGH FLYING

Earlier that day, Sam, Lodak, and Danielle were in the dome, going over maps and accounts of ancient journeys, and long books on certain geological formations. There was one large map that Lodak had found a few years back in Quannak, that he had kept from Cornar and had quickly sent to Varneerah. It detailed the whole of what was now Anaraquan—Where the Great Quan Rules—but was, at the time of the map's making, a landscape of massive cities separated by vast areas of protected nature. Many of the cities were, of course, at locations where the ruins had been discovered and exploited by the Great Quan. But there were many more cities indicated, that had not yet been discovered by the Great Quan, and Lodak wanted it to stay that way. Most importantly, though, the map extended far beyond the borders of Anaraquan and included the Hidden Valley.

"Look here, Saammmm." Lodak pointed to the indication of a great precipice. "This is where the hunting party said they found you."

"And there's the river," Danielle pointed out.

"Well, assuming the river's direction hasn't changed much in the hundreds of years since this map was made," Sam said, "and knowing that we traveled for only a day, I would say that the ruin we found would be just about here."

"But, why do you think, Saammmm, there is no indication of it on this map?"

"Ah, well, good question, Lodak. Possibly because it's not really a ruin of a city. Maybe it was a research facility out in the middle of nowhere."

"That could be, I suppose."

"Oui, très probable." Danielle dripped out some French irony.

"What did she say, Saammmm?"

179

"Oh, only that she agrees with me."

"Sorry, Lodak. Yes, I agree with Sam. But what this map does not tell us, is how hard it is going to be to get the generator, and everything that goes with it, and us, and provisions, and blackclads for protection, over the mountain to make this trip. Not to mention how long that trip will be. And if Bertram figures out things, as we fear he might, the Great Quan's forces may be there waiting for us."

"Yes, Dan-el, that is a dilemma. But if there are wondrous things to discover at this ruin—"

"We don't know that for a fact, do we Sam?"

"Well, I think it's a good possibility."

"Do you? *Je suis sceptique.* Oh, sorry, Lodak. I mean, I am not so sure. Possibly, we could better spend our time building defenses and fortifications for Varneerah."

"Ah, no, Dan-el. We could never build anything that would stand against the full force of the Great Quan. It is better to fight them over there, on their land, in the forests, even on the rivers. We cannot deliver a big blow, but we can give them many small hits and possibly wear them down."

"Well, it has worked for fighters in our world," Sam said.

"And if there is any chance that, at this ruin, we can find more help like your gunpowder, we must take it."

"But the problem remains, can we get there in time?" Danielle, the philosopher of time, asked.

"How do you say depressing in French, Danielle?" Sam asked.

"*Réalité,* Sam."

"If only we had your Nautilus, Saammmm."

"What?"

"*Quelle?*"

"Your *barge of the air* that you told me about."

Sam and Danielle had both forgotten this little canard.

"Oh, yeah, sure," Sam said. "That was just a story, Lodak, that we made up, because—"

"You did not yet want to reveal that you came from the stars."

"Yes, of course. We did not then know how perceptive you were and—"

"It is too bad. A barge of the air that could make it over a great body of water, could possibly make it over a great mountain."

"*Putain de merde!*" Danielle exclaimed, crudely if prettily, as she stood up and started to pace.

Sam got it and stood up himself. "Could we?"

"Why not? This medium is so versatile. *On pourrait en faire des ballons, n'est-ce pas?*"

"But where would we get the helium?" Sam started to pace as well.

"No, no, Sam! *Pensez Montgolfier pas Von Zeppelin.*"

"Hot air!"

"As you say, hot air! *L'antithèse de la bonne science,* but damn good for *élévation!*"

"Dan-el, Saammmm, what…?"

"Lodak," Sam said. "Here, let me draw it out for you."

Sam grabbed a map, turned it over, and quickly, to the best of his ability, drew a picture of a river barge attached to a huge balloon, with a receptacle of fire below it, sending up hot air to lift the balloon into the sky.

"No, no, Sam. It can't really be a barge," Danielle said. "But a…a barge glider. You know with elevators and a rudder and things to control direction. And something for, oh—*pousser ou tirer,* push or pull. You don't want to be at the mercy of the winds."

"Ah, yes, exactly! Something for acceleration."

"*Oui!*"

"So, we could, I think…"

They were excited, these two human children pacing before the adult Saur, who, like adults in the human universe, possibly in all universes, sat and smiled, and took delight in their excitement.

III

The Varneerah barges of the air were not pretty. But after some quick-paced trial and error, experiments of many sorts, and figuring out how they were going to pilot the crafts, they turned out to be quite functional.

They first created and tested sheets of flexible medium of various thicknesses until they found one that held in the hot air and expanded well. The first great balloon they created might not have been recognized by Montgolfier, being more bladder than balloon in the traditional sense and possibly a gallbladder, but that did not seem to matter.

At first, they thought they would be able to attach the great bladder onto modified river barges. But those turned out to be made of a wood that was far too heavy. There was another wood, a village carpenter said, that came from a grove of trees only half a day away. It was a light but strong wood. A crew was put together. They marched to the grove and decimated it. They cut the trees into great planks, loaded them onto wagons, and brought them back. They built a prototype barge. It was light relative to the river barges, but was it strong enough? Would it hold the weight required? Then one of the medium masters that Lodak had trained suggested they should paint the barge with a varnish of liquid medium. He felt it would strengthen the wood without adding weight. He was right. And it had the added benefit of being a fire retardant.

Figuring out how to pilot the air barge was a challenge. But Sam applied basic physics and Danielle, who had once flown ultralight aircraft for kicks, applied her experience. Implements were designed, built, and attached. Soon, their prototype was rising into the air and moving to the whims of conscious minds and not the mercy of random winds.

Below, on the ground, the village Saurs stood still, their eyes never leaving the air barge as Sam, Danielle, and Lodak flew above them. They were amazed. They were amused. But most of all, they were emboldened. If one can fly above the world, they must have thought, then one could control it.

But now the task was to construct more. Sam called upon his inner Henry Ford and created an assembly line to build the air barges. Soon, the Varneerah air fleet was finished.

During this time the blackclads continued military exercises. More dornishes were trained, more seedpod grenades were fashioned, and more standard armaments were made, while Danielle trained pilots for the air barges. Sam and Lodak's newly designed hydroelectric generator was built and tested. Sam and Lodak could only hope that it would be sufficient for their needs, even if their needs were in a hidden conflict.

And where was Lara during all this? She cracked the long books she had borrowed, scratched her head, scratched equations onto paper, fell into deep and dark confusion, climbed up towards the light, and, on occasion, celebrated quick flashes of illumination.

Then, the day arrived when they knew they were ready. They could not think of anything else they could do to prepare. There was only one choice. To go.

They had made ten barges of the air, the original prototype, and nine more. One barge was for the generator. Another was for all the subsidiary equipment it would use, including yards of conduit, to connect with the Dark Lady. There were also, on this barge, materials that could be turned into molds if any part or tool needed to be improvised, along with a store of scrap medium and the pots to heat it in. Seven of the barges held the blackclads, their weapons, seedpod grenades, and cages containing dornishes. The final barge was the command barge upon which Lodak rode, along with Sam, Danielle, and Lara (who had insisted on bringing a stack of long books). And Cuz, of course. To have left Cuz behind would have been to forget John.

A contingent of blackclads and a stock of seedpod grenades were left to defend the village if somehow Bertram had convinced the Great Quan to send troops through the vortex to find and destroy them.

The ten air barges, in a predetermined order, fired up their pots of flame, filled their huge 'gallbladders' with heat, and rose gracefully into the sky. Then, following the command barge, they moved away from Varneerah.

Despite knowing that some of them would not return alive, all the Saurs, not to mention the humans, grew giddy with the delight of flying. Especially in this manner—slow, steady, almost casually, and elegantly over a landscape they had previously known only from the ground.

They made their way to the mountain range, spotted the smallest peak, and navigated toward it, hoping it was small enough to fly over. They were in luck, it was, but just barely. The river barge poles came in handy here.

Once over the mountains, Sam and Lodak studied the ancient maps and the charts they had made from them, looking to match up the real with the represented. Their fear was that the ancient maps were so ancient, the geography of the land might have altered over the years, the great river may now flow along a different path, and the destination they were heading for, their assumed location of the 'ancient ruin' Sam and company had discovered, would prove to be barren of any such structure—thus barren of hope.

Their fears proved to be justified; much had changed in the landscape. The river's path had altered. But—and Sam took this as a good omen, not that he had ever believed in such things—by not so much that they could not spot from the air, from their perspective of height, off in the distance, the massive ring of the Dark Lady, made prominent by the fact that within her circumference there still existed a portion of the Mojave Desert. It was a desert with the creep of this world's lush green growth, but not so much green, that the dry and scrubby brown of desert dirt had been completely covered.

"Saammmm," said Lodak, who had taken more than a minute to look at and consider what he was seeing. "This is not a ruin of the ancients."

The moment had come. Sam always knew it would. And he was prepared. "No, Lodak, it isn't. I didn't want to tell you the truth in case we couldn't find it. What it truly is the outpost we put here to be our base for our studies of your planet. We were trying to get back to it when we were captured."

"An outpost?"

"Yeah. Our home away from home, so to speak."

"It is huge for an outpost of five humans."

"Oh, yeah, that it is, but—"

"Is it a vessel? Camouflaged? Did your landing destroy all of that forest?"

"Well, um—"

"Will it take you back to the stars?"

"No, Lodak, it's not a ship. But we have things in there that, with power, we can use against the Great Quan."

"I look forward to seeing these things."

It was the first ironic and incredulous statement Sam had ever heard Lodak make, and the pit of his stomach seemed as surprised by it as he was. "Well, as soon as we get the generator assembled at the river and hook things up, then—"

"*Merde!* Sam, Lodak, look who's here," Danielle, leaning over the side of the air barge, pointed down and off to their right with great urgency.

Lara, holding tight onto Cuz, looked as well. Despite flying high over the land, she suddenly felt a sinking feeling.

TWENTY-EIGHT

LIGHTING THE DARK LADY

Heading through the forest was a contingent of soldiers of the Great Quan, being led by a relatively small, beautifully-robed individual astride a suunar.

"Well, if that isn't the silliest thing I've ever seen," Sam said.

"Is that...?"

"Yes, Lodak, that is Bert-ram. Or possibly, he now calls himself Bert-ram the Bold. He was always good at marketing."

As ten flying barges passing overhead are hard to miss, even peering up through forest flora, Bertram and his troops soon became aware of them, as evidenced by pointing fingers and exclamations of surprise and shock.

Except on Bertram's face, whereupon a knowing smile and a slight look of admiration rested.

"The irony is," Sam said to Lodak, Danielle, and Lara. "Judging by their direction, I think they would have missed our outpost."

"And now, all they have to do is follow us," Danielle completed the thought.

"We're like a big signpost in the air," Lara lamented.

"So, we know we have a battle coming." Lodak looked at the humans with a stern face they had not seen before. "This is no change from what we assumed might be. A certainty is better than an assumption. We should celebrate this knowledge. Rodash would have been thrilled!"

///

Eight of the air barges landed within the circumference of the Dark Lady, her hump making a natural fortress. The two barges transporting the generator and accompanying equipment landed close to the river shore, carefully negotiating themselves away from trees. The barges were quickly unloaded, and a force of blackclads swiftly climbed up and over the hump, releasing dornishes into the sky. A contingent of blackclads moved into the forest, to engage the soldiers of the Great Quan. At the same time, another went off to protect the generator at the river, and a third set themselves up in defensive positions on the hump.

Sam and Lodak went to the generator to oversee its assembly in the river. Danielle and Lara stayed with the blackclads on the hump.

Soon, sounds of battle could be heard—the shouts of warriors, the clash of weapons, the explosions of the seedpod grenades. Even though the Great Quan's soldiers now had seedpod grenades, the blackclads soon defeated them and captured those who were not dead. The soldiers of the Great Quan did not have dornishes and relied on tossing the grenades by hand. Something, it seems, they were not adept at.

When the blackclads returned with their prisoners, it was quickly reported to Sam that Bertram was among them.

III

Sam found Bertram restrained by several strong blackclads, yet he stood up straight and defiant in his precious stones-and-gold-nugget-encrusted robe.

"Hello, Bertie!" Sam said cheerfully. "Nice robe. Seems I've seen it before."

"You will address me as Savaan," Bertram said.

"I will address you as Dipshit if I want. You are our prisoner, after all."

"I am still the Savaan of the Great Quan and should be treated respectfully."

"And just how did you get this office? Can I assume, by the untimely death of your predecessor?"

Bertram smiled, took in a long breath, and then exhaled it slowly. "When the wounded under-captain reported on your violent theft of the property of the Great Quan—and of your continued existence, when the Great Quan had thought you dead—naturally, the Great Quan wanted to know how this could be so. The Savaan That Was had no answer. And then, when your clever little bombs were reported on, naturally, the Great Quan wanted to know how he could acquire such a weapon. Again, the Savaan That Was came up short with knowledge. I filled in these gaps of knowledge."

"With what? Assumptions?"

"Sure, easy ones. It became obvious that the vortex was a path to somewhere hidden, a refuge—a real somewhere, not some mystic afterlife. Am I right?"

"That does seem to be self-evident, yes. I thought you would have figured that out before now."

"Oh, I did. But I couldn't get the Savann That Was to accept the idea. You and I both know the power of irrational beliefs. And the bombs, well—basic chemistry I knew you would know. I blame the under-captain's pain and loss of blood for not fully reporting about your unique Air Force. Otherwise, I would have investigated that. But be that as it may, the Great Quan was delighted with my assumptions and assurance that I could build him as many bombs as he wanted."

"And so, he had the Savaan's head lopped off?"

"Yes. An efficient transfer of power. I was given the Robe of Office, which I had Agfa alter to fit me, as you can see. I think it looks good."

"You can gold-plate shit, but it's still shit."

Bertram smiled his amusement. "The Great Quan wanted me to find this hiding place immediately, but I impressed him greatly by telling him I knew exactly your plans and where I could find you. Why should we now go to you when you were coming to us? He was delighted and instructed me to do so—and to kill you."

"Well. Sorry that his delight will turn into disappointment."

"Things aren't over yet, Sam."

"They are for you, Bertie."

///

Feeling safer, everyone went about their assigned duties. They constructed the generator at the most rapid flow of the river, then concentrated and intensified that flow by funneling it through a penstock. A conduit to carry the electricity generated was connected and taken through the forest to the Dark Lady. After looking at the connection, Sam and Lodak saw they needed an adapter. One was designed, molds were made, the medium was boiled, poured into the mold, and soon they had their adapter.

"Well," Sam said, "it's a bit makeshift, but if it doesn't blow up or fizzle, I think we'll get our power."

"START HER UP!" Lodak yelled toward the river, an order passed along by several blackclads spaced along the conduit.

Lara and Danielle were on top of the hub, looking down into the dark hole of the escape tube. The sound of circulating air reached them first, and then they watched as the Dark Lady developed an inner glow.

///

Sam, Lodak, Lara, and Danielle, accompanied by several blackclads, explored the interior of the Dark Lady. It was fortunate for Lodak that the Dark Lady was built with high ceilings—when one builds an underground facility, you do what you can to stave off claustrophobia. Still, had Lodak been much taller, he would have had to stoop—as the Scale blackclads had to.

"Let's check the kitchen first," Danielle said.

"The kitchen? Why?" Lara asked.

"Because I'm French."

"That's a silly answer."

"*C'est la vie*"

They found the kitchen as they had left it. Lodak found it strange and genuinely alien. He was fascinated by the refrigerator, which emitted a not-unpleasant hum. He hooked a finger in the handle and—

"Don't open that!" Lara and Danielle shouted in unison.

But it was too late, and they were presented with a foul smell.

Lodak swiftly shut the door.

Danielle checked the pantry and was pleased to find what she came for—jars and canned foodstuffs still suitable for consumption, including some of John's applesauce. She grabbed one, opened it, and smelled it. She smiled, stuck two fingers in, pulled some sweet sauce out, and ingested it with glee. "*Belle compote de pommes*," she said. "It is all I thought about on our journey here."

"Is this why we had to come to the kitchen?" Sam asked. "So, you could get an applesauce fix?"

"And other reasons, Sam. You guys go on. I must confer with our security detail."

On their way down the hall, they passed an open doorway with a sign next to it saying: LOUNGE AND LIBRARY.

Lodak peered in. "Ah. Those look like compact little books. Can I look at them?"

"Of course," Sam said. "I don't know what they all are. Let's see."

They walked in and found a section of science books, a section of pleasure reading—mysteries, science fiction, and even a romance novel or two—and a section of large photo books from National Geographic and Scientific American, as well as some photo essays detailing life in various countries.

"Why don't you look these over, Lodak, while we check out what we think we can use against the Great Quan."

"Yes, I would like that."

Finding no furniture he could comfortably sit on, Lodak sat on the floor, crossed his long legs, and reached for books. He grabbed many and set them down by him.

Danielle caught up with Sam and Lara just as they left the library. The three then continued, going down the hall to Lab Station Scorpion. They were greeted by computers that were on, emanating steady light, and displaying exactly what they had all been staring at when their world had blinked out of existence.

III

They went to their stations, checked their computers' operations, and found everything as it should be. Then, Sam called Danielle to his station to discuss some computations and asked Lara to check John's computer.

"This isn't right," Lara said after a few minutes.

"What?" Sam asked.

"This computation. Here, look."

Sam and Danielle walked over to John's station.

"This isn't supposed to be a three. It's supposed to be a five."

"Are you sure?" Sam asked.

"You had me memorize everything. John wouldn't have made a mistake like that. He was obsessed with checking inputting. I mean, I had him check my inputs, remember? Just before—"

Sam shot out of the lab without explanation. Lara and Danielle took one second to question each other with a look, then ran after him.

They found him in Bertram's office, at Bertram's desk staring at the monitor, at the mirror of John's computer display, at the 5 that should have been a 3, at the cursor mark blinking just to its right.

Sam looked up at the two women, livid with anger but soft-spoken when he said, "Get me, Bertram. Have them bring that bastard to me."

///

Bertram and the soldiers of the Great Quan had been taken over the hump and guarded, while a pen to hold them was quickly constructed against the side of the hump. Despite the Geneva Convention not existing in this world, Danielle insisted that the prisoners be treated humanely and decided they must be fed. She had cans of Spam—and only cans of Spam—delivered to them. Bertram was eating Spam with his fingers when two blackclad Scales came into the pen. They picked Bertram up between them with no preamble and carried him away, his feet dangling in the air.

His feet were still dangling as the hunched-over Scales carried him down the hallway to what was once his office, his home away from home. The door was opened. The Scales judged the distance, width, and force required. Comfortable with their conclusions, they tossed Bertram through the doorway, and he landed in a heap on his office floor.

Recovering himself and sitting up, he noticed Sam at his desk, in front of his computer, which was alive and incriminating.

"You son-of-a-bitch!" Sam exclaimed. "You caused everything. Everything!"

TWENTY-NINE

QUANTUM MEMORIES

Bertram stood up. He brushed off his robe and adjusted it for perfect presentation. He then locked his stance into an erect, yet not stiff, posture. Finally, he looked at Sam and said with a very slight smile, "You always did have these strange leaps of the surreal, Sam."

Bertram stood up. He brushed off his robe and adjusted it for perfect presentation. He then locked his stance into an erect, yet not stiff, posture. Finally, he looked at Sam and said with a very slight smile, "You always did have these strange leaps of the surreal, Sam."

Sam turned in the chair and pointed to the blinking cursor on the monitor. "I can see what you did."

Caught but unconcerned, Bertram asked, "How do you know that change is what caused it? How do you know it wasn't you, mucking around with the building blocks of existence?"

"My experiment was finely tuned. I knew *exactly* what I was doing. That change caused exponential quantum shifts."

"I thought it would just make your experiment come up a bust. I had no way of knowing—"

Sam stood up quickly and stepped towards Bertram. "I could kill you!"

Bertram would have much preferred to have leaped back in response and given way to a full-flight reaction. But he managed to control the instinct. Nor did he fight, for that would have been useless. Besides, neither reaction was worthy of a thinking man—a calculating man.

"Yes, you could," Bertram responded casually to Sam. "And you should. You have that power. But power is not something you know how to effectively…execute."

He was right. Sam knew that. But then, the real power, as the old saying went, was knowledge. "Well," Sam said as he sat down again. "At least now, I know what went wrong. That gives me a greater potential to calculate a reversal."

"*Now I have become death, the shatterer of worlds.*"

"Don't quote Oppenheimer to me, you asshole!"

"*The Bhagavad Gita*, actually."

Sam just shook his head and turned to the monitor to study the situation.

"What you're planning to do is far worse than what I did," Bertram said, moving over to the couch and sitting down. "I had a momentary lapse of judgment and altered a colleague's experiment out of—I'll admit it—jealousy. But I did not *intend* to destroy our universe. I did not *intend* to wipe out everything we knew, to erase it from existence. But you are making a conscious and, if I may say so, rather cavalier decision to destroy this universe."

"Which has only existed since we got here," Sam said, keeping his eyes on the monitor.

"My God, what an ego! This universe is here now, and it's been here for billions of years. And these people are here now and have been here for millions of years. Whereas we poor *Homo sapiens*—what there is left of us—have been around for only thousands of years. And yet, you would commit genocide upon this ancient race to satisfy your rather infantile desires."

Sam turned to Bertram, sitting there in his jeweled and gold-nugget-encrusted robe, looking damn silly, and yet all Sam could see was Bertram's lively, but cold, steel eyes. "And what are your desires?"

"Me? Power. I won't hide it. I'm not a liar and hypocrite like you. With my knowledge in this primitive setting—there's no limit. And did you ever consider that, with that power, I might be able to do these people some good?"

"Excuse me if I take a cynical attitude towards the idea."

"But you have to admit that it's possible."

"If improbable."

"But, possible. Whereas, what possible good are you going to do these people?" Bertram smiled a self-satisfied slime of a smile.

And it was that smile, as much as anything Bertram had said, that smacked Sam's conscience—or good sense or intellectual honesty or maybe simple common humanity—and affected the change.

Sam stood up and commanded Bertram to do the same. Bertram

did so. Sam went to the door, opened it, returned to Bertram, grabbed him by the scruff of his neck, and then pushed him into the arms of the two blackclads waiting outside. Then, he exited the room and started down the hall, calling back to the blackclads, "Bring him!"

///

In Lab Station Scorpion, Sam found Lara and Danielle huddled over the monitor of Lara's computer, discussing some matter in soft voices. Lodak was there, watching what they were doing with some fascination, wondering exactly what wonders the illuminated rectangle had that could take their attention. They did not even know he was in the room. He had come in because he had wanted to talk about several books he had in hand, books of stunning revelations to him.

"Okay, look, stop," Sam said as he walked in, followed by Bertram, who was tossed in by the blackclads and, again, found himself on the floor.

"*Pourquoi? Quel est le problème?*" Danielle was a bit irritated over the interruption, her mind wanting to be back in communion with Lara.

"Saammmm?" Lodak himself questioned, Sam's agitation being opaque.

Sam approached Lodak. He looked up at Downy, whose face he had gotten to know so well yet was now *seeing* for the first time. "Lodak, I owe you an apology."

"Why?"

"Because I was planning to kill you."

"I do not understand."

"You and your whole world. I was planning to wipe you all out. Look, Lodak, we are not from the stars. And this is not an outpost, it's—it's called a superconducting super collider. We are from another—universe—another reality—another existence. There are probably a hundred other words you could use, but none of them would be adequate. We are from that which was but is no longer because we destroyed it. And in destroying it, we created this reality, which is made from the same basic stuff of existence. We somehow reconstituted the stuff of our reality into this reality, which has millions of years of history for your people. But, for us, it has only been months."

"Well," Bertram said as he stood up. He tried to recover a dignity no one in this room would have been impressed by. "Time is relative."

193

"Shut up!" Sam commanded.

Lodak was, not unexpectedly, confused. He looked at the large blow-up of the aerial view of the Dark Lady on the wall. So like, and yet unlike, what they had viewed from the air barge, he pointed to it. "This image. Is it this place as it existed in your world?"

"Exactly. It was in the middle of a hot and dry place."

"And now it is here."

"It might be said that it made here," Sam said.

"*It?* Not *you?*" Lodak asked.

"Yes, sorry, the Dark Lady—that's what it's called—is just a tool. A tool to conduct experiments to discover what makes up the universe and how the universe works. Lara, Danielle, John, and I were experimenting with time, and there was an accident. An accident caused by Bertram."

Lodak turned to Bertram, looking at him with eyes that questioned, but not without some pity in them.

"Yes, I fiddled with Sam's fantasy a little," Bertram said, his arrogance intact

"You sabotaged it, is what you did!" Sam wanted to make it clear. "Causing this—this alteration, this parody of our reality."

"This *parody* is Lodak's only reality. It is rather unkind of you to call it names."

Bertram was right. Not for a righteous reason, but he was right.

Sam turned away from Bertram to the large Downy, who must have been feeling much but conveyed nothing of those feelings.

"Lodak, I'm sorry. I lied to you about—well, about everything, I guess. I wanted to come back here to try to reverse what had happened. I wanted to see if I could break it down again and rebuild it to what we had lost, back to our reality. But in doing so, we—I—would have killed you. I would have destroyed your reality. I had thought I was only setting a mistake right, correcting something. But…Danielle and Lara have been trying to talk me out of it. John, I think, would have vigorously joined them in that."

"And they have succeeded?"

"No. No, as persuasive as their arguments were, I was determined. But *Bert-Ram* has pointed out that if I go forward, I'll be a bigger son-of-a-bitch than he is. And that I cannot live with. So we, Danielle, Lara, and I, are now committed to this reality—to you. And although the Dark Lady is not full of weapons that will help you, there are things we know and can do to help you prevail. The first is keeping Bertram and his knowledge away from the Great Quan. That will give us a huge advantage."

"So what are you going to do, Sam? Kill me?" It was a taunt more than a challenge.

"No, Bertie. I'm going to put you to work on a farm."

Bertram's arrogance may have slipped a little, for Danielle and Lara noticed a slight jerk of his held-up-high head and a slight widening of his eyes, consistent with the sometimes subtle sting of fear. Sam did not see this, for Lodak had commanded his attention.

"Saammmm, this reality of yours is what is in these small books?"

They were not small to Sam, of course. Lodak put down the three coffee table books he had been holding. They were part of the *Daily Life In....* series of photo journals, documenting the wonders, the glories, the mundane, and the shame of various countries.

Sam looked at them, thumbed through them, and felt pangs he would have preferred not to have felt. "Yes, Lodak. These books have images—created through a mechanical device—that show our reality in detail and accuracy. This one, *Daily Life in America,* is where we come from."

"*Excusez-moi...*"

"Except for Danielle, who comes from France, which is a whole separate reality."

Lara laughed, thinking it was a good thing that Sam could joke.

Danielle, who did not think it was as funny as Lara did, punched her softly.

"*Pardon,*" Lara said quickly.

Lodak watched all this with little interest. He was much too concerned with something else. "And all this, all these images of your reality, of things and people and creatures of your world—these are all gone now?"

"Yes, we're pretty sure it's all been... Well, like medium, it's been melted down and cooled into your reality, your world, you."

"Then you have nothing to apologize for. You were fighting for your home just as I am. If you can recover it—how can I ask you not to?"

"It's no good, Lodak. Either your home exists, or my home exists, but they can't both exist."

"I'm not so sure about that," Lara said.

Sam turned to Lara and Danielle.

Danielle picked up some notes with calculations that Lara had been working on. "Lara has been doing some rather exciting work in the field of parallel universes," Danielle said as if they were casually chit-chatting at a scientific conference in Boston. She handed the notes to Sam.

Sam took them, glanced at them, and saw calculations combined with musings, flights of fancy combined with solid math.

"Are you saying that you think we just—jumped from one universe to another?"

"No. No, I think we did destroy ours. You put it well. I think we did melt our universe and inadvertently formed this one from it," Lara said. "But that means that possibly every quantum bit making up this universe has a memory of what it once was. And I've been working on something—"

Lara's voice was filled with excitement, which was familiar to Sam, if not recently experienced. It was an excitement that quickly spread and was easily adopted.

"Well, you see, I got some of the concepts from the long books Lodak gave me. The Saur ancients had been dealing with this. I'm not there yet, but I've gotten clues and hints that I think are leading me in the right direction."

"Direction to where?" Sam asked.

"To where we could recover that memory—and make a copy of it."

Bertram, the arrogant asshole that he was, was still a scientist. "Are you saying you could make a copy of our universe and split it from this one?"

"I think so. But I don't know. I still have a lot of work. If John had still been alive to help me…"

"He was brilliant at this stuff," Bertram said, not without some residual human sadness.

"Yes, he was," Sam said. "When he was being purely theoretical, his mind leaped universes like puddles."

"Well, let's not get *poetic* about it, Sam," Bertram scoffed. "It is still just a matter of matter."

"And information," Danielle added.

"Yes! Matter and information. If we think of it as one thing—matter-information, like space-time, then replication…" Sam's mind started to leave the room.

"With time," Lara said, "maybe we can—"

"You don't have time," Bertram said bluntly. "Do you think that puny force I was heading up is the only one coming at you? I left behind designs for simple delivery systems for the seedpod bombs. And an assembly line to make them. A well-armed force is probably coming at you now, led by the Great Quan himself."

"*Merde!*" Danielle said.

"Crap!" Lara said.

"Shit!" Sam said. Then to Lara: "How clear are those long books of Lodak's?"

"They're dense and complex and in another language, but I'm pulling things out."

"Okay, if we all concentrate on it—" Sam started.

"If only we had John," Lara said.

"Well, John taught me everything he knew," Sam reminded her.

"John taught us both, Sam," Bertram said. "Let me help."

"Why would you want to?"

"To get rid of you. And to have you leave this universe in my capable hands."

Sam said nothing. Why did he have to worry about Bertram's sincerity in considering his offer instead of just getting to work?

"Yes, Bert-ram," Lodak broke the silence, taking the decision away from Sam. "You can help. And I will take my force of blackclads and engage the Great Quan before he gets here. We will hold him back as long as we can, to give you time, relative or not."

"No," Sam said. "That's the same as if we destroy your universe. I won't allow it."

"Sam, you're being—"

"Not unless Bertram pledges to let you and your troops escape, Lodak."

"Why would I do that?"

"Because if you don't, we will stay here and help Lodak defeat the Great Quan, free his people and all of his slaves. Except for one, of course. How do you think you'll look in a Yellowsack? Do you know how much dinosaur shit there is to shovel in this world?"

Bertram forced a smile to beat back the intimidation. "Sounds like a good job for a *tight-ass bureaucrat.*"

But Sam did not join him in smiling. "Bertram?"

"Okay. I agree. If Lodak survives his encounter with the Great

Quan, I'll ensure he can leave unharmed."

"And all his people."

"And all his people—assuming any of them are left alive."

"Fine. And you will also show Lodak, on our charts, the route the Great Quan and his army are taking so that Lodak and the blackclads can go and—*welcome* them in the most advantageous location possible."

Bertram smiled in acquiescence. "Smart. But then, it's pretty much what I would have asked for in your place."

"Well, we are fucking PhDs, you know."

Sam turned to Lodak. "Hold the Great Quan and his troops off as long as possible. But when you must retreat, do so, get back here. If we are gone, and Bertram is a man of his word, return to Varneerah, move everybody, find a new sanctuary, then—what will be, will be."

"We will prevail, Saammmm. Eventually."

"I wish I could be by your side."

"You will be. You will be my parallel. We may never meet again, but we will always be side-by-side."

There was a moment between the two, with human eyes looking up and Downy eyes looking down in a deep connection. It was like a quick tableau of a parent and a child, but only physically. Emotionally and empathetically, equality was unquestioned. Lodak turned and started to leave. Then he stopped, turned back, went over to the *Daily Life in...* books and picked them up, pocketed them, smiled, and left.

Then, it was time to get to work.

"Bertram, this will be like when we were Ph.D. candidates. You'll get so far and then not have the imagination to make the necessary leap," Sam said.

"You've always had enough imagination for the both of us. But, without my meticulous work—"

"Doctors!" Lara stopped them. "We don't have time for this."

"Then we'll just have to *make time*," Sam said in confident defense.

THIRTY

IMPRESSIONS AND IMAGININGS

What followed remained in certain minds as mere impressions:

…Of breaking into two teams.

…Of Lara and Danielle, setting themselves up in the library, bringing in dry-erase boards from various offices.

…Of Sam and Bertram, working in Lab Station Scorpion, pushing computers to collaborate.

…Of Danielle, working at the boards, filling them with equations, as Lara poured over several opened long books, translating on the fly for Danielle.

…Of Cuz, making a corner of the library his own and finding a taste for Spam.

…Of Sam, studying the equations on the boards in the library and growing frustrated when their flow suddenly stopped and bunched up into incomprehension. Of him flinging an eraser across the room and having it lodged into a bookcase, wedged between the top of some random mysteries and the shelf above. Of Bertram looking up from the magazine he was relaxing with, Danielle looking over from another board, at which she was doodling to free her mind, and Lara looking up from her long books, where she was trying to divine an answer. Of the three of them quickly applauding a feat Sam could never have repeated, then just as quickly returning to what they were doing. And of Sam, sighing, walking over to the bookcase, retrieving the eraser, and returning to the board.

…Of meals shared. Of the applesauce, the eating of which became like a ritual. Of Vienna sausages, many, many little Vienna sausages. Of crackers and their crumbs, which clung to all.

…Of emergency bathroom breaks because these complex minds ignored their simple needs.

...Of the moment when things changed. Of Lara alone in the library, almost in a twilight sleep, yet still reading from the ancient books as Cuz slept on the table near her. Of slowly translating whole paragraphs at a time, contemplating them, as her head nodded under the weight of closing eyelids. Of her head suddenly jerking up in a desperate ascent into wakefulness. Of rubbing her eyes and slapping herself in the face to jumpstart alertness. Of one last nod and one last jerk up, this time not just into wakefulness but into illumination.

...Of Sam and Bertram arguing bitterly over some fine point in an equation on a board in Lab Station Scorpion, when Lara ran in, clasping awkwardly an open long book which she threw onto the floor, then fell before it in near-worship, and started to read out loud. This stopped Sam and Bertram's argument. This got Danielle's attention away from her monitor. The information, the thoughts, the leaps to conclusions, the application of all this to their thoughts and leaps, had them all speaking rapidly to each other, as the board was erased clean, then filled with new equations, with speed and clarity and *ah-hahs*!

...Of the moment Sam turned to Lara, grabbed her, hugged her, and kissed her in an act that seemed as natural as the formation of stars.

///

Before all this, though, Bertram did confer over charts with Lodak. Then, Lodak gathered his blackclads outside the Dark Lady and formed them into marching order, including his 'air force' of dornish handlers, with their flying partners perched on their shoulders. Bertram even joined Lara, Danielle, and Sam in a final goodbye, an official send-off, an unnecessary ceremony, but one all seemed to feel the need for. Emotions sometimes must be felt.

And sometimes, the game still needed to be played.

Lodak looked at Bertram and said with a certain sad hopefulness, "Join us."

"Will you give me absolute power?"

"No."

"Then, I thank you for the offer, but no thanks."

"I should kill you right now."

"But you won't."

"Why not?"

Bertram quickly looked to Sam and then back to Lodak. "For the same reason, I will let you escape—if you survive. But after today, you will receive no further accommodations from me."

"We will prevail."

"You will try. Then, to quote our mutual acquaintance here, *what will be, will be.*"

Bertram turned and started to return to the Dark Lady when Lodak called out, "Bert-ram." Bertram turned back to the Downy. "When I do kill you, it will be with mercy."

"Oh, no, Lodak. If you get the chance, which I doubt, show me no mercy. Make it a glorious death."

Lodak smiled and ordered his blackclads to march. Soon, their presence was known only by the sound of their movement through the forest.

"That was a bit melodramatic, wasn't it?" Sam chided Bertram, as they climbed up the ladder to the top of the hump.

"If you can't be melodramatic to a talking dinosaur, who can you be melodramatic to?"

III

What happened in the forest that day? Sam, Lara, and Danielle would never know. All they had were their imaginings. Imaginings of the mass movement of macro beings and objects that did not abate, just because their minds mostly dwelled among quanta. They knew that Lodak had decided to confront the Great Quan and his forces in a broad break in the forest if they could get to it in time. The blackclads would remain hidden in the forest, and as soon as the Great Quan Army was exposed, they would rain upon them arrows and spears, and, most devastatingly, they hoped, seedpod grenades dropped from the sky. Then, as the Great Quan's forces flailed about in confusion, they would attack in force.

But they also knew—because Bertram delighted in telling them—that the Army of the Great Quan was now equipped not only with seedpod grenades of their own but with personal hand-carried catapults of Bertram's design that, like all good tools, extended the natural ability of the user. In this case, it would make the soldiers of the Great Quan powerful and accurate throwers of death. Plus, they would be prepared for the dornishes this time, Bertram having initiated training in archery aiming at flying targets.

So, it was not hard to imagine:

The Army, led by the Great Quan, enters into the break of the forest. Once in, shrill whistles are heard. A contingent of soldiers grab bows and arrows, point them upward, and find and follow flights, aim and release. Some of the dornishes will fall, and some will hit their targets. Explosions in the field will be followed by explosions in the forest from catapult-flung grenades. Some of the Great Quan's disciplined soldiers will form defensive postures; some will make offensive forays into the forest. The blackclads will have no choice but to attack and engage in the field to keep the soldiers there, fighting as long as possible.

It will be a bloody mess.

Bertram would have imagined the overwhelming numbers of the soldiers of the Great Quan devastating the blackclads, killing every last one of them. But not before—he may well have imagined—the fall of the Great Quan himself, which would undoubtedly smooth Bertram's path to power.

Sam, Lara, and Danielle retained hope, imagining that the rightness of Lodak's cause and the spirit of the blackclads would see them, if not prevail, at least complete their mission to delay the Great Quan as long as possible, eventually beating a hasty and strategic retreat, disappearing back into the forest to return to the Dark Lady in such a way as to not lead the Great Quan directly to them. There, they would discover if the scientists had been successful and if their friends were gone. If not, they would gather up the disappointed three, fire up the air barges, and escape to Varneerah to plan an exodus.

And if they found Bertram alone?

THIRTY-ONE

RETURN FROM WHERE

Never once did the four of them think they were doing something audacious. After all, they had already unwoven one universe and weaved another in its place. That, of course, had not been their intention, but how much in human history had been accomplished that was never intended?

What was intended now? To find the memory of the unwoven universe within this universe, making a copy of it, and divorcing it from the reality they now lived in. How? A greater mind than the one reporting on these events would have to reveal that. And maybe only other great minds would even understand what was being conveyed. So, we are left with the intention. An admirable one? We can agree that it was. And, audacious, despite none of the four thinking of it that way. Three just wanted to get home, like all travelers in unknown realms, whether it be the center of the Earth, Oz, Pellucidar, or a far-flung future. And, one just wanted to get rid of the other three to make a home, a substantial nest, for himself.

Simple intentions. And they all hoped for no unforeseen accomplishments.

"Are we ready?" Sam asked the other three.

"Just a sec," Lara said as she and Danielle finished a last check of everything inputted into the computers, especially what Bertram had inputted.

Bertram stood to the side with a particularly telling smirk on his lips. "You're wasting precious time," he said.

"Those who do not learn from history…" Danielle said, then turned to Sam. "*D'accord, tout va bien.*"

"*Merci,*" Sam said in a very American way. He looked to Bertram. Are you sure you don't want to go with us?"

"Sure, I'm sure. You're either going to succeed, or you're going to rewrite the laws of the universe, creating something we can't exist in. If it's the latter, we might as well say goodbye here. If you succeed, why would I want to return and be nothing but a 'tight-ass bureaucrat' when if I stay here, I'll sooner or later be the Great Quan?"

"A rather diminutive Great Quan," Sam said.

"Size, like everything else, is relative."

"Okay, stay if you want. But you will keep your commitment to Lodak, right?"

"I will keep my commitment to Lodak."

It was said with blunt sincerity, and Sam did not doubt Bertram's word. He offered his hand. Bertram took it.

"It has been like old times," Sam said.

"Which were both good and bad."

"Doesn't that define all times? Old, new, and yet-to-be?"

"Is this any time to get philosophical?" Bertram asked.

Sam smiled in agreement. "You're right. Get out of here, you son-of-a-bitch."

"Fuck you, you bastard," Bertram said lightly. "And—goodbye."

They shook hands one last time, and then Bertram turned and left. They all waited, listening for the sound of the door closing on top of the hump to reverberate down two stories and down the hall to them. They gave it a few more minutes beyond that to give Bertram time to climb down from the Dark Lady's hump and get a safe distance away. Then, Lara and Danielle were ready, but Sam was unmoving, lost in thought.

"Sam?" Danielle called to him.

"What?"

"Are we ready?"

"Sure, sure. No *time* like the present."

"Sam, stop with the time jokes, *s'il vous plaît.*"

Sam crossed to his computer station, inputting the final instructions, and then he put his finger over the ENTER key. He addressed the two women. "If this is our last moment of existence—know I love you both."

"And if this is not our last moment of existence?" Danielle wanted to know.

"Then know that I admire you both as hard-working colleagues."

"Sam," Lara said, picking up Cuz and holding him close. "Just push the damn button."

Sam turned to the keyboard, focused on the ENTER key, gently laid his finger on it, and pushed.

///

They fully expected to lose consciousness for several days, as they had the first time. But this time, they knew it was coming, their brains knew it was coming, so they didn't shut down in response to the twisted, information-scrambling signals that were hard to differentiate, discriminate, and coordinate. Colors became sound, sound became shapes, and shapes became observable in twelve dimensions. Textures became words, shouting and whispering, and light revealed itself as streams of photons, hitting them. They could see shouting shapes redirect themselves, and they jumped out of their chairs, amazed at the solidity of the floor, even though they could not find it. They recognized each other and yet found each other completely strange, a new experience. They found themselves not being themselves but possibly forces to be reckoned with. Danielle and Sam began to think, no, feel, no, understand, no, imagine, no, hurt, no, trickle away, away, away into some things not Danielle and Sam. But Lara did not; Lara held Cuz, warm, furry, unconscious but breathing in, out, inhaling, expelling. Cuz was Cuz, and Lara remained Lara. She looked around. The lab was coming back into focus again. Lara screamed although she heard nothing, for there was John. John at his station, a ghost-like John just as he was the moment before, the moment before… And there was Danielle, Sam, and herself, all at their stations, all ghost-like but struggling to come into being.

"SAM!" Lara yelled at the bearded, blackcladded Sam, standing close to her, yet miles away. She heard nothing coming out of her mouth. She then moved, or willed, or thought herself over to Sam and butted against him.

He turned to her, looking at her with great curiosity.

She pointed to them all seated at their stations, just as they were when all this started, in their scientist clothes—non-uniform, casual, each to their tastes, probably bought online, the uniforms of their time, that time—instead of being blackcladded in resistance warrior garb.

Sam suddenly understood but could not convey it. He grabbed Lara and pushed her over to herself. He grabbed Cuz, limp but alive, and set him on the desk. Then he took Lara, his immediate Lara, blackcladded with short hair, and moved her to sit within her ghost self, the self at the computer, manipulating her to match precisely the pose of her ghost self.

Danielle observed this and saw the logic. She moved to her ghost self and became one with it. Sam did the same, precisely aligning his body with his ghost outline, instinctively knowing he could not be even one centimeter off.

Then everything went turquoise. *Turquoise? Why turquoise?* Sam wondered, knowing there would be no answer, but comforted that he was able to wonder.

Then, with a cosmic *chunk,* reality reappeared, and all was as once before, not so long ago. But that, of course, was relative.

Sam, Danielle, and Lara immediately noticed that they were now human hybrids, part themselves from before, part themselves as they had become. The women had heads of hair, both long and short, in crazy quilt patterns; Sam had patches of beard spotted over his face. And their clothes were not very attractive combos, crazy quilts, in fact, of what they had worn that day and their blackclad warrior outfits. And, sadly, their shoes were now horribly uncomfortable, being part of this world and part of their custom Saur footwear.

"Damn!" It was John. John as he was in the *then* they had just recaptured, John whom they all loved, concentrating on his monitor, paying no attention to anything else. "It's a bust, an absolute bust! I don't think anything happened. I mean, we'll have to check the atomic clocks but—"

He was cut off by Cuz, who had awoken to the image of John in his line of sight. He jumped up, jumped over, and excitedly jumped into John's lap.

"What the...?" John leaped out of his chair, brushing this giant "rodent" away. Before he could question the incident, he was suddenly surrounded by the other three humans in the room. The women gave him hugs and kisses, and once they were done, Sam gave him a big bear squeeze. Sam held on tight to this man, this mentor, this friend, who had always kept Sam grounded and was, indeed, grounding him at this very moment.

"All right, I hope you've gotten what you wanted because the morning dirigible is here." It was Bertram, walking into the lab, remarkably well-pressed suit and straight-tie-looking for someone who had slept on a couch in his office. "I've got a crew coming in, and I

need you all to leave. You can check your clocks on the way out—"
Bertram stopped when he noticed something wasn't right and strange
things were filling his vision.

Sam wanted to give Bertram no time to consider the strange.
"Come on, you heard the man, let's go. Pack it up, pack it up, make
sure you get the data backup."

Danielle and Lara moved quickly, packing cases and putting on
coats. Lara snatched up Cuz and tucked him into her bag.

"Sam?" John was still standing in a whirl of surreal.

Lara wrapped John's coat around him, handed him his bag, and
hustled him out of the lab. "No time to talk, John. The morning
dirigible is waiting."

Sam, briefcase in hand, approached Bertram. "Well, thanks for your
generous hospitality, Bertie. It's been a pleasure. And look, now that
we've reconnected, we must stay in touch."

"I don't stay in touch with practical jokers and clowns. Would you
leave, please?"

"I'm serious, Bertram. *I'll* be in touch."

///

They entered the airship's cabin and settled themselves. John, for
whom time had shrunk and reality had altered, was on the verge of
hyperventilating as he sat and stared at his now very weird-looking
companions.

Lara took Cuz out of her bag and placed him gently onto John's
lap. "It's okay," she said, as John wanted to draw away. "This is Cuz;
he's a friend. Pet him." She took his hand. "Come on, pet him. He
loves it."

John started to pet the primate, who curled himself into a burrow
in John's lap, quite satisfied.

Lara went over and sat next to Sam. Together, they watched as the
dirigible lifted off and elevated out of the hangar, reoriented its
position, and started its slow float over the Mojave Desert back to
Tysontown. Down below, they could see the Dark Lady recede as if
shrinking into nonexistence.

"Sam?" Danielle, from across the cabin, called for his attention.

Sam turned to her. "Yes?"

"Do you think it's still there? *L'autre univers?*"

"I don't know. But it doesn't hurt to believe it is. You did get the backup, right?"

Danielle held up two small pods, identical except for their colors. "Twice. One's encoded DNA, the other is quantum."

"Good thinking. Well, maybe the answer is in those."

"Or maybe not," Danielle said.

Sam looked over to John, who had taken refuge in Cuz's warmth. "Then we'll search elsewhere. We owe it to *him*."

"Oh!" Lara suddenly joined the conversation. "By the way, I almost forgot."

"What?" Sam asked.

"I'm pregnant."

Danielle laughed.

Sam's mouth opened then closed, then opened again, wanting to ask Lara if she was sure, but no words came out.

It didn't matter. Lara understood, and she nodded her head in acknowledgment.

Sam looked to Danielle and mouthed; *did you know?*

Danielle laughed and shook her head.

Then Sam sat back to think, to look at Lara very deeply. Lara looked right back and smiled. Sam thought for a moment more, then called out. "John?"

John looked up from Cuz. "Yes?"

"Bit of news. Lara and I are getting married."

Lara entwined her arms into Sam's and rested her head on his shoulder.

"Would someone please explain to me what the hell is going on?"

"All in good time, John. All in good time."

EPILOGUE

You have just finished reading my account of my brother and his companions' journey to Where the Great Quan Rules. The question now is not whether you believe it but how you came to read it. For the powers that be, powers most potent and virulent, have tried their best to quash it. In any case, I congratulate you for your courage in reading such a subversive work. And I apologize for my brother that you had to make the effort, for he is, of course, once again, to blame.

When Sam, Lara, and Danielle returned to this universe, there was obviously a period of a few days when they had to go through a kind of decompression, filled with moments of wondering if it had all been a dream, or a shared hallucination, or some kind of weird quantum trip. But the physical evidence was there, not the least being the little creature, Cuz. And then, there were the insistent questions from John, who would not relent in his interrogation of them, in wanting to know what had happened, and he kept pressing the experience back into their minds, detail after detail.

What they told him profoundly affected John, especially the small fact of his death in the Saur universe, the details of it, the violence of it, and the *why* of it. John became obsessed with the Saur universe. He began to wonder out loud if there would be a way to return to it, to avenge his own death, and fight again for the oppressed. But, as he could do nothing on his own, he stopped asking questions and found comfort in caring for Cuz.

After this short period of decompression was over and they began to feel normal again, they looked up from their self-regard to appreciate their universe again and were shocked to find they had not entirely succeeded in recreating it. It was close, a close copy, a casual look-see at the men and women and material, at both mundane and monumental activities, would not necessarily give them a clue that something most horrible was fundamentally different from the universe they had known. But a few days of *living* in this world did.

That was when my brother secretly communicated with me.

Everybody knew of the modern underground railroad, which ferreted questers for freedom to our tiny Bay Area nation. But only a few knew how to access it. Fortunately, I was one of the few. Soon, Sam, Danielle, Lara, and John were with me in San Francisco, telling me their stories to establish their veracity and justify what they planned to do next.

But first, they told me of the universe, of the Earth, of the United States they had left. It was more unbelievable than the story of their journey.

In their universe, the fallback from freedom, the embrace of authoritarianism, had never occurred among the liberal democracies of Earth. They told me there had been much flirting with authoritarianism in the liberal democracies, and they had, in fact, found it rather disconcerting. For it had been preceded by years of the denigration of knowledge, the discounting of facts, and attacks on the sincerity of the intelligences who gathered and documented the data to back it all up.

Scientists, of course, caught the brunt of this, they being the main generators, analyzers, and interpreters of data. There had been concerted efforts from several fronts to demonize all scientists as either Frankensteins, know-it-all elitists, or secular atheists determined to make war on religion and to destroy people's faith, or virulent anti-capitalists whose pesky data (pointing out dangers to health and the environment) was really just a bunch of fake fact chains meant to shackle good CEOs—who were, of course, the heart and soul of the nation—from doing their jobs.

Despite all this, the four had assumed the principles of free expression established in the Enlightenment and certain laws and traditions codified, especially in the Constitution of the United States, would eventually prevail.

But that was *then*, in their universe, not *now*, in ours.

In looking closely at this altered universe they now occupied, they realized that in trying to recreate their universe from the memory locked into the stuff of the Saurs' universe, a glitch had occurred. That, except for a few pockets of resistance and freedom, such as the Bay Area nation, this Earth was under the control of a handful of authoritarian dictators who worked in concert to create and perpetuate a pyramid of privilege where only the best and brightest in their estimation—not to mention the most fashionably dressed—would reside at the point of the pyramid, while the base would be crowded with the masses, straining to support the top, while wallowing most happily in their ignorance.

Sam and the others were shocked, stupefied, almost paralyzed. The alteration of reality as they had known it was so monumental to them that they didn't know what to do: save, possibly curl up, and ignore their surroundings. A very difficult pose for scientists.

Then, a small item of information, one individual fact, maybe even just a factoid, spurred them to uncurl and act. They discovered that in this world Harvard University—an institution none of them in their universe had attended, but one they revered nevertheless—only offered two advanced academic degrees. One was a PhD in Christian Reverence. The other was a master's in business administration.

When they finally reached me here in San Francisco, I had much to do to calm them down. I had much to do, to take in and understand their stories of the two other realities they had come from. I had much to do, to remain objective and disinterested, and professional. I had much to do to accept. It was a struggle. But I succeeded.

Or had I been infected by their perfect madness?

In the middle of my tests and physiological evaluations of Sam, Danielle, Lara, and John, Bertram showed up at my door.

If Sam and the others were disconcerted by suddenly finding themselves in a reality so like what they expected, yet fundamentally so different, imagine what Bertram felt. He did not have the background of having journeyed to and living in the Saur universe. Reality for him, despite being a physicist, was as it was for most people living in the mundane day-to-day, rock-solid and irrefutable. But Bertram was the consummate adapter and, keeping his shock and thoughts to himself, quickly and brilliantly improvised competence in his new role—not just as the head of America's superconducting super collider, but also as a Major General in the United States Army. But he was plagued by a need to understand what had happened. And he knew the answer lay with Sam—it was the only conclusion he could come to.

Bertram looked for Sam and found that he had abandoned his home, leaving everything behind—furniture, clothes, cans in the pantry. He tried to contact Danielle in France and found she had been reported as missing. The same was true of Lara and John. It didn't take him long to figure out where they all must have gone. And so, using his status in this world, he secured permission to travel to the degenerate Bay Area nation. Once here, he came immediately to me.

You may think that this world we are living in would be a perfect fit for the Bertram I have portrayed in my account of their journey to Where the Great Quan Rules. But that turned out not to be true. Bertram found that the Bertram he was supposed to be in this world, while an extremely loyal functionary of the authoritarian President-for-Life of the United States, was also a scientist and so came under unending suspicion. And he was tasked with not just unlocking the secrets of the universe via the Dark Lady, but also the powers hidden within those secrets. His sacred duty, as he was reminded by the Secretary of Force, was to advise how to best harness those powers for the benefit of the United States. How, for example, might dark energy and dark matter become the driving force of the enhancement of the nation through overwhelming military power? Bertram was appalled, or so he told us. But he was most disturbed at finding himself a puppet on a string.

Sam was happy to see Bertram. Bertram expressed no similar joy. He had questions, and he wanted them answered. But he was in no position to make demands, despite the superior demeanor he threw at everyone. He was told that answers would be provided and the story would be told, but only if he submitted to my questions and evaluations. He was reluctant at first, but as Sam and the others revealed what they knew, he became an enthusiastic participant.

What Bertram could tell me about the journey before and after was helpful and confirmed that part of the story. He even confessed to his single-digit responsibility for setting the whole thing in motion—confessed but not apologized.

The five I was now playing host to were collectively the most unusual and strangest humans on the planet.

Where are they now? You may well ask, and I wish I knew for certain. All I can tell you is they felt the desire for freedom, for the satisfaction of intellectual curiosity, for the simple comforts of home and place. They needed to survive, to strive, and to know.

I tried to talk them out of it. I tried to tell them that our world—my world—needed them and their story. They laughed at me—gently, but still... *Who's going to believe them?* they asked. But if I thought the story was useful, then they suggested that I write it up. But they themselves—they had to go.

Defeated, if not convinced, I secured for them lab space and equipment at the old Lawrence Livermore National Laboratory.

I have not seen them since.

Three weeks after they had moved to the lab and, indeed, moved *into* the lab, having never left it day or night, ordering in meals charged to my bank account, and putting in the odd request that I send them tins of Spam, there was a small, contained implosion. The lab was destroyed. No other part of the building it was in was damaged.

Their bodies were never found.

Where are they now? You may well ask.

You may as well ask: *Where are we now?*

END

THANK YOU FOR READING

JOURNEY TO WHERE

ABOUT THE AUTHOR

Photo by Amanda Martin

Before publishing thirteen critically acclaimed works of fiction, award-winning and Amazon Bestselling author Steven Paul Leiva spent over twenty years in the entertainment industry as a writer and producer. He worked with such talent as Academy Award-winning producer Richard Zanuck; director Ivan Reitman; literary legend and screenwriter Ray Bradbury; *Star Wars* producer Gary Kurtz; Looney Tunes legend Chuck Jones; and Animation Feature Academy Award-winning director Brad Bird. He even lent his voice to the Academy Award shortlisted (placing in the top ten) animated short, "The Indescribable Nth."

Leiva produced the animation for the original *Space Jam*, starring the very tall Michael Jordan and the relatively short Bugs Bunny. For this production, Leiva put together an ad hoc animation studio for Warner Bros and executive producer Ivan Reitman in three days over the phone

During this time, he wrote novels and a play, *Made on the Moon*, which premiered at the Edinburgh Festival Fringe and received a four-star review from *The Scotsman*.

After *Space Jam*, Leiva decided to concentrate on writing novels. Since 2003, he has published twelve novels, a novella, and a book of essays.

His work has been praised by literary great Ray Bradbury, Oscar-winning film producer Richard Zanuck, *New York Times* bestselling author and Pulitzer Prize finalist Diane Ackerman, *New York Times* Bestselling Author Jonathan Maberry, comedy great Phil Proctor of The Firesign Theater, *USA Today* Bestselling Author Jean Rabe, *Star Trek: Enterprise* actor John Billingsley, Australian philosopher Russell Blackford, and British physicist and author Stephen Webb. He has received the Scribe Award from the International Association of Media Tie-in Writers

You can find Steven Paul Leiva on Facebook and read his blog, The Emotional Rationalist, at https://tinyurl.com/ydgpkps8

BOOKS BY STEVEN PAUL LEIVA

Blood is Pretty
The First Fixxer Adventure

Meet the Fixxer—with wit and aplomb, he works the fruitful fields of Hollywood fixing the sins and correcting the stupidities of the denizens therein. In *Blood is Pretty,* he comes to the rescue of "the most beautiful woman I have ever seen" to extricate her from the grip of the soul-sucking sexual desires of a producer born in slime, and takes on the task of buying off with money and muscle a film geek who won't cooperate with a director of minuscule talent who simply wants to claim "V"—the geek's "Holy Grail" of a film treatment—as his own.

Hollywood is an All-Volunteer Army
The Second Fixxer Adventure

What those in the know in Hollywood really know is that if they need a dark deed done, if they need a sticky personal or professional problem "fixed," they can call upon the mysterious and dangerous Fixxer. Whether you are a successful comedy film director whose "Art" has never truly been appreciated because the country's most important film critic has held a grudge against you since college or you are a neophyte and naïve screenwriter who resents the professional blackmail she has just suffered, you call upon the Fixxer.

Traveling in Space

A unique first contact novel from the aliens' point-of-view. The last thing the factfinders—who call themselves Life—expected to find while traveling in space in "The Curious" on a mission from their planet, The Living World, was other life. But one day, they stumble upon the third planet out from a backwater sun and find it teeming with a vast diversity of life, including one sentient and cognizant, if primitive, species that they dub Otherlife. Being not only from The Curious but inherently curious themselves, they begin to study the Otherlife and their alien culture, discovering such strange things as marriage, intoxicating drinks, weapons of minor and mass destruction, the gleeful inhaling of toxic substances, two-parent families, layered language, genocide, non-nude bathing, and—the strangest thing of all—religion.

This first contact between Life and Otherlife, disconcerting for both, has moments of humor and moments of horror—and neither escape the encounter unchanged.

12 Dogs of Christmas
A Novelization

Winner of the Scribe Award from the International Association of Media Tie-in Authors

Based on the beloved independent family film.

12-year-old Emma O'Connor is sent to live with her "aunt" in the small town of Doverville. Emma soon finds herself in the middle of a "dogfight" with the mayor and town dogcatcher. In order to strike down their "no-dogs" law, Emma must bring together a group of schoolmates, grown-ups, and adorable dogs of all shapes and sizes in a spectacular holiday pageant. *The 12 Dogs of Christmas* is a fun, heartwarming story featuring a diverse canine cast and is perfect for all those who love dogs, kids, and Christmas.

By the Sea
A Comic Novel

A modern comic adult fairy tale with an ensemble cast of Cinderellas. Instead of a kingdom by the sea, our story takes place in and around a residential hotel by the sea. The architecturally eclectic Briers Hotel is situated on Leech Beach, a not particularly inviting beach that is often fog-bound and always scruffy. But it's the perfect setting for our Cinderellas, male, and female, who put up with the scruffiness of life while striving to make it through their various personal seaside fogs. Theater; art; antiques; old movies; sex; more sex; death; fast and slow cars, chicken shit, and cow poop; military bearing and erotic emissions—not to mention the wicked witch, the sea serpent by the sea shore, the village ogre, the village idiot, and several Prince Charmings—all figure into this merry tale with a multitude of happy endings.

The Definition of Luck
Or
The Post-Modern Prometheus

Khadambi Kinyanjui, a 6-foot-five-Kenyan who grew up in London, is from a wealthy family. Joe Smith, quite a bit shorter, is a red-headed orphan who grew up with his Aunt Liz in a hole in the California desert. Both are brilliant scientists. One is a neurobiologist, the other an astronomer, who first meet in 2049 under the Tommy Trojan statue at the University of Southern California. They become the best of friends but a very odd couple. And yet, their brotherhood is more robust than most actual brothers.

Then tragedy strikes the pair. Death is near for one of them. What can fend it off? Can the mind, the *self*, be uploaded to some digital realm? Can one become more than a human and far less than an animal? Or will the fix be something unexpected and mysterious? Can this human survive? Can humanity? Can friendship?

IMP
A Political Fantasia

Thomas P. Powell's ascension in politics was both unusual and yet very American. From traffic cop to Vice President of the United States, his climb up the ladder of public service was often due to the push of random acts and not-so-happy accidents—although Thomas held the opinion that it was due solely to his singular innate moral authority. What matters is what's within, that's the Powell political philosophy. Then, on the cusp of his grasping the last rung of the American political ladder, something truly within suddenly appears. A horrible homunculus, an impetuous imp, climbs out of Thomas's right ear to bedevil his nights, confuse his days, and take him on a crazy, wild, nauseating, and nuclear journey. It's as if *The West Wing* was done as a *Twilight Zone* episode.

And you thought our last political nightmare was surreal.

Journey to Where
A Contemporary Scientific Romance

When a radical experiment into the nature of time is sabotaged, the scientific team finds themselves in an alternate universe where humans never became the dominant life force. Instead, dinosaurs evolved into intelligent bipeds, developing language and societal structures.

The scientists must learn to communicate with this alien species, who view them as unusual pets, and figure out how to recreate the original experiment in a non-industrialized world so they can go back home—assuming there's a home, or even a universe, to return to. But the scientist who sabotaged them is trapped in this new world with them. And he's looking to rise to power, even if his quest means the death of his traveling companions.

A contemporary scientific romance in the tradition of H. G. Wells and Jules Verne

Creature Feature
A Horrid Comedy

There is something strange happening in Placidville

It is 1962. Kathy Anderson, a serious actress who took her training at the Actors Studio in New York is stuck playing Vivacia, the Vampire Woman on Vivacia's House of Horrors for a local Chicago TV station. Finally fed up showing old monster movies to creature feature fans, she quits and heads to New York, and the fame and footlights of Broadway.

She stops off to visit her parents and old friends in Placidville, the all-American, middle-class, blissfully normal Midwest small town she grew up in. But she finds things are strange in Placidville. Kathy's parents, her best friend from high school, the local druggist, and even the Oberhausen twins are all acting curiously creepy, odiously odd, and wholly weird. Especially the town's super geeky nerd, Gerald, who warns of dark days ahead.

Has Kathy entered a zone in the twilight? Did she reach the limits that are outer? Has she fallen through a mirror that is black? Or is it just—just—politics as usual?

Bully 4 Love
A Rather Odd Love Story

Adolphus Seruya is a happy, middle-aged, unambitious bachelor and a history professor at a prominent community college. Then suddenly SHE walks into his classroom. Lavinia Carson is beautiful in a unique yet compelling way. And radiant almost beyond description. Thus begins a rather odd story of love rejected, love ignored, love found— and cuttlefish pizza.

Extraordinary Voyages

What if a man wanted to go to the moon from the time he was an infant? Not a toddler, not a child, not a young man, but a babe in his mother's arms?

What if Baron Munchausen traveled from 1790 to1641 to take Cyrano de Bergerac to Mars?

What if the man who wanted to go to the moon from the time he was an infant wrote some rude poems?

What if the author of this book wrote his own Wikipedia page that he was sure Wikipedia would never publish?

What if you bought this book and found out?

Includes the critically acclaimed novella *Made on the Moon.*

The Reluctant Heterosexual
A Tragicomedy in Four Movements a Prelude and an Interlude

With *The Reluctant Heterosexual,* Steven Paul Leiva concludes his thematic trilogy: **The Love, Sex and Pursuit of Happiness Novels**. All three novels look at these essential aspects of the human condition, with each novel focusing on one of the three. *By the Sea: A Comic Novel* looks at our unease when unhappy. *Bully 4 Love: A Rather Odd Love Story* takes a skewed view of this most revered emotion. And now, *The Reluctant Heterosexual,* as the title predicts, concerns sex, which is not always the same as love, nor is it always a happy situation.

Subtitled *A Tragicomedy in Four Movements a Prelude and an Interlude,* each section of the novel, as in a musical composition, has its own tempo, mood, and form as it tells the story—and stories—of Robert Leslie Cromwell and Sandy Smith. Two *Homo sapiens sapiens* surviving and striving in the late 20th century.

Robert and Sandy are intelligent, creative, not unattractive, wealthy, married to each other, and in love. And yet their procreating bodies might as well be standing naked on a savanna in Africa in the late Pliocene Era.

It's the sometimes comic conflict between ancient bodies and modern culture. Can there possibly be a happy ending?

Right
A Portrait of Controversy

In a 1980s America different from our own, both familiar and not, Congress passed and President Henshaw signed the Birth Cessation Act. Once it became law, no one would be allowed to have a child for twenty-five years, any woman under 24 weeks pregnant was required to have an immediate abortion, and all men were called up to report for a vasectomy.

"Conscious regulation of human numbers must be achieved." Dr. Paul R. Ehrlich wrote in his 1968 bestseller, *The Population Bomb*. By the early 80s, the government had statistical projections that the population growth was outpacing the available resources needed for all in America to live a comfortable and secure life. A situation that would inevitably lead to the chaos and violence of extreme civil unrest.

Most Americans, liking comfort and security, supported the government's action. Most, but not all. And those who didn't, including a world-famous female billionaire entrepreneur inventor film producer, a major appliance salesman from Queens, a well-to-do Manhattan college radical, an unwed mother in Los Angeles who protests most horribly, America's premier pundit-columnist, and a young man who talks to his dead brother, became loud enough to start a fresh new controversy in America.

This is a portrait of that controversy.

Searching for Ray Bradbury
Writings about the Writer and the Man

Includes the title piece written for the *Los Angeles Times*, and "The Man Who Was Himself," Leiva's memorial appreciation of Bradbury commissioned by the Science Fiction & Fantasy Writers of America for the Winter 2012/13 edition of their quarterly magazine, *The Bulletin*. Other pieces were originally written for *Neworld Review*, KCET.org, and his personal blog.

With a special foreword by Hugo and Nebula Award-winning

www.ingramcontent.com/pod-product-compliance
Lightning Source LLC
Chambersburg PA
CBHW020323200626
46814CB00006BB/2391